COME NEXT WINTER

*To Sandra,
Follow your dreams!*

Linda Hanna

Deborah J. Dilworth

Seasons of Change Series

Book one: Come Next Winter

Come Next Winter

Seasons of Change Series: Book One

**By
Linda Hanna
and Deborah Dulworth**

Come Next Winter
Published by Mountain Brook Ink
White Salmon, WA U.S.A.

All rights reserved. Except for brief excerpts for review purposes, no part of this book may be used in any form without written permission from the publisher.

The website addresses recommended throughout this book are offered as a resource. These websites are not intended in any way to be or imply an endorsement on the part of Mountain Brook Ink, nor do we vouch for their content.

This story is a work of fiction. All characters and events are the product of the author's imagination. References to real locations, places, or organizations are used in a fictional context. Any resemblance to any person, living or dead, is coincidental.

Scripture quotations are taken from the *Holy Bible*, *New King James Version®,* NKJV® Used by permission. All rights reserved worldwide.

ISBN 978-1-943959-20-4
© 2016 Linda Hanna and Deborah Dulworth

The Team: Miralee Ferrell, Nikki Wright, Cindy Jackson
Cover Design: Indie Cover Design, Lynnette Bonner Designer

Mountain Brook Ink is an inspirational publisher offering fiction you can believe in.

Printed in the U.S.A. 2017

Endorsements

Come Next Winter is a wonderfully written tale wrought with emotional ups and downs, snippets of real-life drama, plenty of humor to offset the pain from loss of a loved one, and an endearing romance. The manner in which Hanna and Dulworth write as a team is a true pleasure to read. Without a doubt, this one goes on my keeper shelf! ~*Sharlene MacLaren, Author and Women's Speaker, River of Hope Series, Tennessee Dreams Series, Forever Freedom Series*

"Come Next Winter," was a delight to read. A story of second loves and second chances for characters that you come to care deeply about, you are reminded to place your trust in Lord in the good times and the bad. ~*Veronica Leigh, short-story author and blogger*

A heartwarming tale of friends, enemies, and eccentric family members. Come Next Winter kept me laughing one minute and wanting to wring Aunt Penny's neck the next. Hanna and Dulworth deliver a delightful story you'll want to read more than once. ~*June Foster, contemporary inspirational romance author including* Ryan's Father

The dynamic writing duo of Deb Dulworth and Linda Hanna deliver a 5-star winner with Come Next Winter. Using a strong dose of comedy and a cast of quirky, whimsical characters, they take us on an emotional roller-coaster with Carol Mason and her loved ones. I cried and grew angry at times by how others treated her, and I cringed when the dragon of the family breathed fire and brimstone. But I also laughed, and even snorted out loud a time or two.

This story is such a powerful and inspirational message of hope and trust in the Lord, and of His promise not to spare you from dark times, but to support and strengthen you as you travel difficult paths. So, you ask do I recommend this book? As Aunt Penny would say, "Of course, I do!" ~*Elizabeth Noyes, author of The Imperfect Series (Imperfect Wings, Imperfect Trust, Imperfect Bonds, and upcoming: Imperfect Lies and Imperfect Love)*

Hanna and Dulworth hit the mark on a wonderful tale in Come Next Winter. The reader's emotions will undoubtedly be drawn in with the allure of the ups and downs of real-life drama. Not only are the characters relatable, but the pain of the loss of a loved one, the feel of an endearing romance and the stitches of humor all combine to make a this a must-read book. This is one book no shelf should be without. ~*Sandra Stein Author/Speaker*

In *Come Next Winter* we are drawn into the lives of recently widowed Carol and her teen aged son, Andy. This novel by co-authors Linda Hanna and Deborah Dulworth explores love and loss, friendship, and family. I enjoyed their humorous descriptions and clever turns of phrases that kept this a light, easy read overall. The flawed, quirky residents of Apache Pointe, Arizona, had me rooting for them as they leaned on God in everything, from serious issues to unexpected mouse sightings and sleigh ride mishaps, throughout this sweet, modern-day love story. ~*Cathy Shouse, Journalist and novelist, author of* Images of America: Fairmount

Dedication

We dedicate this book to the Author of our faith, Jesus Christ, who has walked with us on this path.

Acknowledgements

Thanks to our husbands, Bill Hanna and Ray Dulworth, for your patience, prayers, and backing each step of the way. Our families have continued to believe in us and supported our dream of publishing Come Next Winter. From the bottom of our hearts, we thank the Marion Writers' Group, ACFW critique group #215, Phi Beta Psi Sorority, and Westview Wesleyan Church for their prayers and encouragement.

Our gratitude goes to our publisher and mentor, Miralee Ferrell, who made this novel possible. Her dedication and hard work set a great example and will always be appreciated.

Linda Hanna and Debbie Dulworth

CHAPTER ONE

Powder Ridge, Vermont
Saturday, January 4

GUILT PECKED AT CAROL MASON'S CONSCIENCE as she dropped the Belgian waffles into the toaster. Would her poor husband forgive her for ruining his peaceful Saturday? A phone call last evening altered his plan to sleep in and leisurely work on his sermon. Maybe the aroma of coffee and bacon would get him moving faster.

Heavy footsteps trudged down the stairs.

"I smell bacon." Bob sauntered into the kitchen and snitched two smoky strips from the platter. "Hey, do you know where my Mukluks are, sweetheart? I've looked in the hall closet and can't find them. If I'm gonna ski with our charged-up youth group, I'm going to need my Mukluks." He kissed her cheek. "And a lot more bacon."

"Relax, honey. They're with the other boots where they're supposed to be." She shook her head and retrieved butter and orange juice from the fridge. "Remember the mudroom?"

He yawned, scratched his belly, and headed for the back porch. "Oh, yeah. How long have we lived here?"

"I'll help you in a minute." She pulled out the baking sheet, added more waffles to the pile, and shoved them into the oven to stay warm. "I shouldn't have said you'd chaperone, especially on a Saturday."

"We agreed not to volunteer each other, but under the circumstances I understand why you did. Here they are."

He took his boots and gloves from the cubby below the coat rack and placed them on the bench. "I'm glad the slopes got six inches of fresh powder last night. It'll be a lot more fun." He grinned.

Carol's heart turned over at the endearing dimple in the center of Bob's chin. His schoolboy smile still charmed her. "That's my man. I toss you an Eeyore moment and you catch Pooh Bear. And while your hand's still in Pooh's hunny jar, thanks for not being upset when I told Jake he could tag along. He's been begging to go with Andy all week."

"Don't worry. It's been a while since the Mason men spent quality time together. Too bad Ethan had to go back to college early."

She stood on tiptoes, finger-combed his rooster tail, and kissed his freshly shaved cheek. "I made your favorite breakfast as a peace offering. Along with the nuked bacon, we have Belgian waffles, blueberries, and coffee. I'm sorry I added to your busy schedule. Forgive me?"

"You should be sorry, you rascal. Just maybe I'll forgive you if tomorrow's sermon notes are typed out while I'm skiing for the Lord." He swept her into a hug, lifted her off the floor, and planted a tantalizing kiss on her lips.

"I smell eau de pork-fume." Andy's adolescent shout came from the hall. "Oops! Hide your eyes, Jake. Mom and Dad are smoochin' again."

Eleven-year-old Jake entered the kitchen, his face scrunched in mock disgust. "Eww, that's gross. Do you have to do that mushy stuff in front of us?" He turned to the toaster and bunny sniffed. "Yay! Waffles. I got dibs on these puppies." He put them on his plate along with a handful of crispy bacon and sat at the table.

Andy dropped his backpack behind a kitchen chair

and grabbed a couple slices of bacon from his little brother's plate. "You took all the waffles. You don't get all this, too."

"Settle down, boys. We have lots more here." Carol opened the warm oven, placed the cookie sheet on the table, and sat next to her husband.

"Let's offer thanks so we can eat." Bob bowed his head. "Heavenly Father, please bless our food. Thank You for this beautiful day, and we ask for Your presence as the youth group enjoys winter fun together. Be with Carol and those helping her with our fellowship afterward. Keep us safe and mindful of Your continuing love. In Your Son's precious name, amen."

"Mom, tell Jake not to embarrass me in front of my friends." Andy frowned at his brother, took a gulp of orange juice, then wiped his mouth. "Last week at school he told Jenna I loved her. Now she always wants to sit with me in the cafeteria."

"Jake, don't hassle Andy, and I want you to promise to not be a daredevil on the slopes. Understand? Stay with your dad all day." She pointed at her husband's nose. "Don't let him out of your sight."

He raised his hand. "I, Bob Mason, do hereby pledge to stick to Jake like mustard on a hot dog."

Jake raised his arm in solidarity. "Yeah, like warts on a toad, right, Dad?" He stood and kissed her cheek. "You can trust me, Mom. Thanks for letting me go today. Love you."

By early afternoon, the temperature in Powder Ridge had dropped. Carol and her best friend, Sue North, lugged several grocery bags to the house and dodged the whirling snow devils which crossed their path. They stomped snow from their boots and entered the mudroom. A brisk wind slammed the door closed behind them.

Carol's teeth chattered as she set her bags on the old bench and took her coat off. "The way the wind's picked up, the front must be coming through earlier than predicted."

"The roads are slick." Sue hung her coat next to Carol's and rubbed her hands together. "I hope the youth group started home from the resort long before now. Has anyone brought chili for the teen fellowship yet? We'll need to heat it up."

"We have two pots in the refrigerator along with a platter of sandwiches. Should be a good start. The other moms will bring everything else around five."

They gathered the grocery bags, hurried to the kitchen, and placed them on the counter.

The phone in her husband's home office rang. Carol threw up her hands. "Not again. I'm going to let it ring."

"Don't you want to know who's calling?" Sue pulled bags of marshmallows, hot chocolate mix, and graham crackers from one of the sacks. "With the bad weather, the youth group might be running late."

The phone went silent.

"You're right. I should've answered it." Carol pressed an index finger on her twitching eyelid. "I'm pretty sure it was one of the moms, and I can't deal with her smother-hood right now. She's called every hour with a different concern. Last time I told her if this trip wasn't properly supervised, I wouldn't have allowed Jake to go."

The shrill ring of the parsonage phone sounded again.

Sue removed a pot of chili from the refrigerator and set it on the stove. "Your eyelid's doing the Mexican hat dance. You might as well talk to her and get it over with, girlfriend. I don't think she's going to give up any time soon. Before I unload the rest of the snacks, I'll scoop snow from the front door."

Carol dried her hands and headed for the office. She lifted the receiver on the fifth ring. "Hello, Pastor Mason's office. How may I help you?"

"You promised the children would be safe, and the roads are treacherous."

"I'm sure they're fine, Betty." She breathed deeply in a plucky attempt to keep the frustration from her voice. "I have no control over the weather."

"I just heard on the news there was an accident at Crystal Peak. Two people were air lifted out. It better not be my Barry, or I'll sue the church, the chaperones, and the resort." Without another word, the agitated mother hung up.

Carol's stomach knotted as she tried to suppress a repulsive thought. Could her boys be involved? She rubbed her neck with sweaty palms as a tingle of uneasiness crept down her spine. "Oh, Lord, please be with the youth group and bring them home safely in this storm." She hurried to the kitchen and turned on the radio.

Sue came in from the mudroom. "The snow's really piling up. Hey, you're as white as a ghost. What's wrong?"

"There's been an accident at the ski resort." Carol tried to swallow the lump rising in her throat. Her gaze shifted to the floor as the eerie hunch continued to niggle at her stomach. "They didn't have any details, but I have an awful feeling. What if Jake or Andy got hurt?"

"Relax. Bob would've called by now if anything happened to our kids." Sue stirred the chili and tapped the spoon on the side of the pan.

Carol blinked the tears away, lifted her head, and

nodded. "Of course you're right, but I'm going to check in with him, anyway." She pressed Bob's speed dial number and waited for him to answer. Her call went to voice mail. "Bob, I need to hear from you. Please call me."

Car lights flickered across the kitchen window. Her heart raced. Were they home? Carol took a deep breath, set her cell phone on the counter, and hurried to open the front door.

The assistant pastor's grim face made her knees weaken as he came closer.

"Pastor Cliff. What are you doing out in this weather?"

He paused with his hand on the doorknob, knocked snow off his boots, and then entered the house. "I thought it best to come see you." He put his arm around her shoulder. "Let's sit down." He removed his gloves and led her into the living room. "Is anyone here with you?"

The question made Carol's stomach pitch. "Sue North's in the kitchen." Feeling the blood drain from her face, she sat stiffly on the edge of the couch and fought the urge to vomit. "Something's wrong. Just tell me."

"I got a call from the ski lodge." The young pastor's voice broke, and he cleared his throat. "There's no easy way to say this." He sat forward, elbows on his knees. "Pastor Bob and Jake were in a snowmobile accident."

"What happened?" Her body shook as she waited for his delayed response. "Cliff?"

His answer was hoarse. "Their snowmobile hit a tree on the way back to the lodge."

"Oh, no." She gripped his arm. "How bad is it?"

"I hate to be the one to tell you." He broke into a sob and rubbed Carol's hand. "They said the doctors did everything they could." He wiped his eyes and cleared his throat. "I'm so sorry, Carol. They died on impact."

A sense of disconnection spun around Carol as her mind grappled with his statement. She leaned against his shoulder. "Where's Andy?" Her voice became high-pitched and hysterical. "Is he okay?"

"He'll be home soon." Cliff's grip on her hand tightened. "Trust me, he's fine."

Sue ran into the room. "What's wrong?"

Shivering, Carol's stomach clenched and a nauseating spike impaled her soul. Her husband and youngest son had been taken in an instant. She grabbed her midsection and squeezed her eyes shut. "Not both of them."

"You're scaring me." Sue knelt beside her in front of the couch. "Did something happen to your folks?"

"Accident." Her breathing was labored, and her whisper thick as she struggled to form the dreaded words. "Bob and Jake."

In a hushed tone, Cliff explained what happened.

Sue released a sorrowful moan and wrapped her arms around Carol. They wept aloud and rocked back and forth.

"They were just here for breakfast. Bob asked me to go over his sermon." Her hands shook as she blew her nose.

"Honey, I'm so sorry." Sue offered her more tissues and gently rubbed her shoulder. "You and Andy won't have to face this alone. Your church family is here for you, and of course, Grady and I are, too."

Carol's chest burned as she leaned on the arm of the couch. Would she ever wake up from the nightmare? Bob and Jake . . . gone? "D-Dear Lord, why did You take both from me?"

"Shh." Sue's voice was gentle. "We'll help you through this."

"You don't understand. It's my fault, Sue. A chaperone for the youth group trip got sick at the last minute. I volunteered Bob without asking him." Her son's young face came to mind. "Jake pleaded to go with his dad." She wiped her tears and stared straight ahead with unfocused eyes. "He wasn't old enough, but I agreed. I knew he'd be safe with Bob. If only I hadn't . . ." She collapsed in Sue's embrace and sobbed.

"You know the enemy always tries to defeat us, so don't let your mind go there." Cliff spoke gently. "Accidents happen. It's not your fault." He gathered both women in his arms. "I'm glad you're here with her. They're taking the teens to the church, and we need to help them deal with the situation. Is there anything I can do before I go?"

Sue shook her head. "Thanks for coming. I know Carol appreciates it. I'll spend the night with them."

Carol stared at them in silence – a silence she couldn't seem to break. Her eyes swept the room that had been so full of life that morning. With slow steps, she went to the picture window and watched snowflakes blow in the bitter January wind. "Jake's only eleven years old. My baby." She dared to look at her friend. "He and Andy are so close." She grabbed Sue's arm. "Oh, no! Did Andy see the accident? He should be home by now. Don't they know I need him? And Ethan. I want him here, too."

"Andy's on his way. Let me have your cell phone, and I'll call Ethan." Sue pushed a stray lock of hair from Carol's face. "After that I'll call your folks."

"Where's my phone?"

"Wait, I think I saw it in the kitchen." Sue left the room.

Bob's sermon outline lay next to his Bible on the end table. Trembling, she retrieved the papers with his final handwritten words.

Today is January fifth, the first Sunday of the new year. What does God have in store for us, individually and as a church family?

We serve an almighty God who rules over the skies and seas. He dwells among the majestic mountains, but He is never too far from us to meet our needs. Our Heavenly Father knows when a single hair falls from our head. In Psalm 68:5 we learn He's a father to the fatherless, a defender of widows—

Widow. The realization of her fate hit like jagged lightning. Carol steadied herself at the edge of a deep, terrifying chasm. She picked up his well-worn Bible, held it close to her shattered heart, and leaned back into the softness of the sofa cushion.

Reach for Me. A calm voice beckoned.

CHAPTER TWO

Apache Pointe, Arizona
11 months later

THEY DIED TOO SOON. CAROL MASON finished the last of her peppermint tea and set the empty cup on the granite counter. Unsettling thoughts of returning home to Vermont weighed heavy on her mind. "Thanks again for inviting us to come out here for Thanksgiving, Mom."

"It's a shame Ethan couldn't come, but I understand college kids have their own agenda. I'm glad you and Andy could get away. It has to be hard to celebrate without your husband and youngest son." Sylvia Drake put an arm around her daughter's shoulder. "Little Jake was always the life of the party."

"Andy and I have been dreading the holiday season this year." She leaned against her mother. "I'm trying to be strong for him. Let's change the subject or I'll be a blubbering mess."

Sylvia gave her an extra squeeze then placed their cups in the dishwasher. "Have any new leads in your apartment search?"

"Not yet, but our needs are always supplied." She knew God would take care of them, but worry sometimes crept in. "We were so spoiled by the large parsonage. Living in Grady and Sue North's garage apartment is cramped, but at least it's rent-free and very temporary. Thanks to you, Dad, and the church helping with funeral costs, I've been able to save a modest deposit to put down on a two-bedroom place."

"Wish we could help more." Sylvia wiped her eyes. "This visit has gone so quickly, it's hard to see you go. I wish you lived closer."

"I've thought about it, too, but Powder Ridge has been home for a long time."

"Remember you'll always have a job at your dad's flower shop." Sylvia's mouth went into a sly pout and hope filled her eyes. "Promise me if you can't find a better apartment or job, you'll consider moving home."

"We'll pray about it, Mom. Right now I have to see if my son's ready to go." She went to the hallway. "Hurry, Andy. Our ride will be here any minute."

"I know. I'm putting my shoes on."

She returned to the kitchen. "I feel sorry for him because he gets sidetracked like me."

Sylvia wiped the top of the coffeemaker and pushed it out of the way. "Are things going better for him?"

"School's been difficult this year because most of his friends have shied away. I told him they probably feel awkward and don't know what to say." She brushed tears from her cheek. "So now he's acting like any other fifteen-year-old. You know the basic eye-rolling, sagging shoulders, and traditional grumpy attitude. I hope it's one of those passing phases."

"The poor kid's been moping a lot this visit, but I know my grandson. He'll come around. He's always been easygoing like you and Bob." She glanced at the clock. "Better get things together. We don't want to keep Pastor Frank waiting. I'm glad you got to chat with him when we went out for Thanksgiving. You both need encouragement after losing your spouses."

"You're right, Mom, it did help. He's very nice and easy to talk to. I liked the way he included Andy in our conversation." She checked her purse for their airline tickets. "Be sure to thank Dad for putting us up in the motel all week. We needed time away from daily reminders."

Sylvia nodded. "I'm sorry our condo only has one bedroom. It would've been nice to have you and Andy stay here with us."

The doorbell rang. A twinge of uneasiness nudged Carol's conscience. That had to be Pastor Frank. She knew exactly how a preacher's life was often interrupted with errands for his congregation. Hopefully they weren't keeping him from anything important. She drew sunglasses from her purse and reached for the handle of her suitcase. "I wish Dad could've taken us to the airport."

"He wanted to, but the flower shop is swamped with two afternoon weddings. He didn't have enough help to get away. Pastor Frank doesn't mind." Sylvia called over her shoulder as she hurried to answer the door. "In fact, it was his idea."

Carol attempted to maneuver her suitcase around the kitchen table as her son bounded into the room. "Could you help me, Andy?"

"Sure, I'll take it to the door."

"Thank you." She followed him to the living room where Frank Bailey was waiting. Her left eye twitched as she peeked over her sunglasses. He wore khakis and a rich purple Phoenix Sun jersey and was better looking than she remembered. Better put the sunglasses on and keep this formal. "Hello, Pastor Bailey."

He offered a friendly smile that accentuated his tanned face. "Hi, Carol. Let me take your luggage out. Andy, grab your tote and we'll get rolling."

Andy ran ahead of them to the car. "Shotgun!"

"Don't think so, buddy." Frank flashed a boyish grin. "The pretty lady sits with me."

Her chest rose and fell unevenly as he lightly squeezed her shoulder and reached for the door handle. Was he flirting or just being friendly? She made sure their hands didn't touch as he helped her into the car. In one swift move, she placed her large black purse on the seat between them as a barricade.

Frank shut the car door. She was so beautiful. Her creamy complexion and the dark lashes touching her cheekbones quickened his pulse. Gorgeous. The thought shook him. Carol Mason was the first woman to capture his interest since his wife's death two years ago. He was tired of being the lonely widower. Could she be in God's plan for his life? Maybe it was time to stick a toe into the dating pool.

He slid behind the wheel and noticed the black obstacle wedged between them. All-righty then. So much for testing the waters. Apparently, she needed more time. Movement in the rearview mirror caught his attention. Strike two. Andy's presence in the car would definitely hinder any private conversation. "It was nice of your folks to include me in their family Thanksgiving plans. I enjoyed getting acquainted with the two of you over turkey." He glanced her way. "Sorry you have to leave so soon."

"Wish we didn't have to, but Andy has school on Monday. I have to work at the bakery and find another apartment."

Andy poked his head between them. "We're living in a dinky place." He sat back and clicked his seatbelt.

"We had to leave the parsonage." Carol straightened her posture. "My best friend and her husband offered the small apartment over their garage until I can find a better place."

"Yeah. Mom sleeps in the only bedroom. I have to sleep on the couch, and it's too short."

"Sorry to hear that, Sport." He stole a look at Carol and pulled onto the street. "Sylvia said if things don't work out, you might move back to Apache Pointe."

"It's not that I don't want to, but, like I told Mom, after twenty years, Powder Ridge is home. Andy's never lived anywhere else, and with all the changes in his life, uprooting him would be my last choice."

"That makes sense." He winked at Andy in the rearview mirror. "Are you driving, yet?"

"I'll get my learner's permit in July when I turn sixteen." Andy crossed his arms. His teeth glistened through a goofy grin. "Me, Tank, and Fuzzy have big plans. We're gonna buzz the mall and check out the babes."

Carol turned in her seat. "Andrew Robert Mason!"

"What?"

Frank released a peal of laughter. "Aren't you ready for that, Mom?"

"I'm attempting to get used to my older son having a serious relationship with my best friend's daughter, Rikki." Carol pulled her sunglasses off. "Andy, if you're not careful, you'll wait an extra year to drive."

"Aww, Mom. I'm just kiddin'."

"Me, too." She handed him her smart phone. "Here, play one of your alien games."

Frank ventured another glance at the petite lady sitting beside him. "Other than finding another apartment with an Andy-sized couch, how are you coping?"

"One of the biggest hurdles is watching another man take over Bob's pulpit. Nearly a year later and I still expect to see my husband there and Jake singing in the youth choir."

"Is it time to attend another church?"

"North Sum—" She choked on the words and tried again. "North Summit Church has been very supportive and will always hold the best memories. How could we go anywhere else?"

He answered with a nod. "I understand. Barb sat in the same pew every Sunday. Her place has been empty for two years now, and at times I still look that way for her validation."

"I didn't mean to bring up sad memories." Carol sent him an apologetic look.

"That's all right. It helps to talk to someone who understands the heartache of losing loved ones." He smiled. "Would it be too presumptuous for me to call once in a while to see how you and Andy are?" Awkward. What was he doing? "Not sure I'd be any help, but I'm a good listener in case you need to talk." As his eyes connected with hers, the car veered to the right, kicking up gravel.

Andy tapped his shoulder. "Eyes on the road, man."

CHAPTER THREE

Powder Ridge, Vermont

THE SECOND WEEK OF DECEMBER ROLLED around far too quickly for Carol. They still hadn't found an apartment even close to their budget or Andy's school.

Once their prematurely packed boxes were pushed out of the way, she hurried to finish her chores before Andy got home from wrestling practice.

She pulled her hair into a lopsided ponytail and pushed up the sleeves of her sweatshirt. With one good shove the love seat moved away from the wall, exposing three crushed soft drink cans and a twisted Cheddar Doodle bag. While dropping litter into the garbage can, the sweeper hose fell from her hand, and the machine released a wheeze, whirr, and whine. Her tug-o-war with the vacuum and Andy's crusty gym sock triggered the involuntary flutter in her left eye.

Carol finished de-socking the beater bar and sneezed from the airborne dust. Her cell phone rang displaying her mother's number. Good! Time for a break anyway.

"Hi, Mom." She gave her nose a quick swipe with the sleeve of her shirt. "What's up?"

"I wondered how things were going. We're still praying for a bigger apartment to open up." Her mother cleared her throat. "By the way, Pastor Frank said you had a nice talk when he took you to the airport a couple weeks ago."

"He assured me what I'm going through is normal

grieving, and I need time to heal."

"Pastor Frank's good at counselling." Sylvia hesitated. "His caring spirit makes everyone feel comfortable."

Carol patiently allowed her to ramble while she wiped the kitchen counter. "Mom, you've mentioned Frank's name at least six times. I hope you're not playing matchmaker."

"Can't say your father and I haven't thought about it." She giggled.

"This is awkward on so many levels. I'm not ready for a relationship." Carol rubbed her forehead. How could she even think of replacing Bob? "Would you mind if we talk about something else?"

The voice on the other line became muffled. Who was she talking to?

"Carol? Say hi to Pastor Frank. I'll let you two chat while I get lunch on the table."

Mothers. Carol crossed her eyes at the phone and waited for Frank's voice. At least he couldn't see her red face.

"Hi, Carol. How are you?"

"Umm, hi." His captivating image flitted through her mind. "I'm fine, but it appears a certain someone has donned her matchmaking cape."

"It's a hazard for any eligible man." He released a lighthearted laugh. "You wouldn't believe the mothers standing in line to marry off their bachelorette daughters."

"Like flies to buttermilk, right?" She rested against the wall. Her mom needed to get out of that parade. "It's far too early for me to even think about dating."

"I know what you're saying. It takes a while. I've only gone out once, and that was a blind date. Her name was Spring and I called her Barb all evening."

She couldn't hold the laughter in. "Oh, Frank. You

didn't!"

"Unfortunately, I did. Seems she took it personally and asked me not to call her again. So maybe we both need to trust in His timing."

She choked down a chuckle. "Sounds like a wise choice to me."

"I'd better go. Your mom's garlic bread is making me slobber like Pavlov's dog. May I call later this week?"

"That would be nice. 'Bye." She turned the phone off, put a pot of coffee on, and headed for the sweeper. Frank had been a nice reprieve, but her problems still lacked answers.

Andy would be home for the next three years of high school. At fifteen, he needed her to be strong more than ever, and she couldn't let him down. How she missed Bob's keen insight and wisdom as they tackled important decisions together. Now it was up to her alone.

Deuteronomy 31:6 popped into her head. *"Be strong and of good courage, do not fear nor be afraid of them; for the Lord your God, He is the One who goes with you. He will not leave you nor forsake you."*

Carol drew a deep breath and bowed her head. "Thank You for my blessings and forgive my doubts. Keep our hearts open as we trust You to direct our steps. Please supply the strength I need to get through the next few weeks."

She tucked a lock of hair behind her ear feeling blessed with great parents, a best friend in Sue, and now Frank—all willing to be sounding boards. Their encouragement had become a lifeline as she struggled to gain a foothold in this new reality.

With the Lord's help, she'd move forward, and take one obstacle at a time.

She eyeballed the refrigerator. Maybe frozen bonbons were a God-thing, too. Hopefully Andy hadn't found her newest hiding place. A stray curl fell to her forehead as she reached for the buried frozen pea bag and then elbowed the freezer shut.

"Yoo-hoo!" The front door slammed. "Are you here? I smell fresh coffee."

Carol yelped. Her arms flew up, the vegetable bag took wing, and chocolate hailstones pelted the floor, scattering hither and yon.

"Oooh . . . chocolate!" Sue North dropped to her knees. "Five-second rule."

Carol pointed heavenward. "No bonbon shall perish before its time." Laughter reigned in the kitchen as she held the pea bag while her blonde friend scooped handfuls of candy into it.

"Caught ya red-handed, didn't I?" Sue's grin exposed a chocolate-covered front tooth.

"I'm on my coffee break from packing and wrestling with the vacuum. I deserve this lip-smacking indulgence." She popped another fudgy bite into her mouth. "What are you doing sneaking up on me, anyway?"

Sue's eyes widened in mock surprise. "There was no sneaking involved. I'll have you know I knocked prior to my 'yoo-hoo'." She got off the floor and brushed her knees, her voice lowered to a whisper. "Your secret stash is safe with me, but you have to share."

"Why, that's blackmail. I recall a few chocolate skeletons dangling in your freezer, too." Carol handed her a cup of coffee.

"Oooh, touché." Sue pointed to a basket she'd placed on the counter. "Well, Miss Stingy Pants, I was sweet enough to bring my specialty from the Pie Hole."

Carol sniffed the air. "Cinnamon! You brought me cinnamon rolls."

"Along with beef stew and a dry shoulder to cry on. I'll

miss you when you move out."

"We'll still see each other at the bakery and have lunch together." She put the stew in the fridge. "Thanks for bringing supper, Sooze. You're so thoughtful. I guess that does merit a chocolate reward."

"Are you sure you can spare it?"

She grinned at her friend. "There's more in the Brussels sprout bag."

"You rascal." Sue nodded toward a stack of boxes. "You sure got a lot done today."

"Yeah, I was feeling really productive until I noticed how little time we have left to pack." She rubbed the back of her neck. "And I'm overwhelmed financially. It's been months since copies of Bob's death certificate and autopsy report were submitted, and the insurance check still hasn't come. I need Grady to look into it."

"I think you need more than that." Sue leaned closer. "What if Grady and I take you and Andy out this evening? You can save the stew for another time."

Spending the evening with Sue sounded great, but Carol dreaded being around her domineering husband. She grimaced and patted her friend's hand. "It isn't necessary. Besides, Andy and I still have lots of packing to do."

"Tomorrow's Saturday. Grady has a rare day off, and I'll be free at noon to roll up my sleeves and help." She wagged her finger. "No excuses, we'll pick you up at six this evening. That gives you plenty of time to get out of Bob's old sweatshirt, shower, and put on something a little more fetching."

"Fetching?" Carol smiled. "Six o'clock works. Thanks." Hopefully, going out would give her a break from the moving madness.

Sue held up her phone. "I have to take this call. See you later." She dashed out the door.

Feeling swamped by the amount of work facing her, Carol plopped into a chair. No matter where she and Andy lived, life would never be the same. Maybe the problem wasn't the actual move but the underlying emotional changes. Sending Ethan off to college last fall was one thing; however, that emptiness was nothing compared to Bob and little Jake's absence.

The rest of the afternoon passed quickly as Carol completed her household tasks.

The clock in the connecting bedroom indicated forty-five minutes to get ready. Grady was always early. She grabbed her robe from the closet and hurried to shower.

Once done, she raced to the bedroom and reluctantly donned her black slacks, wishing she could lounge in her sweat pants all evening.

The front door slammed. "Mom, I'm home. What's to eat?"

She pulled on a blue cable knit sweater and stuck her head out the bedroom door. "Nothing. Grady and Sue are taking us out for supper. You only have enough time for a *quick* shower before they pick us up. Your clean clothes are in the basket on the couch."

"Oh, great." Andy grabbed his underwear and stomped to the bathroom. "We're in for a crummy night of Grady's lawyer jabber, and I don't like the way he's been gawking at you since Dad died."

"Thanks for telling me. I thought it was just my imagination. I'll keep my distance."

A few minutes later, he emerged with a towel around his waist. "Grady stares at Mrs. Garr at church, too."

"Keep it to yourself." She shook her head and hunted

for a missing earring. "Now, hurry and get dressed. I want you to wear that green button down shirt and your new church pants. The Norths always dress up, and we don't want to look shabby." Maybe she should alert Sue about her husband's roving eye. A shiver sprinted up her arm.

"S'pose we'll go to a snooty restaurant and choke down snails and frog legs again?"

"Even so, mind your manners, and don't you dare do Kermit imitations this time. Think of it this way—we don't eat out often, and you're not stuck with leftover spaghetti for supper."

"Point taken!" he yelled from the living room.

"Let's hurry. They'll be here in about ten minutes." She looked into the dresser mirror, dabbed on a touch of makeup and combed her hair. Andy's comment echoed in her mind. 'I don't like the way he's been gawking at you since Dad died.' She'd have to thwart any passes Grady tossed her way.

CHAPTER FOUR

A BLARING CAR HORN SET CAROL'S nerves on edge while she slipped into her leather boots. Grady North was in the car, ready to go.

Andy waited in the living room. "Sounds like 'da Bear's' got his skivvies in a knot."

"Be nice, Andrew." She squeezed his arm as they stepped from the apartment to the stairs in the garage. "*Please* don't embarrass me this evening." They climbed into the backseat.

"My idea's better, Sue." The lawyer's voice was intense as he spoke to his wife. "We'll go with that." He turned around to greet them. "Evening. Since Andy's with us, I thought Slippery Slope Pizza would be a nice change of pace."

"They have a small arcade." Sue grinned at Andy.

"And cute waitresses." Andy wiggled his eyebrows and rubbed his hands together. "I'm ready for games and dames."

Carol gaped at her baby-faced teen. "Where did you hear about dames?"

"Grandpa Drake has some fine old gangster movies."

"That's vulgar language, Andy." Grady glanced over his shoulder. "Real men treat women with respect."

Carol firmly pursed her lips, locked eyes with Andy, and hoped he got the message to keep quiet. The atmosphere remained gloomy as they drove across town. If only she'd followed her instinct to stay home in her sweats to eat stew and cinnamon rolls.

When they reached the pizza parlor, a van pulled out from the front row of the parking lot, and Grady claimed the prime space. "Lady Luck is on my side tonight."

The tantalizing aroma of hot pizza and breadsticks lured them inside. Andy fell in line behind the cute blonde waitress through the noisy, teen-infested restaurant. She led them to a booth near the arcade. Carol and Sue scooted in first. The server passed the menus, and threw a dimply grin the boy's way. His color blossomed into a bright red.

When Grady ordered iced tea all around, Carol caught Andy's grimace and patted his knee. Poor kid hated tea. She sat up straight and glanced at the girl's name tag. "Sunni, would you make one of those drinks a root beer, please?"

The waitress licked the tip of her pencil and nodded. "We've got a special on our Cavorting Carnivore Deep Dish and the Slippery Slope Salad DeLite."

Grady adjusted his tie, rubbed his closely trimmed beard, and glanced from the menu to the server, staring at her a little too long for Carol's comfort. With a sly smile, he winked at the young girl. Had Sue caught that blatant flirtation?

The waitress turned her attention to Sue. "Have we decided yet?"

Grady's voice boomed over the surrounding clamor. "The boy and I will have a large Carnivore, and the ladies want your salad special. We'll need a family order of breadsticks, too."

Without a chance to order, Carol compressed her lips. The jerk. She handed the useless menu to the waitress. Rabbit food now, Sue's beef stew later. One good shrug and she removed her jacket and laid it next to Andy.

Rock music boomed from the jukebox, and the table vibrated as Andy beat out the rhythm. "Mom, I'm bored.

Can I have change to pick a song, please?"

"Here you go." Grady shoved a pile of quarters to the boy. "Save a few for the arcade."

Before Andy could slide out of his seat, the waitress arrived with their breadsticks and drinks. The boy beamed as Sunni handed him the breadbasket.

Grady intercepted the garlicky handoff. "Do you think we could say grace before you delve into those, Romeo?"

"Oh, yeah, sorry." Andy shrugged.

After a short prayer, Grady whispered, "Amen," and snatched four breadsticks. He kept two for himself, handed one to each of the ladies, and gave the half-filled basket to Andy. "That's called survival of the quickest. Okay, let the feeding frenzy begin."

Sue was her usual stunning self, dressed in a lavender pantsuit. She delicately dipped her bread into the cheese sauce. "I have a surprise announcement, and I'm really nervous about it. Even Grady-Bear doesn't know the results, yet."

"Oh, Sooze!" Carol gasped. "You're not—?"

Grady threw his half-eaten breadstick on the table. "Absolutely not. I won't hear of it." He took a quick assessment of his grinning wife. "You're too old, right?"

Andy sat with his cheeks bulging like an overfed chipmunk. "Not what?"

Sue twisted the ends of her golden hair. "Yes, it's true. I have a bun in the oven." She giggled and wiped her mouth. "Get serious, people. My bakery really took off when Crystal Peak Resort became my new client. Since I needed more space, Grady suggested I purchase The Muffin Man Bakery." She grabbed his arm. "The bank called today. The loan went through."

Grady wiped his brow. "Whew! Now, *that's* good news."

"Congratulations." Carol squeezed her friend's hand. "I'm so happy for you. You're not going to keep the

Muffin Man name, are you?"

"No, my customers know The Pie Hole." Sue sipped her sweet tea. "I've been swamped with orders for large groups, so the industrial kitchen will be a blessing. Now I'll be able to offer you a full-time job, Carol."

"What a relief. I'm so thankful." She dabbed her eyes. Her job hunt was over. She'd soon have a new apartment and a less stressful life.

The waitress placed the pizza and two salads in front of them.

Andy eagerly grabbed the first two pieces, stacked a larger one on top, and contentedly stuffed his face.

"Let's get down to business." Grady cocked his head. "Andy, I'm thinking you and Ethan will help with deliveries next summer when the new place is up and running."

The teen stopped mid-chew and his face drooped.

How presumptuous of the arrogant man. Carol squinted hard to suppress the tremor in her left eye.

Sue lowered her fork, glanced at Carol, then her husband. "It would be nice if you asked Andy instead of ordering him, Grady-Bear."

"We're the adults, he's the child." A scowl etched his face. "He follows our directives."

No wonder Bob always complained about the man's authority issues. Carol's stomach curled as her son slouched lower in his seat.

"Great. Sounds like my life's all planned." Andy halfheartedly bit into his pizza.

Carol whispered in his ear. "Let's not have a scene in public. We can talk about this later, but you'll need something to do next summer." She tapped his plate. "Finish your pizza so you can play Galaxy Wars."

He nibbled around the edge of the slice in hand and then scarfed it down. With her blessing, the teen escaped to the small arcade. A loud belch from Andy's direction rose above the buzz of diners' voices.

Carol's face heated as she glanced at the boy. He delivered two thumbs-up. She shook her head. "That's my boy, always the gentleman."

A giggle escaped Sue's lips. The mirth ceased when her stern husband's forehead creased into its customary frown.

"Do you want me to speak to the lad about his lack of social graces?"

"I think Carol can handle it."

"Thank you, Sooze." She threw him a dark look and loaded her fork with unwanted mixed greenery. "Remember, he's a kid, but I'll talk to him when we get home. The most pressing thing on my to-do list is finding an apartment."

Grady huffed, drummed his stubby fingers on the table, and then rubbed his beard. "I have the answer to your living arrangement dilemma."

Big surprise. He *always* had the answer. Carol faked a smile. "I don't want your money."

"Keep an open mind, okay?" Sue reached in her purse. "I told Grady to find a clean, efficient place. The realtor's flyer is right here."

Grady rested his elbows on the table. "I spoke to a client who knows someone with available accommodations. I've gone over the lease agreement. He says you can move in any time you want between now and Christmas." He winked. "I took the liberty of paying your first month's rent. I know you want to be independent, so we'll come up with a way for you to reimburse me." Grady's hand went up to stifle any further discussion. "Case closed."

Carol's eyes widened as she waited for any reaction from Sue.

"I haven't seen the place." Sue chased a crouton around her salad bowl. "But Grady said it's a pretty chalet-style duplex with two bedrooms and one and a half baths."

"Wow. You've given this a lot of thought." She tried to smile with an appreciation she didn't feel. Of course, Sue had the best intentions, but she questioned Grady's objective with the generous offer.

Sue threw her an enthusiastic grin. "And this is your answer."

Grady smacked the table and reached for Carol's hand. "Then it's settled."

She pulled away. "I need to know what the rent is and check it out before making a commitment." At this point, she didn't have the energy to disagree with the couple. She was out of options. All she had to do now was finish packing and break the news to Andy.

CHAPTER FIVE

THE NEXT MORNING, CAROL'S HEAD THROBBED as her car meandered through accumulating mid-December snow in the high-priced housing division. The interior of the chalet duplex was extravagant and beautiful. Grady had to know anything in this area was completely out of her budget. Good thing she'd checked it out before mentioning it to Andy.

A few months ago, Grady insisted she and Andy move into the apartment over his garage, but what did the man hope to gain this time? More power over her? His sly wink at the restaurant suggested another bile-producing possibility. She pounded the steering wheel. No way would she be anyone's concubine!

If only Sue could get her nose out of the bakery's flour bin long enough to recognize her husband's carnal pursuits. On the other hand, what could she do to rein him in? Grady was so intimidating, no one dared stand up to him. Not even his wife.

Carol pulled into her space in the garage, slammed the car door, and trudged up the stairs.

The temperature of the apartment was glacial. Carol left her coat on and checked the thermostat. Fifty-three degrees? She stomped her foot. Grady tinkered with it twice last week, and big surprise, the thing still wasn't fixed.

They were in the middle of a snowstorm with no heat and very little food. Her mind raced. Better get extra blankets out and let the faucet drip so the pipes didn't freeze before going to the store. Burning candles might add a little warmth to the place. Carol dashed down the steps to the garage and gaped at the mound of packing boxes. She threw up her arms and kicked the nearest carton. Why didn't anyone think to write 'candles' on the side of the box?

Her throat ached as pent-up tears surfaced. She rushed to the bedroom and dropped to her knees by the bed.

"Dear Heavenly Father, I'm doing the best I can. Working part-time, apartment and job hunting, paying bills, housekeeping, packing, not to mention all the legal details from Bob's passing. It's been too much." With shaky hands, she covered her face. "I know You wouldn't put us through this misery without a reason. Please give me strength to go through it or provide a way out. I want to thank You—"

"I'm home, Mom." The front door slammed. "Do we have anything good to eat?"

Caught off guard by Andy's early arrival, Carol wiped her eyes and nose. He shouldn't see her blubbering like this. "I'll be out to help you find something in a minute."

Floorboards creaked in the hall, and within seconds, Andy knelt on the floor beside her. He put an arm around her shoulders. "What's wrong, Mom?"

She couldn't tell her son about Grady's plan to set them up in a luxurious condo. No matter which way she turned, they were still under Grady's self-proclaimed superior command.

"I'm sorry you caught me crying. I'm overstressed and needed a chance to pray about things." She drew a deep breath. "What are you doing home from school?"

"Coach cancelled practice because of the snow." Andy stood and helped her up. "Don't worry, things'll get better, Mom. Remember the verse Dad always quoted?"

He cleared his throat and imitated his father. "'James 4:8. *'Draw near to God and He will draw near to you.'*" His voice returned to normal. "Maybe we need to do that more."

Her heart soared. She embraced her son and patted his back. "Will you help me talk to the Lord about it?"

"Let's do it now, Mom." Andy bowed his head. "Dear God, You know how Grady gets into our business. Please help us find a place to live far enough from Grady so he can't bother us. It doesn't have to be fancy, just calm like when Dad was still here. Help us keep our cool and trust You. In Jesus' name, Amen."

She held him tight. When did his shoulders get so broad? "Thanks, Andy. I'm so proud of you, and your dad would be, too."

"Okay." His face reddened. "I'm gonna get a snack."

Many prayers supported them, but Andy's petition was more precious. She wished they lived near her parents so they could witness his growing faith.

A spiritual thump on the back of the head brought another thought. Why couldn't they live near her parents? Going home to Arizona might be the way out, and if it was, He would handle all the details. New hope lifted her spirits. Andy didn't need to know yet. He had to deal with too many upheavals as it was.

Carol headed for the living room. "I hear 'Chicka Chicka Boom Boom' music."

"It's your phone, Mom."

"Great. Will you stop changing the ringtone, Andy? It's not funny anymore." She followed the sound until the singing phone was in sight.

"Hello?"

"Hi, Sweetheart. It's Mom."

Carol sat on the arm of the couch. "Hi, what's up?"

"You'll never guess who stopped by." Her mother

cleared her throat. "I'll give you a hint. He was asking about you."

"Oh, let me see. Pastor Frank, right?"

Mom giggled. "He said you've talked to him on the phone."

"Yes, Frank's checked up on me a couple of times. I have to admit; he's helped me deal with anger issues I've been holding in."

"You've had a lot of stress this past year. It's good to share your feelings with someone who understands." Her mother paused. "Since things are going better, think you and the boys can come here to celebrate Christmas?"

She hesitated. "We'd sure like to, Mom, but it's only two weeks away, and we were just there for Thanksgiving. Ethan's coming in a couple of days to stay until mid-January. He's going to help us with the move."

"I didn't expect you to come, honey, but we miss you so much, I had to try. We haven't seen Ethan for a long time."

"I'm sorry. I promise we'll visit as soon as possible."

The sound of shattering glass came from the kitchen followed by Andy's adolescent squawk. "Moth-er! I need your help in here!"

The sharp scent of pickle juice emanated into the room. Carol moaned. "Sounds like Andy made a dilly of a mess in the kitchen, Mom. I'll talk to you later. Say hi to Dad for me. Love you." She hung up and smiled. So, Frank was asking about her, huh?

CHAPTER SIX

Carol gave the pickled floor one last swipe, tossed the mountain of paper towels in the trash, and hurried to change her clothes.

"Why hasn't Grady fixed the furnace? He's the landlord." Andy huddled beneath blankets on the sofa.

"I think he had a case in court today." She turned the kitchen light off and joined Andy in the living room. "I'd call Fix-it Freddie's Heating and Cooling, but I have to get Grady's okay."

Goosebumps sprinted down her arms as she retrieved her cell to leave a voice mail for the reluctant landlord. According to the weatherman, another four inches of snow was due to hit Vermont's Green Mountains overnight. Bad timing for a broken furnace.

Andy tossed an extra blanket to her. "When are we going apartment hunting again?"

"When the weather permits. I promise." Carol leaned over and hugged him.

"I can't wait to get our own place where it's warm, and I can sleep in a real bed." He looked up and grinned. "And no Grady-Bear breathing down our necks."

She couldn't blame him. For seven months da Bear had growled about increased utility bills, their social activities, and the quality of Andy's friends. "You do realize putting a deposit on a place will take most of our savings, so our Christmas shopping will be limited."

"Me and Ethan talked about Christmas being tough this year without Dad and Jake." He rubbed his nose with a handful of blanket. "Ethan being at college is like losing another brother."

Her throat tightened. "Only a few days until he's home. How about we get a small tree and the two of you decorate the living room?"

"It won't be the same. He has his girlfriend, Rikki." Andy's damp eyes searched hers. "Everything's different this year, and I don't like it."

"Life constantly changes. I'm trying to adjust like you are, so we have to be strong for each other. Remember, I'm here anytime you need to talk."

"Yeah, Mom. I know." His teeth chattered.

A rerun of 'Chicka Chicka Boom Boom' resonated from her hip pocket. Andy put his hand over his mouth and smiled through his tears.

Carol grabbed the cap from his head, and playfully smacked his shoulder with it. "You rascal. It's Grandpa, so be quiet." She cleared her throat and answered her phone. "Hi, Dad. I'm glad you called."

Andy yelled, "Hi, Grandpa Drake!"

"Say hi to Andy for me. Listen, I know you spoke to your mom a little while ago, but I have a little problem." He hesitated. "Your Uncle Stuart's doctor said they can't put off his hip surgery any longer. It's scheduled for this month."

"That's awful."

"He'll be laid up at least six weeks." Her father took a deep breath. "I hate to ask this, but, if I pay your way, could you come help me run the flower shop?"

"What? I told Mom we wouldn't be able to come."

He laughed. "Yeah, I know, but I need Scott and June to help me fill the orders. During the Christmas rush we like to have at least two workers in the showroom. My list of dependable people is at a dead-end, and I'm desperate. If you can't come, I'll have to ask your Aunt

Penny to step in." His low groan was mournful. "Oh, Carol, the thought of my brother's wife working here makes my teeth itch. You know how we get along, and not only that, she bungles delivery addresses."

She frowned. "What about Mom and Millie?"

"Your cousin's busy working all day in the church office."

"Has Mom helped you any?"

"Let's just say it doesn't work out. I can't afford to have her in the shop. She supplements every arrangement with extra ribbon, candles, and doodads. To make matters worse, she always forgets to add sales tax."

"I totally understand. When Aunt Penny's there you lose customers, and with Mom, you lose inventory and profit. Hold on, Dad." She glanced at a nearby calendar, her mind clicking off the days of Christmas break. Her eyes met Andy's. "Wanna go to Arizona for Christmas?"

His face brightened as he nodded vigorously and gave her a thumbs-up.

Carol smiled. "We could come for two weeks while Andy's on Christmas break. Then we'll have to get him home for school."

A brief silence followed. "I wish you could be here on a permanent basis, but I appreciate any help you can give me. Maybe by January, Stuart can handle paperwork at home. Anyway, it'll be great to have you here for the holidays. I'll make arrangements for your flight. Will Ethan be coming, too?"

"I seriously doubt it, Dad. He'll want to be with Rikki. Who can compete with a girlfriend? He has a job over Christmas break, too, and he needs the money." She glanced at Andy's disappointed face. "We can leave this Saturday. Does that work?"

"Great. Thank you! A customer walked in, so I've got

to go. Love you. 'Bye.'"

"Poor Ethan's gonna miss the fun." Andy grabbed Carol's arm. "Can I go next door and tell Fuzzy about our trip?"

"Sure, but be home by five. And bundle up, it's cold."

"No colder than it is in here."

Carol rubbed her arms, returned to the thermostat, and tapped it harder. How she hated to call Grady for repairs, especially a second time. That constituted nagging to his narcissistic way of thinking. She'd either have to demand the furnace be fixed or live with terminal goose bumps until they left for Arizona.

Andy zipped his coat, put up the hood, and opened the door. "Mom, Sue's here."

"Yoo-hoo!" Sue shook a white bakery bag. "I have treats."

"Save me some!" The teen hurried out.

"In your dreams, boy." Carol swiped the bag from her friend. "You'll stay for coffee and help me eat these, right?"

"Hello, that's why I brought them." Sue chuckled. "Brr! It's cold in here. Have you been dealing with hot flashes again?"

Carol frowned in mock anger. "Susan Eulala North! Hot flashes? You brat. The furnace is out again. I've tried to contact Grady, but he hasn't returned my call."

"That's terrible. You and Andy can't live like this. I'll see something gets done." Sue rubbed her hands together. "Grady's been working late at the office and on weekends, too. Now he's home still preparing for that demanding trial. It's made him grumpier than usual, so I came here for human contact."

"Yikes! Grumpier than usual?" Was that even possible? "Is everything else okay?"

"Not really." Sue's eyes lowered. "Maybe it's my

imagination, but I've noticed signs that Grady might be fooling around. I'm pretty sure that's where the bum was over the weekend."

"Oh, Sooze. I'm sorry." Apparently her best friend hadn't been oblivious of his wandering eye after all.

"I've noticed red flags for a while, but I kept making excuses for him." Sue pounded the counter with her fist. "If I ever find out who that tramp is—" She wiped her eyes. "Will you visit me in prison?"

"I can do better than that. I'll help you dispose of her body, and we'll never speak of it again." She poured two mugs of coffee and motioned for Sue to sit at the counter. "Seriously, you're always in my prayers. I'm here if you need to talk."

"I knew you'd be there for me." She perched on a stool and reached for the creamer. "That makes me feel better, thanks."

"Speaking of being there for you—" Carol cleared her throat and sat down. "My Uncle Stu's having surgery so Dad needs my help at Floral Scent-sations for a couple of weeks." She reached into the white bag, pulled out a gingerbread man, and crunched off a spicy foot. "Sorry I won't be able to help at the bakery, but if you ever need to talk, I'm only a call away."

"Don't worry, family needs come first. Ethan and Rikki will be home by then and can take your place." Sue dunked a smiling cookie head into her coffee. "When will you leave?"

"Dad wanted me to stay six weeks, but I can only stay two since Andy has to go to school. So the plan is to leave this Saturday and be home after New Year's."

Sue finished her cookie and dabbed coffee from her chin. "Wait, I have an idea. Ethan will be staying in your apartment while you're gone, right? Andy can fly home by himself, hang out here with his brother, and go to school. We'll keep them warm, fed, and even keep an eye on Andy until Ethan goes back to college in mid-January. That gives you two extra weeks to help your dad and you can be home to see Ethan off."

"That's a great plan. You'd actually do that for me?"

Sue threw a wadded napkin at her. "Well, you offered to bury bodies for me."

"That's why we're such good friends." Carol tossed the napkin back. "As usual, you've come up with a perfect plan. What would I do without you? Andy will love having down time with his brother for a couple of weeks, especially if he can sleep in my bed." She licked her finger and dotted up cookie crumbs from the table. "Still, I need to talk it over with him. He likes to think he has a say, too. It's a man thing, ya know."

Sue grinned. "For sure. I'm going to let Grady think he came up with the idea." She glanced at her watch. "I've got errands to run and only have a short time."

"Look, I hate to mention this again since Grady's in a legal snit, but we need heat. If he can't get to it now, could he hire someone?"

"I'll tell him right away." Sue pulled the keys from her purse and strolled to the door. "See ya later."

Carol returned the creamer to the refrigerator. She wasn't the only one who grieved the loss of Jake. Andy and Ethan missed their little brother, too. They needed this together time and would require plenty of food while they took a stab at bachelorhood. She'd have to add to the grocery list and make it to the store before the weather got worse. First she needed to phone her dad with the new plan.

After the call, Carol shrugged on her heavy coat and scurried to the door. While reaching for the doorknob, her mind went to Andy. The poor kid was out of the decision loop again. She went to the table and scrawled a note. *EMERGENCY: ANDY WE NEED TO TALK.* Once the message was securely propped against the sugar bowl, she hurried out the door.

As she backed the car from the garage, large icy snowflakes hit the windshield. The second wave of the storm had arrived right on schedule.

While driving to the store, her thoughts wandered back to Sue's plan to watch over Andy. It dawned on her that she couldn't allow Grady to be in charge of her son. Maybe Fuzzy's mom would let him stay over there while Ethan was at work.

Harried shoppers crowded the aisles as Carol maneuvered her cart to the canned goods. She smiled. Great. Keano-Beanos were on sale with no purchase limit. Her boys loved them. She scooped numerous cans from the shelf and into the basket and hurried down the aisle. Andy still liked Pasta-Hoopies, even though it was beneath Ethan to partake of such childish delicacies. Once the last item was crossed off her list, she made her way to the checkout and paid for them.

Snowdrifts had formed while she shopped and traffic had nearly come to a standstill. "Dear Lord, please let Grady have the furnace running."

After thirty minutes of skidding on slick roads, she turned into the cleared driveway, pulled into the garage, and honked the horn. Hopefully Andy would help her with the groceries.

When he didn't come out, she honked again. He'd better not still be at Fuzzy's.

With a groan, Carol half-lugged and half-dragged three of the loaded plastic bags up the garage steps. When she set the groceries on the landing to open the door, Grady's deep voice thundered from the apartment. If Andy wasn't inside, she'd give in to the sudden urge to flee. Instead, her inner mama bear kicked in.

As she rushed inside, Andy bolted into the bathroom, and slammed the door.

Grady stood by the thermostat in the kitchen. "It's about time you're home, Carol." He crossed his arms and targeted her with razor-sharp eye daggers. "Maybe you can hammer a little common sense into that kid of yours."

She clenched her teeth. "What's going on?"

"It's just one of his childish moods." His eyes narrowed as he moved closer. "The boy will get over it soon enough if you don't coddle him."

Oh, how she'd love to tell the blowhard off, but that would only complicate things. Carol counted to ten as she headed to the landing to retrieve the grocery bags. "Want to help me?"

Grady followed her, grabbed two of the bags, and took them to the kitchen counter.

"Now, what happened between you and Andy?"

"I gave him the note you left on the table. He blew up when I told him we were going to babysit while you're in Arizona."

Carol clenched her fists. "Oh, Grady. You used the word babysit? No wonder he's upset." She huffed and stomped her foot. "I need to talk to him."

"Aw, let him cool down, first." Grady reached into the toolbox. "Remember, Bob's not here, so you need to step up and take charge. Andy's the child, and you're the parent. Whether he likes it or not, *you* make the decisions for him until he's an adult." He sniffed and returned to his work.

"That's right. I make the decisions for my son, not you." Grady's parenting philosophy wasn't something Andy needed to hear. Neither did she. Friend and landlord or not, his constant interference added another layer of brick to the wall between her and Andy.

Her cell sang out. She quickly turned the phone off and slipped it into her hip pocket. Grady didn't need to know any more details of her life.

She hurried to the bathroom. "Andy?"

He kicked at the door. "I'm not comin' out till he leaves."

"Impertinent brat." Grady shook his head, grunted, and began putting his tools away. "Keep the temperature below seventy. Anything else you want me to look at?"

Only a growing list, but she needed him to go. "Not this evening. Thanks for working on the furnace. I've got to fix supper." She slammed a can of Keano-Beanos on the counter.

Carol turned her back to him, hoping to expedite his departure. The can opener whirred, releasing the sweet scent. She dumped the contents into a pan and snatched a wooden spoon.

Inserting the spoon, she caught a glimpse of a suspicious clump on top of the bean pile. Her heart raced as she nudged it with the utensil. Was that pork fat? She carefully lifted the foreign object, held her breath, and looked closer. A little leg dangled in front of her nose.

Mouse!

She gasped for air as her chest tightened. The room spun into blackness as strong arms grabbed her, and for a moment she sank into the warmth of Bob's protective embrace.

Haziness slowly swirled into clarity as hot breath blew against her neck and the embrace became intense and forceful. Bob?

"Oh, Carol." Grady turned her around to face him. "We've waited a long time, baby." His beard raked against her lips like steel wool.

Fear robbed her breath. She jabbed his eye, kicked his

shin, and gave him a forceful shove. "Let go!"

Grady's face paled as he covered his eye and released a string of profanities. "You asked for it. You fell into my arms, missy." An arrogant expression appeared as he took a step toward her.

"Leave her alone!" Andy ran from the bathroom and jumped on the man's back and pounded his head.

Grady scowled as he tossed the teen to the floor and then grasped Carol's jaw. "If one word of this gets out, I'll tell Sue you came on to me." He snatched his tools and stormed from the apartment.

Andy's scrutinizing eyes focused on her. Carol tensed and reached for her son.

He sidestepped her hug, snatched his coat from the hook by the door. "How could you let this happen, Mom?"

"I didn't . . ." Her chest tightened. "Andy, we need to talk about this."

The door slammed.

CHAPTER SEVEN

Growing more impatient, Carol scraped the thick frost from the living room window with a thumbnail and continued to watch for any sign of Andy. This was the first time he'd ever run off, but with four inches of new snow, he couldn't have gone far. Helplessness seeped into her bones. She looked up. *Please keep my son safe and help him recognize this wasn't my doing.* Then wiping her eyes, she decided to give Andy another half hour before making any calls.

Her son's biting question echoed in her memory. 'How could you let this happen, Mom?' She covered her ears with her hands. Sue and Bob were always a buffer between her and Grady. She never had to deal with the brute on her own before. Grady knew Bob's death left her insecure and broken, so he made sure to take every opportunity to intimidate her.

The past year had severely stretched Andy's ability to cope, too, but this afternoon's drama had pushed him beyond that capacity. The need to move from the Norths' apartment had never been more evident.

Was there anyone at church she and Andy could feel comfortable enough to stay with until they left for Arizona? The Gordons had offered the use of their basement. She shuddered as freeze-framed images of the bean-covered mouse came to mind. Not a chance in this catawampus world would she ever consider living in a basement.

For several minutes she paced through the yellow and

white kitchen, exhaled slowly, and returned to the living room window to continue her vigil.

When the door slammed, Carol spun around and released her pent-up breath. She glanced heavenward and mouthed, "Thank You." Her mind flickered through a jumble of emotions and finally settled on gratitude mixed with irritation.

Andy marched into the room, his wet hair blown by the harsh wind. He plopped on the couch and defiantly crossed his arms.

"Where have you been?" She hurried to wrap an afghan around his shoulders. "Look at me, young man. You've been gone for over an hour and it's dark. I've been so worried." Worried? Ha! The kid had pushed her a mere eyelash away from a nervous breakdown.

Andy wiped tears away with his thumb. "I needed to talk to my dad."

She gasped as the blunt remark hit home. Her heart broke. Poor kid. "You went all the way to the cemetery in this ice and snow?" She brushed hair from his face. "That was a dangerous thing to do. What were you thinking?"

His eyes narrowed as he sprang from the couch. The afghan fell to the floor. His curt voice lashed out. "I was thinking my mother was kissing my dad's friend."

"Watch your tone." Carol lifted her chin, and met his icy scowl. "Let's get one thing straight, Andy. I did *not* come on to him. First of all, I've never liked the man. Second, Sue's my best friend, and I wouldn't hurt her for the world." The words spilled out in a rush, and her lungs drained of air. "What you saw isn't what you think."

"I know kissing and touching when I see it." He headed for the bathroom.

Before he could lock himself away, she grabbed his

coat sleeve, yanked him to the stove, and pointed to the tainted pan of beans. "I want you to understand what really happened with Grady. Take the lid off the saucepan."

Andy's eyes challenged her authority as he reached for the pan. The lid stuck for a moment then popped open. He did a double-take, gagged, and jumped back. The metal cover clattered to the floor. "Oh, man! Is that a mouse?"

"Meet Stuart Little. You know me and creepy crawlies. I passed out." She grabbed the lid and re-covered the preserved cadaver. Tears stung her eyes. "Unfortunately I was in Grady's clutches when I came to. He took advantage of the situation and kissed me. Then you walked in."

"And I thought you were . . . well, you know." Andy lowered his head and peeked at her. "Sorry, Mom."

She nodded and sealed her forgiveness with a hug.

"I can't stand that bum." Andy bared his teeth and slammed his fist on the counter. "I'd like to bash his hairy face in."

Her hand restrained his arm. "As tempting as that sounds, it won't solve anything."

Andy pulled away. His cheeks grew deep red, and his expression took on the universal teenage glare. "You keep letting him take over, and now he thinks he owns us." He huffed and planted himself on a kitchen chair.

She sat beside him and caught hold of his clenched fist. "Your dad and I always talked things over before making decisions. All these new responsibilities bogged me down, and I couldn't focus. Since Grady's our lawyer, I naturally went to him for advice."

"His advice was for us to move here, and he had to keep coming back to fix the furnace." Andy jumped up and shoved his chair against the wall. "The creep probably faked the whole thing to be with you."

"Come on, Andy. Sit down." A lump formed in her throat. *Please Lord, help me be strong for my son.* "Grady never physically came on to me before, and we were desperate to find a place to live. When they offered to let us live here rent-free, we had no choice but to grab it."

He shifted in his seat. "I wish we'd gone to a shelter instead of here."

"Don't be a smart aleck. I promise to work on being a single parent and standing on my own two feet, but don't be surprised if I make a few more mistakes along the way." She lowered her voice. "Will you be patient with me?"

"Sure, but will you let me be a part of the decision making? I'm almost sixteen."

Carol laughed. "Your birthday is several months away. What if we hold family meetings to get your input before I make any decisions?"

"Sounds good. Can I say something now?" Andy rested his elbows on his knees, hands folded. "You're not safe around Grady, and I might not be here to help you next time."

"I'll be fine. Remember he didn't get off unscathed. He has to explain his black eye to Sue." She ruffled his hair. Moving day couldn't get here soon enough. "So he probably won't bother me again."

He growled as he stood. "You're *so* getting one of those zapper things for Christmas."

Carol pulled the reluctant boy close. "I'll call Grandpa and tell him we can only stay during Christmas break, then you won't have to come home early and deal with Grady alone."

"Thanks, Mom." His shoulders relaxed, and he returned the hug. "Hey! I know. Why don't I go online and search for a place to live?"

"That's an excellent idea." She nodded to the stove. "Since you still have your shoes on and are so willing to be man of the house, please be my knight in shining armor and remove the corpse from my kitchen."

Andy laughed and lifted the pan off the stove. "Get rid of the pan and spoon, too?"

"Naturally. By the way, don't expect Keano-Beanos ever again." She tossed him the car keys. "On your way in, would you bring the rest of the groceries from the car?"

Carol eyeballed the fifteen cans of beans still sitting on the table and grimaced. So much for pinching pennies. She pushed the offending cans aside. Now to find time to return them.

Remembering a call had come earlier, Carol pulled the cell phone from her pocket and sat on the bed. Frank. Good, he left a voice mail. She hit the button.

"Carol, this is Frank Bailey." His mellow voice was comforting. *"Just calling to see how you are. Give me a buzz when you can. Bye."*

She needed a confidant to talk about what happened with Grady, but Frank Bailey was not the person. Her problem was too personal to share with anyone, especially a man she didn't know that well. Maybe she'd get enough nerve to talk to her mom when they arrived in Arizona, but for now Sue was on her mind. The future of their relationship had been severely compromised, thanks to Grady.

She had two options. Be the first to tell Sue and get the sordid truth out in the open, or keep her mouth shut and pray he had the sense to do the same. The trip to Arizona provided an opportunity to clear her head, but would Grady have the smarts to keep his trap shut while they were gone?

Thoughts of leaving Vermont for good revisited her

mind. Was it God's plan for them to stay in Arizona *permanently*? She reached for a pen and paper to make a pro/con list.

The pro list would be easy. She scratched her head and quickly jotted down:

1. Away from Grady's negative influence.
2. Permanent job at Dad's flower shop.
3. Family close by.
4. Better living arrangements.
5. No more parsonage fishbowl existence.

Now for the con list.

1. Take Andy out of school and away from his hometown.
2. Leave Sue, friends, and church family.
3. Major cost of moving.
4. Scorpions, snakes, lizards, and dealing with stern Aunt Penny.
5. Sue might perceive it as guilt.
6. Bob and Jake are buried here in Vermont.

She set her pen down. Great. That didn't help. More cons to moving than pros. She bowed her head and whispered out loud. "How can I drag Andy across country when I'm not sure it's Your will? If this is what You want us to do, could you have him suggest the move first?"

Carol put the worthless list away and a sense of relief washed over her. She pulled bread and peanut butter from the cupboard.

The door slammed. Andy kicked off his shoes, set the groceries on the counter, and pulled a snack bag from a sack. "We have more Cheddar Doodles." He tossed his coat to an easy chair in the living room.

"Yes, but don't you dare get into them until you disinfect your hands."

When Andy returned from the bathroom, they both sat

at the table. Following a short prayer, he took a bite of his sandwich. "Are you still going to work for Sue after today?"

She wrinkled her nose. "Would you?"

"Just wondered." He shrugged and chomped on a Doodle.

"It appears job hunting is in my immediate future."

"What if you can't find one?"

"Then we might have to move out of town." She grabbed a napkin and wiped orange Doodle dust from her fingers.

"Where would we go?"

"I've heard of work opportunities in Timber Falls. It's only a half-hour away." She rubbed her throbbing temples. "You sure got quiet. What are you thinking?"

"I'm sorry about our argument." Andy wiped his mouth with his hand. "You know how we're going to Arizona for Christmas?"

She glanced at her son. "Yes?"

"I've been thinkin' a lot about us living there since Pastor Frank mentioned it at Thanksgiving. You could work at Grandpa's flower shop full time."

Carol's jaw slacked, and her heart beat a little faster. This had to be divine direction. She hadn't expected it to come so quickly.

"Everything around town reminds me of Dad and Jake, and it makes me sad." Andy stared at his hands. "We had to move out of our house, Grady's taking over our lives, and I'm so over using the couch for a bed."

"Do you realize what a move like that means? A new school, new friends?"

"Yeah, I know, but nobody wants to hang out with me anymore. Even Tank and Schwartzy treat me different. Might as well make new friends." He turned to face her. "Think about it, Mom. It also means no more Grady.

Besides, Grandma and Grandpa are gettin' old. They probably need our help."

"They aren't ancient." Her snicker triggered a snort. "They're only in their early sixties."

"That's what I'm sayin'. So what do you think about moving?"

"For your first man-of-the-house decision, it's a pretty big one. I asked God to help both of us be willing to leave Powder Ridge if that's His will."

The boy grinned broadly, and his eyes brightened. "Guess we're gonna move."

"Guess so." She glanced at her wedding ring. They'd buried Bob and Jake less than a year ago. Andy still felt the need to run to his dad's grave this afternoon. Could they honestly let go of their loved ones and move across the country? *Dear Lord, forgive my doubt and insecurity, but may I have one more sign, in black and white so I don't miss it?*

By eight-thirty, Carol's shifting emotions had produced a tension headache. While Andy showered, she put things in the cupboard and tidied the apartment. On her way to the living room, she noticed one of his gloves at the front door, and next to it was an unaddressed envelope.

She was still holding the letter when Andy emerged from the bathroom.

"I'm still hungry, Mom." He ran his hand through his wet hair. "Can I finish the Cheddar Doodles while we watch my movie?"

"Of course. By the way, you dropped these by the door." She handed him both items.

"The glove's mine, but the letter isn't." He gave it back

and headed for the kitchen.

Carol tossed the unopened envelope on her dresser. Andy witnessed Grady coming on to her, but he didn't need any more information. She joined him in the living room to watch the latest space alien movie.

While he was glued to the raucous sci-fi adventure, questions about that note swirled in her mind. Not hers, not Andy's. Who else had been there? Grady. Maybe he'd dropped a love letter to or from a girlfriend. Her stomach curled. Or, what if he returned and left a threat? No, a lawyer would be smarter than that. More likely a plea bargain.

The next two hours were miserable. No matter how hard she tried to garner interest in Martians with laser guns, her mind kept darting to the letter. Curiosity trumped fear. She had to know what was inside.

"That was the best movie ever." Andy reached for his soft drink can. "Did you see when he dropped the Alpha Gamma Ray Spectrometer?"

"Yes, that was exciting." Carol handed him the empty snack bag. "Let's clean this place up before we have devotions and go to bed."

"Go to bed? How am I supposed to sleep after watching a Kelly Quasar movie?" He gulped the last of his drink. "Can you imagine if da Bear had X-ray vision?"

"Thanks a lot. That pretty much spoils my sleep, too." Carol turned from him. She'd try to avoid nightmares of her grizzly landlord with spinning X-ray eyeballs.

"Sorry, Mom. Why do you think Sue married him, anyway?"

"Love is blind, Andy. Grady wasn't as outspoken and rude when she met him in college. Hurry and brush the orange crud from your teeth. I'll get the Bible and study booklet."

When their short Bible study was over, Andy prayed

for the Lord's leading in their future. An overwhelming peace filled her heart. Regardless of Grady's comment, Bob would be pleased the boy was off to a good start on his road to manhood.

Following goodnight hugs, Carol trudged to her bedroom to face the letter. Her eye twitched as she ripped the envelope open and saw Sue's slanted handwriting.

Carol, what have you done? Grady confessed your growing attraction to each other, but I couldn't believe it. Now I find you're the one who's been having an affair with him. I understand you're still mourning the loss of Bob, but how could you betray me?

We've been best friends for over twenty years. Your Ethan and our Erika plan to be engaged soon, and we often dreamed of sharing grandchildren. When Bob died, Grady and I graciously took you and Andy in when you had no place to go. We even supported both of you by giving you jobs in lieu of rent.

You've ruined my marriage, compromised the relationship of our children, and shaken my faith in God. It's time you leave. I never want to see or hear from you again.

After rereading the letter, it fell to the floor. Totally on impulse, Carol hurried to the living room. Even if this was the black and white sign she'd prayed for, she still needed to convince Sue that she was not Grady's lover. "Andy, I need to check on something. I'll be back in a few minutes."

She inhaled deeply and left the apartment, her mind set on the mission. Her knees shook and arrhythmic heartbeats banged against her ribs as she pounded on the Norths' door.

A smirking Grady answered and stood with his arms crossed.

"I want to see Sue." She found the courage to raise her eyes to his.

"Sue wants nothing to do with you." His hand roughly squeezed her face as he lowered his voice. "And neither do I."

With stiffened shoulders, Carol applied the sternest voice she could muster. "Your wife needs to know the truth!"

"You and the kid have one week to vacate the premises." The door shut.

Taking the stairs two at a time, she entered the apartment and tiptoed to her bedroom.

She dropped to her bed in stunned silence as disbelief, followed by grief swirled around her. She rocked back and forth. "I've lost my best friend, Father. I never dreamed confirmation of our move would come like this." She wiped her eyes. "But now I'm sure of Your will. Prepare us for what's ahead."

CHAPTER EIGHT

Apache Pointe, Arizona

MILLIE DRAKE HUMMED *GOOD KING WENCESLAS* and plugged in a ceramic Christmas tree. A pine candle flickered in the window adding the festive ambience she wanted for the church office. She held up a spray of mistletoe her mother suggested she hang over the old copier. Too obvious. Where could she put it without appearing as desperate as she felt? After scanning the room and not finding a better place, she schlepped to the closet to get a stepstool.

Once the sprig of hope was tacked in place, she returned the stool and wondered if Pastor Frank was her true destiny as Mother maintained. Millie glanced at the clock. She had time to read another chapter of her romance novel before he got to the office. She removed her red-rimmed glasses, huffed on the lenses, and cleared every smudge with a tissue.

"Oh, my darling," *Lady Ashley whispered as Sir Stone came ever closer, prepared to slay dragons for her honor. She would be safe from the dastardly Duke's vile plans.*

Millie licked her finger and quickly flipped the page.

Sir Stone released her shackles and Lady Ashley flung herself against his armored torso. His breathing was ragged as he lifted her effortlessly into his arms. She swooned—

The office phone's shrill ring caused Millie to nearly swallow her Sassy Lassie breath mint. Her book tumbled from her hands and knocked over the paper clip box. She pushed the mound of fasteners aside, and managed to answer the phone on the fourth ring.

"Apache Pointe Community Church. This is Millie Drake. How may I help you?"

A harsh voice answered. "Millicent, this is your mother. I'm so mad I could spit nails."

Millie sighed, scooped the paper clips up, and dropped them into the box. "So, what did Dad do this time?"

"I'll get to that later. First of all, your cousin Carol is coming tomorrow."

"I know. She's going to help Uncle Max in the shop while Dad recovers from surgery."

"You don't understand. She and Andy are moving to Arizona . . . *permanently*."

Millie squealed. "She is? That's wonderful. What's the problem?" She sketched a heart on a sheet of paper, and added her name to Pastor Frank's in a decorative flair.

"I swear! You're forty-two years old and don't have the good sense God gave a stump, Millicent. Don't you think she'll horn in on your chances with Pastor Frank? Of course she will."

"What makes you say that, Mother? Bob hasn't been gone a year yet. I seriously doubt if she's looking." Millie took a deep breath. "Now what did Dad do?"

Her mother's voice lowered. "Millicent, you know I'm the paragon of hospitality, however, your father invited Carol and Andy to live with us until she finds a place of her own."

"Uh-oh. You've never cared for her, have you?" She drew curlicues and flowers around the Frank and Millie Bailey names. "Remember she's family."

"Be that as it may, when Pastor Frank comes to woo you, she'll be right there working her womanly wiles."

"Woo me? Oh, Mother, from your mouth to God's ear."

She studied her caricature of Pastor Frank standing under the mistletoe. The forehead was a little too pronounced.

"I don't mean to be prickly, but Carol's always showed you up with her pert little smile and perfectly straight teeth. You mark my words. She'll be flashing those pearly whites and ruin everything—and just when you almost have him in your hip pocket. What crummy timing."

"Carol and I have always been best friends. She'd never do anything to hurt me."

Her mother laughed. "She's flirty like Tawny Lamour on *Crest of Love*." Her voice jumped half an octave. "Don't you realize she'll leave you eating her dust? Of course she will."

"This isn't a soap opera, and besides, she's nothing like Tawny. I've got to go. Pastor Frank pulled into the parking lot." She quickly folded the paper with the name doodles and slid it to the side.

"Pinch your cheeks, dear. Suck in your stomach and compliment the man."

Millie rolled her eyes and cleared her throat. "'Bye, Mother."

Pastor Frank stopped at her desk, balancing a tray of two coffee cups on his day planner.

The aroma of mint chocolate and coffee tickled her nose. Her heart soared. He remembered her favorite. She licked her lips, sucked in her stomach, and swiveled her chair to face the object of her affection. Remain shy and demure like Mother said.

"Good morning, Pastor Frank." She pointed to his tartan plaid tie. "What a dashing Christmas tie. Is it new?"

"It's a couple years old." He set the cardboard tray on her desk.

Millie ripped a sticky-note off the computer screen and waved it in the air. "Miranda Blevins canceled her appointment at ten."

"She said that might happen." Pastor Frank looked at the clock. "I could've stayed longer with Pastor Russ at Java Joe's this morning. Here, I have something for you." He took a cup from the tray and offered it to her. "I felt guilty about all the extra work I piled on you this week, so I bought you a Mint Chocchiato with extra foam."

"Thank you. How thoughtful. This will taste great with the sugar cookies you brought in yesterday." When she reached for the Java Joe's cup, the doodle paper fell to the floor. She gasped as it wafted to the preacher's shoe. Her face warmed, and her brain screamed, don't look at it . . . don't look at it.

Pastor Frank leaned down to retrieve the paper and placed it on his planner. "Hey! The New Year's Eve party is coming up. You wanna go?"

Millie's heart soared at the implication. At long last, the handsome prince asked her out. Frank stood at the desk waiting for a reply as the wedding march pounded in her skull.

"Millie? Are you okay?"

Her tongue froze to the roof of her mouth. Fortunately, she managed a stiff nod.

"It'll be fun. Our copier guy, Lou Blythe, and his quartet will be singing." Frank's white teeth sparkled against his deeply tanned face.

Millie squirmed and eyeballed her confidential sketches still in his possession. He'd see her doodles! Her heart went into explode mode as the pastor picked up his coffee cup and started for his office with her paper. She shot up from her chair and headed his way. "Wait! My notes."

"What notes?"

"The paper you picked up." Her itching fingers snatched the self-incriminating material from the top of his planner. Did he notice the elaborate calligraphy? "This is mine." Triumphant relief surged through her, making her knees go weak. She plopped into her chair.

"Sorry. I'll be in my office. Enjoy your Chocchiato."

She stuffed the folded paper into her novel. "By the way, the copier's messed up again."

"Maybe it's time to think about getting a new one. Why don't you call Lou, and let me know when he gets here."

Millie waited for his door to close before retrieving the treasured paper. She would've absolutely died had he caught sight of the artwork. She flipped the switch to the shredder and inserted the paper into its grinding teeth.

Pastor Frank could be described in a single four-letter word. HUNK. She loved how his deep penetrating eyes crinkled when he smiled. His dark brown hair, lightly graying at the temples, gave him an air of wisdom. She hugged herself and grinned. Mother was right. No other man enhanced a golf shirt better.

He'd been widowed for two years and Millie, like every other single woman within a fifty-mile radius, did her best to win his heart.

However, she had a definite advantage. She worked side-by-side with him in the church office. Mother said he was only being coy because he'd ignored her availability thus far. Maybe he needed more time.

Millie, happy her work was finished for the moment, carefully removed the plastic lid from the steaming Java Joe's cup and waited for the repairman. Was there anything more soothing than reading a good novel while sipping a Mint Chocchiato from the man you love? Absolutely not.

The front door groaned open right as she'd reached the middle of the chapter. Lou Blythe, the six-foot repairman, entered the office and approached her desk. She'd never noticed how the navy-colored uniform accentuated his blue eyes.

His deep bass voice greeted her. "Morning, Miss Drake." He set his tool case on the floor and cracked his knuckles.

Millie offered a smile. She'd grown accustomed to his face turning beet red when he spoke to her. "Good morning, Lou. I'm sorry we have to keep calling you."

"Bet you're tired of seeing my ugly mug, aren't you?" He ran his fingers through his dark brown hair and glanced away.

She hated when he put himself down. Lou might not be overly handsome with his prominent brow and low hairline, but he certainly didn't scorch the retinas, either.

"Don't say that! But come to think of it, maybe we should put you on retainer." Millie motioned to the adjoining room. "You know where the copier is."

As Lou walked to the room her stomach dropped. The mistletoe. Would he think it was there for him? Her brain skipped into fantasy mode. She envisioned the repairman's lips in a pucker as he scooped her into his sinewy arms. Pastor Frank, dressed in shining armor, would ride up on his ever-faithful steed and snatch her away to safety. Her unfurled locks flowed as the gallop of hoof beat—

The galloping grew louder and brought her out of the trance. What? Hoof beats? She sighed. Only the copier's death rattle.

The machine's cover snapped open as she alerted Pastor Frank of Lou's arrival. She loitered around the corner of the copy room. Would her name come up in their conversation?

The pastor spoke first. "Hey, Lou. Is it time to get a

new copier?"

"In all honesty"—Lou's deep voice answered—"this old gal needs to be put out of her misery. It's getting hard to find parts for her."

"You're a fair businessman. I trust your judgment."

"We've got some real beauts at the shop."

"Speaking of beauts—" Pastor Frank lowered his voice, and Millie leaned closer, straining to hear. "Any progress on the lady we discussed earlier?"

"Not yet, sir." Lou cleared his throat. "I plan to take your advice, though."

"Good. I'm sure everything will work out. Just between the two of us, maybe you could help me pray for a gal I'm interested in."

The repairman chuckled. "Will do."

Millie's mind whirled. Pastor Frank was genuinely interested in her. She'd heard it with her own two ears. No more wishing, hoping, and praying. Better call Mother with the news when Pastor Frank went for lunch . . . unless he asked her to join him today.

The cover to the machine snapped shut bringing Millie out of her euphoric jubilation. She scampered to her chair and pretended to be occupied with a stack of paperwork.

Pastor Frank led the repairman to her office. "Millie?"

She raised her head. "Yes?"

"Could we interrupt you for a moment? Lou needs to talk to you about a new copier." He put his hand on Lou's shoulder. "Why don't you grab a cup of coffee from the break room first, and Millie, maybe you could share those Christmas cookies?"

Lou smiled and set his tool box down. "It won't take long, Miss Drake."

"Please call me Millie." Her eyes gravitated to his dimples, so deep a girl could get lost in them. She took a sip of Chocchiato. Dimples-schimples. Frank was finally showing interest in her, and she wasn't about to be diverted by such frivolity. Besides, Mother would flip if she lost Frank to the pack of wild spinsters nipping at his heels.

"I'll get my coffee and then ask you a few questions." He cracked his knuckles. "Would you like some, too, umm, Millie?"

She held up her Java Joe's cup. "No, thank you. I'm good."

Pastor Frank waited until Lou was out of earshot. "I'd like that project finished this afternoon." Then he winked and placed a sprig of mistletoe on her desk. "By the way, we found this on the copier."

He winked at her! A power surge revved Millie's pulse as she mentally reeled her chin from the floor. The afterglow of his attention had her fidgeting in the chair. She pulled herself together long enough to throw him a demure smile. "I'll make copies of your project this morning if the copier works. Don't forget Uncle Max needs me to help at the flower shop this afternoon."

"That's fine. Reverend Foster is going to call, so I'll answer the phone." Frank stopped at the office door and turned. "You and Lou are on your own."

Lou returned with his coffee and sat near her desk. "Before we get started, I wondered if you were going to the New Year's Eve party."

Ha! A pack of wild pigs couldn't keep her away. "This will be my first time. My cousin, Carol, is coming with me." Her face warmed. "I hear you're going to be there."

"Yeah, my quartet's singing a medley. We have to go early to set up."

She sipped her minty drink. "I look forward to hearing your group."

"Is it okay if I save a table for you near the stage?"

"That would be great." Millie nodded as an epiphany hit. Everyone would see she was Pastor Frank's chosen, and then Lou and Carol would connect. He was kind of cute, with those dimples and all. She loved when plans came together.

Later that day, Millie rubbed her ankle as the last customer left the flower shop. "I'm exhausted, Uncle Max. I'm glad Carol is coming tomorrow to take my place."

"That large delivery from Clements' Kaleidoscope of Blooms kept you working like a one-toothed beaver all afternoon." Max Drake locked the front door to Floral Scent-sations and returned to his niece. "I'll clean up, so why don't you go ahead and leave? I appreciate you standing in for your Dad."

"Happy to help."

"I know working both jobs hasn't been easy for you." He kissed her forehead. "Thanks again."

Millie's feet ached as she drove home. She couldn't wait to get her legs elevated and return to that steamy romance novel, *A Snowy Knight Surprise.* With a hot cup of chamomile tea in hand, she hobbled to her bedroom with thoughts of the cookies Pastor Frank shared last week. She smiled and pulled the zippered bag from her nightstand. Two left. Perfect.

The fringed pillows had to be just right before she could comfortably escape into a world of passion and romance—which had been denied her in real life. Millie envisioned Pastor Frank as the virile answer to a damsel's wish and, oddly enough, she was the meek recipient of his affection. She bit the cookie, snuggled deep into the large pillow, and removed the laminated photo of the handsome preacher used as a bookmark. Before long she was immersed in the stimulating plot.

Sir Stone's husky voice called, "Be that ye, Lady Ashley?" He paused at the door. "Come hither, into the light, lass."

Lady Ashley emerged from the shadows. "I have naught else to give thee for thy chivalrous rescue but Cristes Maesse pudding and nog. Dost thou approve?"

"Oh, Lady Ashley, 'tis most splendid!"

"I'm pleased thou liketh it." She looked into his deep brown eyes, windows to his soul.

"Verily I loveth it." His firm lips covered hers. "And by my troth I loveth thee, too."

Millie turned the page, her pulse racing. Why couldn't men talk like that today? So passionate and alluring. She hugged the romance novel tightly to her chest and envisioned herself being swept into Friar Frank's smothering embrace.

Her mind popped out of the medieval reverie. Maybe by this time next year, she would be Mrs. Rev. Frank Bailey.

CHAPTER NINE

"Thank you for your order, Mr. Wilcox. We'll have it delivered by tomorrow morning." Carol placed the receiver on the old wall-mounted phone. In her first two hours at the family-owned flower shop, she'd processed at least fourteen Christmas orders.

Finally, a lull in the telephone activity gave her time to price the countless packages of mistletoe. She held up a crinkly cellophane package. Bob used to bring sprigs home every year to hang them in the most unpredictable places. How she missed his kisses under each one. A flurry of loneliness returned as if on automatic rewind.

"Sounds like we've had a lot of phone calls. I hope they were all orders." Dad checked the sales book. "Did you and Andy get settled in at Penny's last night?"

She forced a smile. "Let's say she took a stab at being pleasant while reciting her list of rules and regulations. We'll do our best to keep on her good side. Breakfast wasn't fun, so we're going to eat our meals here. *Please* be on the lookout for another place for us."

"I will. In the meantime, you and Andy will eat your suppers with us. You hear? We'd better get back to work." He kissed her cheek and returned to the workroom.

The little bell over the shop door jingled. Carol looked up as a familiar face with an irresistible grin came her way. Feathery laugh lines crinkled at the corners of his brown eyes.

She pushed the heaping box of mistletoe aside and

returned his smile. "Good to see you again, Pastor Frank."

"Welcome to Apache Pointe, Carol." His baritone voice was rich and powerful. "Why don't you call me Frank like you do on the phone?"

"I thought it might sound better to be formal in public."

"Maybe you're right, but when it's just us . . ." His eyes went to the door of the adjoining workroom where Carol's father stood. "Oh, hi, Max."

"Hey there, Pastor. Thought I heard your voice." He went to the refrigerated case and added a festive red and white arrangement. "I'll bet you're here to pick up the usual Christmas gift for your mother-in-law, right?"

"Yes and no. She's visiting her sister in California, so I'll order two and have you send them there." He winked at Carol. "I need help picking out a couple of smaller ones for my daughters, too. Unfortunately, neither of them can make it home for Christmas."

Max shook his head. "Anything wrong?"

"Lisa's baby, Shea, has chicken pox. My youngest daughter, Gwen, works at a hospital and can't get this holiday off."

"A double whammy. That's too bad." Max slipped his arm around Carol's shoulder and squeezed. "Gotta get to work, so I'll leave you in this pretty lady's capable hands."

"Catch you later." Pastor Frank turned to Carol. "I want something to make my girls ashamed for leaving me alone on Christmas." He laughed. "I'm not talking Jewish mother guilt, but maybe a planter with sad, puppy dog eyes?"

She snickered. "A little parental persuasion never hurts, does it? You're a man after my own heart."

His chocolate-brown eyes twinkled with humor. "I'm

glad you identify with my plight."

"My oldest son is home from college. He plans to enjoy Christmas vacation with his soon-to-be fiancée and her family."

"Life changes, doesn't it?" He picked up four cards. "Is the planter from the church ready for Stuart? I'm headed to the hospital next."

"It is. I used the ceramic Model T Uncle Stu loves."

"Great choice." He signed the cards.

Max brought in a brightly wrapped package and set it on the glass counter. "Here's a box of Stu's favorite candy to go with his flowers. It's to help him take advantage of the peace and quiet at Apache Pointe Memorial. Penny doesn't need to know." He looked out the front window. "Uh-oh. Speaking of trouble."

Penny's imposing figure loomed at the door. The sequined black outfit accentuated the lines of her square body, and her maroon-colored hair was meticulously piled on top of her head. The heels of her black shoes pounded like a judge's gavel as she stormed into the shop three steps behind her hearty cologne.

Max slipped the chocolates to Frank. "Carol, my love, you help the pastor." His voice was barely above a whisper. "I'll take one for the team."

Penny's eyes lit behind her red-framed glasses when she noticed Frank. "How nice to see you, Pastor." She forced her way between the clergyman and Carol. "My Millicent was thrilled you bought her a Mint Chocchiato. You're such a dear man."

With a hand on his sister-in-law's sequined sleeve, Max pulled her aside. "Can I help you, Penny?"

"I need a centerpiece for the family Christmas dinner." Penny shot a scalding glance Carol's way. "She said she'd pick something out, but, you know."

Max pasted on a plastic smile. "You'd rather pick it

out yourself, right?"

"No offense, Carol dear." Penny turned to Pastor Frank and smiled like a used car salesman about to seal the deal. She leaned close, her perfume as disagreeable as her temperament. "Too bad my Millicent isn't here to help me. Her taste is impeccable."

Pastor Frank coughed and took a step back. "I hear Stuart will be released in a couple of days. I'll bet you'll be glad to have him home."

"As long as he doesn't want me to fetch and carry 24/7." A quick uneasy laugh followed. "He told me you accepted the invitation to our Christmas dinner. We'll expect you promptly at five o'clock."

"I'll be there."

The unflappable woman deposited her purse on the counter. "Now, Maxwell, about my centerpiece. I want blushing poinsettias, not the common red this time."

"Whatever you want, *Penelope*."

Frank's gaze returned to Carol, and he offered a pained smile. "Do you have a catalog so I can choose arrangements for my girls?"

"There's one over here." She led him to the far counter while Penny ripped fern filler from a sample display, scattering the narrow leaves on the floor.

Carol opened the large book and turned it his way. "First, thanks for the call last week." She kept her voice soft. "So many things needed my attention right then, I couldn't find time to get back to you."

"That's okay. We'll chat more often since you've moved here."

She raised an eyebrow. "I'll need a break from you-know-who once in a while."

"Outings it is!" The minister kept his laughter low and pointed to his choice of flower arrangements. "Let's get three of these and that one for Barb's mom."

After quickly writing the order, she nodded in her aunt's direction and shrugged. "I'm sorry Aunt Penny's so harsh. We're always dodging barbs, but she's family."

"Actually, it's my third invitation, and I ran out of excuses." Frank shook his head and handed her a credit card. "Besides, Stuart invited me, and who can say no to him?"

"Maybe it won't be too bad if you come prepared to talk about sports and cars with Andy." Carol grinned. "Mom and I will try our best to keep the ladies talking about their romance novels or soap operas. In other words, we'll have your back."

The tenderness of his smile suggested interest. "You're going to be there, too?"

She crossed her eyes. "I live there." Her face warmed as she returned his card. "My role in this family is to be the buffer between Mom and Penny, so my presence is in great demand."

"Entertainment, too." Frank released a lighthearted chuckle. "Now, I can honestly say I'm looking forward to this shindig."

Her eyes widened. "Shh! She'll hear you."

"I'm on my way to the hospital. See ya later." He took the planter and candy, then left.

All it took was a simple, brief encounter for joy to bubble inside Carol once more. Her smile faded as Aunt Penny's scowl produced an early frost in the room.

The older woman pursed her lips and raised her voice in the vacant shop. "I've taken the liberty of setting an appointment for you to see an apartment at noon. Here's the address. You will try to be on time, won't you?" She shook the paper for emphasis and laid it on the counter. "Of course you will."

CHAPTER TEN

The aroma of roasting turkey filled Penny's kitchen and made Carol's mouth water. She put an arm around her petite mom as her aunt dipped the edge of a spoon into the fruit salad. She tasted it and promptly turned up her nose.

The angry woman dropped the deli container on the island. "Millicent and I prepared an elegant Christmas meal, and *you* have the audacity to bring a chintzy salad from Dandy Dan's?"

Sylvia's face flushed as she bit her lower lip. "I brought it for Stu. He says it's his favorite, and he never gets it at home." She closed the cabinet door a little too forcefully.

Great. Carol winced. It only took one shot from Penny's verbal arsenal to turn her good-natured mom into a door slammer.

She slowly poured pepper into a crystal shaker which produced three successive sneezes.

Penny turned to Carol. "Don't just stand there depositing your germs everywhere. Take the dishes and help Millicent set the table. By the way, put the plastic one where your Mother sits. It's only fair, since she broke my good China plate last year, and now I don't have enough."

A cabinet door banged.

Carol retrieved the floral dishes and eyed the pink child's plate. "Look, Mom, it's Benny Bunny. I haven't seen this in years. May I use it for old-time's sake?"

"Be my guest."

Penny's resounding grunt came from behind them.

Millie carried the tray of crystal goblets, silverware, and folded lace-trimmed napkins. "Come on, Carol. Let's set the table."

On the heels of her cousin, Carol scurried out of the viper's den and into the Victorian-inspired dining room. She drew in a deep breath. The mauve flowers on the wallpaper matched the crushed velvet draperies and linen tablecloth.

"Nice to see Aunt Penny's mellowed over the years." She kept her voice low and positioned the bunny plate. "At least she's going to let Mom sit at the big girl table."

"That's only for Pastor Frank's benefit."

"I'm sorry you and Uncle Stu have to put up with so much drama."

"I love my mother. I do." Millie set the tray down and placed a goblet at each setting. "But living here is beyond stressful."

"I don't know how you do it. I've been here less than a week, and my other eye has developed a major tick, too." Carol laid a comforting hand on her cousin's arm. "You definitely need your own place, Mills."

"I'm trying to save up enough money." Millie exhaled and arranged the over-sized blushing poinsettia centerpiece.

"After Andy and I move out, you can crash at our place when things get too hairy here. I promise not to decorate with anything pink or ruffled."

"And nix on doilies, wallpaper, and beadwork. Bless your heart, Carol. I'll look forward to that." She set the napkins beside the plates. "We were close when we were young, weren't we? I've really missed you."

Carol nodded and followed with the silverware. "Remember the time we glued the last three pages of your mom's novel together?"

"She was seething." Millie covered her mouth and laughed. "It's been thirty years, and she *still* brings it up. Speaking of novels, you can borrow mine any time."

"I don't know." What could she say that wouldn't hurt Millie's feelings? "Are they like your mother's?"

"Yeah, she passes them down to me. We have stacks of romantic pulsators."

"No thanks, Mills, I don't care for that kind of story. Bodice rippers pulsate a little too much."

Millie toyed with the lace of her napkin. "I've never had that passion in real life, so I live it through those stories."

"I'm sorry, but you deserve more than a fairy tale. I'll help you pray that God brings a special man into your life."

Millie managed a timid smile. "There is someone. He's asked me to our church's New Year's Eve party." Her face reddened. "It's our first date, and I'd rather not tell Mother yet. She'll embarrass me and scare him off."

Carol quietly clapped. "That's wonderful. I promise not to say anything."

"The party isn't too formal, but I don't have a pretty outfit to wear, and shopping's not my strong point. Would you help me choose something? I'm tired of dressing like Mother."

The Hallelujah Chorus reverberated in Carol's mind. "Why don't we make a day of it? Next Saturday?"

"How exciting. Sounds fun." Millie cleared her throat. "Maybe one more favor? I'm meeting my date there, so would you go to the party with me for moral support? I'm so nervous."

"Me? I've been gone for so long I wouldn't know anyone. You'd be off with your fella, and leave me sitting alone to stuff my face with pigs-in-a-blanket."

"That's not going to happen. You're so outgoing, people naturally gravitate to you."

"Sure. I'll go with you."

Millie squared her shoulders and nodded to the kitchen. "Ready for round two?"

Carol rose from her chair. "Sounds like the chaos has settled between our mothers. Matter of fact, it's too quiet. Let's check for casualties." She expected frostbite when she entered the kitchen's icy atmosphere. Their mothers worked in opposite corners of the room, their backs turned to each other.

Hating to break the silence, Carol picked up a serving bowl. "Would you like me to put the sweet potatoes in here, Aunt Penny?" She clenched her teeth, placed the bowl on the counter, and closed her eyes. Uh-oh. How could she forget the semi-annual tuber debate? The yam-bomb had been dropped and would detonate in three . . . two . . . one . . .

On cue, Penny spun around, hand on her hip. "Yams, Carol. You *know* they're yams."

"Who cares?" Sylvia, brandishing a stick of butter, turned to her sister-in-law. "For Pete's sake, Penny, let it go."

Max poked his head into the kitchen. "Hey, will you gals quit yer yammering? We hear you all the way in the family room." He winked at Carol. "Yammer, get it? Good one, huh?"

Amazed at her dad's kamikaze pluck, Carol quickly shooed him to safety as her aunt reached for an unpeeled sweet potato—or was it a yam? Either way, flinging tubers would definitely put a damper on their holiday merriment.

"Millicent, after you finish the mashed potatoes, put them into the large poinsettia bowl. Sylvia, your fruity stuff can go in my pretty crystal bowl. At least it'll look decent."

The food was arranged per Penny's directives. She removed her pink and purple plaid apron and sashayed into the dining room. "Stuart, you sit at your usual spot at the head of the table. I'll be on your right and, Millicent, dear, you sit next to our esteemed guest, Pastor Frank." She stood and headed for the kitchen. "I smell the dinner rolls."

A sly smile adorned Sylvia's lips as she hurried to complete the seating arrangements. "Andy, stay there and I'll sit beside you." Her voice was meek, but firm. "Max, darling, you sit on the other side of Andy, which leaves Carol next to me."

With the precious bunny plate in hand, Carol changed places with her father. Once seated, she glanced up, and a pleasant jolt surged through her. Pastor Frank sat directly across the table. Sylvia patted her hand.

Oh, her mom was good.

Millie squirmed when her mother insisted everyone hold hands while Pastor Frank returned thanks. She'd never held his hand before, but it felt so right. Her heart quickened, and she was afraid of passing out. Was she experiencing early onset vapors like Miss Charlotte in *Yankee of My Heart?*

Following the prayer, Pastor Frank released her hand and unfolded his napkin. "I really appreciate the invitation. I wasn't looking forward to spending Christmas alone." He took the poinsettia bowl from Millie's shaking hands. "Everything smells so good."

"Thank you." Penny beamed as the pastor plopped a heaping scoop of mashed potatoes onto his plate. "I must say, Millicent has whipped those potatoes to perfection, like always."

Could her mother be any more obvious? Heat rose in Millie's face as she rearranged the food on her plate. Her stomach churned like a cement mixer as Frank and Carol chatted across the table. They had so many things in common. *She'd* been a pastor's wife, and both were widowed. Carol was so pretty and friendly, why wouldn't Frank like her?

As if reading her thoughts, Penny nudged her arm and nodded toward the couple. "See?" she whispered. "Tawny Lamour."

A lump of turkey lodged in Millie's throat. Mother was right. Frank couldn't keep his eyes off Carol. How could she break into their conversation? Surely she could do better than shop talk like Mother mentioned. Her cheeks warmed as a horrible awareness hit. She had nothing to say.

Her mother leaned close to whisper in her ear. "Speak up." Another nudge. "They're talking about coffee. Mention Java Joe's."

Millie straightened in her seat and took a deep breath. "I-I-I'm-fond-of-Java-Joe's." She cringed at the monotone uttering. Silence. Would anyone notice if she slid under the table? She peeked at her mother, whose eyes pierced her soul.

Frank's face crinkled in a smile. "Java Joe's is good, but Chug-a-Mug's closer for me." His attention returned to Carol. "They have two outstanding holiday flavors, eggnog and gingerbread. I'll take you there sometime."

Every Drake head turned to Penny as her scowl deepened.

Max cleared his throat. "Hey, Stu, we got a double shipment of mistletoe from Clements'. Any ideas what we should do with the rest of it?"

With a playful grin, Andy asked, "How long does the mistletoe magic last?"

Carol laid her fork down. "And you're asking this because?"

"C'mon, Mom, I'm fifteen. I need to know this stuff."

Frank winked at Carol. "Yeah, Mom, inquiring minds want to know."

"Andy's posed a legitimate question." Stuart took a drink. "Legend is every time a young man kisses his girl, he pulls off a berry. When the berries are gone, so is the magic." He grinned. "How many cases should we put you down for, son?"

Millie lowered her eyes. She'd love to get her first kiss under the mistletoe. How romantic. Frank's strong arms would pull her close and send operatic arias rushing through her veins. The kiss, surprisingly gentle. He'd raise his mouth from hers and gaze deep into her soul before going for that second and maybe third mistletoe berry.

"Millie?"

"Huh? I mean, yes?" Millie turned toward the pastor.

"Would you have your mother pass the sweet potatoes, please?"

Again, heads turned to Penny as her obstinate streak broke surface. She lowered her red-rimmed glasses to make her not-so-subtle point. "Yams, Pastor. They're *yams.*"

"I stand corrected." Frank grinned and straightened his shoulders. "Would you pass them, please?" He winked at Carol.

He was flirting with her. Millie's mouthful of turkey disintegrated into sawdust. How could he? Right here at her parents' Christmas table, and with the whole family watching? At least good ol' Carol had the decency not to respond. Did mother see that wink?

Her mother's dramatic scowl peered over her red-framed glasses.

Question answered.

With a huff, Penny reached for the bowl and thrust it into Millie's hand. "Here." Then, her frown converted into a crooked smirk as she looked at the clergyman. "Don't you think my daughter will make a wonderful wife someday, Pastor Frank? But of course you do."

His fingers touched Millie's hand when he took the bowl. "I do."

Millie's breath caught at the two magic words. This time next year, she'd hear them again—at the altar. A bevy of butterflies went into a Flamenco frenzy in her stomach.

He spooned the orange vegetable onto his plate. "With her pretty eyes, she'll have the lucky guy wrapped around her pinkie in no time."

Penny's smile oozed satisfaction as she peered at Sylvia.

Face burning with embarrassment, Millie lowered her head. As long as the family pit bull was in the picture, any chance of significant pinkie wrapping was nil. Wait, Frank said she had pretty eyes. She smiled and popped a bite of roll into her mouth and resisted the urge to bat her lashes in the pastor's direction.

Her dad relaxed in the chair and patted his belly. "I'm about ready for a large piece of mincemeat pie and a mound of my canned whipped cream."

"Sounds good." Sylvia nodded. "Holiday desserts are my favorite. Why don't we start clearing the table?"

Penny wiped her mouth with a cloth napkin and nodded in Frank's direction. The only sound was his fork clicking on the china plate. They all watched as his lips slowly surrounded the final yam bite.

"Now that everyone's finally done, we'll have dessert."

Penny stood. "Sylvia, you and Carol take the plates to the kitchen, and I'll bring in the pies." Her voice became more rigid. "Andrew, get the bowl of whipped cream from the refrigerator, and keep your fingers out of it."

"What would you like me to do, Mother?"

"You may get the dessert plates from the buffet, Millicent."

Frank's head bumped the crystal chandelier as he sprang from his seat and took the stack of plates from Carol. "You've got an armful. Let me help you take them to the kitchen."

"I think my niece is fully capable of one simple task." Penny pointed to Millie. "Millicent could use a hand, Pastor."

"No worries. I'll help them both."

⁂

Carol tensed as Pastor Frank leaned in front of her to place dishes in the sink. Aunt Penny and her flaring nostrils had scrutinized their interaction all through dinner. She certainly wouldn't appreciate any accidental touching over dirty plates.

As the preacher turned around Aunt Penny shoved two pies at him. She grabbed a third pie and handed it to Sylvia as she entered the room. "Take these in and we'll bring the coffee."

Both complied with her commands.

"And now—" Her aunt stood nose-to-nose with Carol by the kitchen sink. "You came on too strong with Pastor Frank and humiliated the family." Her eyes narrowed into slits. "I don't know how things are done in Vermont, but it's not proper here."

Carol's body stiffened at the well-aimed barbs. She

clamped her mouth shut to avoid any reaction that might add fuel to Penny's fire. Let the old windbag blow herself out.

The kitchen door opened and Frank appeared with the turkey platter. Carol cringed. Had he heard the terrible accusations? The jarring thought made her want to hide.

He set the platter down. "Stu wants the whipped cream in a can."

"He can eat my Chantilly Cream like everyone else." She gave an uneasy laugh. "I mean, uh-h-h, it's in the refrigerator."

"Aunt Penny, would you please excuse me? I have a headache and need to lie down for a little while. You can have Millie call me after dessert, and I'll come help."

"Load the dishwasher first, dear. We all have to work together." Penny took the wrapped leftovers to the refrigerator and muttered to herself as she made room for them.

Tears formed as Carol offered her hand to the preacher. "Nice to see you again, Pastor Frank. Merry Christmas." She mouthed the words, 'I'm sorry,' then turned to the sink and scraped food from the mound of dishes.

Frank spoke in a soft voice. "I enjoyed talking to you, Carol. We'll have to do it again, soon. Sorry about your headache." He checked his watch as Millie entered the kitchen. "I hate to eat and run, ladies, but I need to get home. My girls are supposed to call this evening. Thanks for everything, Penny. You and Millie are wonderful cooks."

"Wait, Pastor." Penny pointed to her daughter. "We haven't had Millicent's mincemeat pie. You don't want to hurt her feelings, do you?" She smiled. "Of course you don't."

"That's okay, Mother. He can take a whole pie home.

I'll wrap it for him."

Penny yanked the pantry door open. "Then let me get a basket so the crust will stay intact." She put the covered pie in the carrier. "Merry Christmas, Pastor Frank. It was so nice of you to join us. Millicent will walk you to the door." Then she tossed a fleeting smirk in Carol's direction. "Don't they make a lovely couple?"

CHAPTER ELEVEN

The dishwasher loaded and running, Carol made a quick exit to her room. Her only sanctuary in Aunt Penny's domain was filled with a distinctive whiff of old romance novels. She closed the door and threw herself face down onto the chenille bedspread. What a dreadful night for everyone. Which was worse? Grady's bear claws or Aunt Penny's bubbling cauldron?

With a sigh, Carol turned over to stare at the ceiling. Poor Frank's testimony had remained unscathed even though pushed to the hilt with the sweet potato-yam skirmish.

As much as she hated to admit it, certain aspects of the pastor were downright intriguing. Frank's lightly graying temples suggested sophistication, and the natural curve of his mouth offered a ready smile.

She groaned and covered her face with a pillow. How could she be attracted to another man so soon after Bob's death? It hadn't been quite a year since the accident.

The 40-watt bulb in the bedside lamp provided minimal light. Taking the Bible from the nightstand, she opened it to Bob's homemade bookmark. Her fingers touched the raised area where pansies were lovingly preserved. Ecclesiastes 3:1 was written in his familiar script: "To everything there is a season, and a time to every purpose under the heaven." She closed her eyes and stifled a sob.

In this new season of her life she needed to be

cautious before entering into a deeper friendship with Frank. Even though she longed for his touch she feared what it might bring. How easy it would be to get swept away.

Meanwhile, Aunt Penny's discovery of Millie's upcoming New Year's Eve date would generate more than enough theatrics to keep her mind off romance. Carol wiped her tears and silently chuckled. How she'd hate to be in the mystery man's shoes.

A knock on Carol's bedroom door was followed by her mother's voice.

"Carol? It's Mom and Dad. We came to say goodbye."

"Just a minute." She opened the door. "Hope I didn't embarrass you this evening."

Her dad held her close. "The only embarrassment in this house is ol' Penelope, and don't you forget that. It was all I could do to keep my trap shut tonight. She needs a tranquilizer the size of a hockey puck."

Sylvia leaned forward. "Andy needs a break from the negative atmosphere. We'd love to have him stay with us for a couple nights." She shrugged. "He can sleep on the couch."

"Thank you. I know he wants out of here. Wish I could go, too."

"So do we." A muscle clenched along Max's jaw. "Too bad we're one couch shy. Sorry I can't put you up in a motel again."

"Don't worry about it, Dad. I'll have Andy get his things together. Is it all right if I bring him over in a little bit? I need fresh air." She melted into another tight squeeze from her father.

"Sounds like a plan. C'mon, Syl, let's get out of here while we're still breathing."

"Mom and Dad, wait." She lowered her voice to a whisper. "Andy and I like Pastor Frank, but I think it might be best for us to go to another church for a while."

"I'm sure Frank will be disappointed." Her dad winked. "I've seen how he looks at you."

"Dad! We're only friends." Warmth bubbled at the thought of Frank's touch.

Sylvia kissed her daughter's forehead. "I understand, honey. Look at all the changes you've had this year. Penny's not the person to be around in stressful times. Go easy on yourself, and let's get through this first Christmas the best we can."

When they left, numbness settled over Carol. This *was* the first Christmas without Bob and Jake, and the shifting lifestyle had briefly taken her mind off both of them. She closed the door softly as guilt once again pierced her heart.

Carol sat on the bed, removed Bob's bookmark from the Bible, and dropped the marker into her purse. She needed to think and pray, away from Aunt Penny's oppression and control. What were the chances of a coffee shop being open on Christmas evening?

Another soft knock on the door. Andy poked his head inside. "Grandma said I could sleep on their couch. That seems to be my destiny these days, but I want outta here. Can I go?"

"I'd rather you be with me, but you need to enjoy what's left of Christmas with Grandma and Grandpa." Carol squeezed him tight. "Sorry, Andy. Things will get better, I promise."

He shrugged. "One couch is as good as another. Besides, Aunt Penny's all kinds of mad, and I wanna get away from all the pink Barbie junk around here."

"I understand. Go get your stuff and we'll leave right now."

Thirty minutes later, Andy was camped on his grandparents' sofa. His contented smile lifted Carol's spirit. Not in a hurry to face Penny's pink pandemonium, she drove around the east end of town. There were very few landmarks she recognized since moving away twenty-four years ago.

She passed a small, dimly lit business then checked her rearview mirror. "Was that Chug-a-Mug? Open on Christmas?" No better time for a quiet cup of coffee.

The heady scent of ground coffee beans mixed with freshly baked cookies and muffins greeted her nose at the door. The comfortable surroundings drew her in like a warm, fuzzy blanket.

The clerk's face brightened as Carol entered the holiday-bedazzled coffee shop. "Merry Christmas. What can I get for you tonight?"

"I'm so glad you're open." She set her purse on the stainless-steel counter. "I'm new to the area. What are your top three flavors?"

"White Choco-Mocho and Chilly Dilly are best sellers." He grinned and handed her a menu. "But the Raspberry Brownie Frappuccino comes in a close third."

A familiar voice called from behind. "We meet again, Carol."

Her breath caught at she turned. "Frank, what are you doing here? I thought you were expecting phone calls."

"I already talked to Lisa, and Gwen will get in touch when she's off work." He shook his head. "After this evening, a shot of high octane beckoned me. I saw your flower shop van parked out front and decided to join you."

"I'm glad." She smiled as the awkwardness lifted. "What flavor do you recommend?"

"My favorite this time of year is Chug-a-Nog."

"I love eggnog. I'm going for it."

"My treat." Frank turned to the clerk. "For here, two

half-caf, double grande, whipped Chug-a-Nogs, please. Could we have it in ceramic mugs?"

The clerk nodded. "We'll bring your order out as soon as it's ready."

Frank pointed to the booth beneath the multi-colored holiday lights. "I'll pay the man, while you grab that corner seat."

As Carol approached the table, thoughts crowded her mind. Christmas was different a year ago. Bob had snuggled her close as they reminisced in front of the blazing fireplace. Who knew it would be their last Christmas together? Tears welled as she twisted her wedding band. This year she was spending the evening with someone else. The desire to recreate a loving relationship stirred in her heart.

She folded her coat and placed it on the seat. Penny's accusation blared in her conscience. *'You came on too strong with Pastor Frank and humiliated the family.'*

Since the Grady incident in Vermont, Carol had doubted herself. She remembered his threatening voice. *You asked for it. You fell into my arms. I'll tell Sue you came on to me.*

She bowed her head. *Heavenly Father, what kind of vibes am I throwing off?*

Footsteps approached as she brushed tears away. Frank settled into the curved leatherette booth. "Christmas dinner with the Drakes was quite an experience, wasn't it? Penny not only ruffles the décor, she ruffles family feathers, too." He grinned. "She's one of a kind, to be sure."

"We're confident she has at least one redeeming qualitiy, but none of us can quite put our finger on it. Dad says she has a black belt in verbal karate." Her napkin went to her mouth. "Oops, did I say that out loud?"

"Verbal karate?" Amusement flickered across his features, quickly followed by rich, warm laughter. "Penny has a nice singing voice, and her good cooking has added a couple of inches to my waist." His eyes grew serious. "Sorry, but I kinda overheard what she said to you in the kitchen. Has she always been so assertive?"

She nodded. "Poor Millie's had to take the brunt of it. At least Uncle Stu stands up for her when Penny goes too far. He rarely says much otherwise. His philosophy is 'a soft word turneth away wrath.'"

"I thought that might be the case."

"The time will come, and soon, when Millie will have to stand up to her mother and refuse to bow down to her. That's the only way she'll ever be her own person." Carol paused when the clerk approached.

"Here's your Chug-a-Nogs. Enjoy." The young man grinned.

"Thank you." Carol wrapped her hands around the warm mug and returned his smile. A gust of cool air hit her feet as a couple entered the coffee shop.

"I know them. They recently started coming to our church." Frank stood. "Be right back."

She nodded and swirled the foam in her coffee with a red stir stick. Now was probably the time to tell him of her decision to attend another church.

Frank rejoined her. "Sorry to make you wait. I needed to greet them."

"Understandable." Her gaze settled on his mouth. What would one little kiss feel like? She erased the thought. "There's something you should know and please don't take offense. Andy and I need to attend another church for a while." She took a deep breath. "Without mentioning any names, someone has compromised my ability to worship. I have to separate myself from certain problems and let God bring healing."

"No offense taken. This someone's been a cross I've had to bear way too long. May I recommend Living Water Chapel on the other side of town? Pastor Foster's a friend of mine."

"We'll check it out. Thanks for understanding." She watched the steam rise from her cup. "Enough of Aunt Penny. How's your granddaughter's chicken pox?"

"Shea's doing better. The good thing is, she's too young to remember all the discomfort. Her mommy, on the other hand, will never forget it."

"I remember going through chicken pox with my three boys. Jake had an extra hard time." She looked away, tentatively took a sip of the hot drink, then wiped foam from her lips. "This is pretty good stuff."

"Told ya so." His mouth curved into a captivating grin as he lifted his cup in a salute. "Barb got me hooked on this place. She had a daring palate and insisted we try every flavor." He chuckled. "One in particular gave us the Mexican Quickstep for two days."

She snorted and her nose burned as the last sip of Chug-a-nog made a startling departure. She grabbed a napkin and took a swipe at the points of exit. "Frank, you're so much fun. I needed a good laugh."

"Our church is having a New Year's Eve party. Would you like to come?"

"Actually, Millie invited me to go with her. She said someone asked her, and she's a little nervous about it." Nervous was putting it mildly, the poor thing was borderline spasmodic.

Frank leaned forward. "Between you and me, the copier repairman has had a crush on her for a long time. Anyway, I prompted Lou to invite her to the party. I'm surprised he did it, he's super shy."

She nodded. "Millie's excited. I'm taking her to get a makeover."

"That's nice." He took another drink and put his cup on a napkin. "Millie needs to experience a loving relationship, and Lou is perfect for her. I've been trying to ignite a fire under him for months. Maybe together we can fan the embers."

"I assume you've prayed about this?"

"Trust me. A pastor's prayer is long and deep."

She laughed. "Then I'm up for the challenge, Reverend Matchmaker."

They sealed the agreement with a high-five across the table.

He looked at her and smiled. "Since we're going to be co-cupids, maybe you should tell me a little about yourself."

She lowered her eyes, then glanced back. "Bob and I pastored the same church in Vermont for twenty years."

"That's a long time. I'm impressed. What part of the ministry was nearest to your heart?"

"I worked mainly with the senior adults and shut-ins." She smiled. "I've sure missed it."

His eyes lowered. "Sadly, since Barb's death, I've neglected that part of my ministry." He dragged a hand over his angular face. "I'm sure they feel abandoned."

"If you don't mind me asking, what happened to your wife?"

"She had a nasty case of flu and couldn't snap out of it. One day she slipped into a coma, and we found out it was bacterial meningitis." He cleared his throat. "They couldn't save her."

"I'm so sorry."

"I was a mess that first year. Pastor Russ and JoAnna from Living Water Chapel kept me from falling into deep depression. My daughters and your folks helped, too."

"It's great you had that much support. Mom and Dad helped me as much as they could. I had a close friend to talk to, but she was pretty overwhelmed with her expanding bakery."

"People gave me all of three months to grieve before trying to set me up with their daughters and granddaughters. Even after two years, that fact has made me leery of dating." He swallowed another gulp of coffee.

"Mom and Aunt Penny have become the top contenders, haven't they?" Her face warmed as she smiled. "Sorry about that."

"They're just watching out for their daughters. I have two girls, and I'd probably do the same thing."

"Sometimes I feel ready to move on, but then I think of Bob and guilt sets in."

"We'll both know when it's the right time." He casually patted her hand. "I understand your husband's accident happened at a youth outing."

Carol bowed her head and took a deep breath. "Bob was chaperoning the event last January. He and our youngest son, Jake—" She choked on another sob as tears blinded her eyes. "Th-they were killed instantly in a snowmobile accident."

He leaned forward and spoke softly. "I'm sorry. Want to talk about something else?"

The line of her mouth tightened. With a nod, she wrapped her slender fingers around the warm drink.

Frank finished the last of his Chug-a-Nog. "So you moved from the snowy Vermont mountains to the dusty Arizona desert. Other than living with you-know-who, how are you and Andy adjusting?"

"We sure miss good old New England winters." Carol smiled. "It doesn't seem like Christmas without snow."

"Hey, if you want winter weather, I could take the two of you up to the White Mountains sometime in January. We can visit Russ and JoAnna at their get-away cabin.

They go nearly every Friday and Saturday, and I have an open invitation."

"We'd love that." She closed her eyes and envisioned frosty mounds of snow. "I haven't been to the White Mountains since I was a teenager." What a blessed escape.

"Good. Then it's a date?" Frank's cell phone rang.

Carol nodded as he pulled it from his pocket.

A date? Uncertainty tripped her heart. Should she go? Andy would love it, and since he'd be with them this trip to the mountains wouldn't constitute an actual *date*. She mentally stomped her foot. So what if it did? According to Ecclesiastes, it was a new season. Time to take one more step out of her comfort zone and make new friends.

"You should wear that smile more often. It becomes you." He leaned forward. "A penny for your thoughts."

Penny. Her heart bottomed out. When the old bat got wind of this, she'd have a cow.

CHAPTER TWELVE

CAROL BEAMED AND CLAPPED AS MILLIE pirouetted in front of the gilded, full-length mirror in her bedroom. "A dab of makeup, a red chiffon dress, and you're ready for the New Year's Eve party. That shoulder-length haircut is perfect for you."

"Thanks for talking me into it. I've never felt so glamorous in my life." Millie reached to hug her. "How can I ever thank you?"

"Simply by having the time of your life tonight. Your date won't know what hit him."

"Can you believe I'm finally going to spend the evening with my handsome prince?"

"Bless your heart. You deserve all the love and freedom you can get." Carol couldn't wait to see Frank and Lou's reaction to Millie's makeover. Would Lou throw his head back and howl at the moon like Frank suggested? She grinned. This was going to be fun. A new life was waiting for Millie. "Are you ready?"

"I think so." Millie crossed her fingers. "Wish me luck."

"I can do better than that, I'm praying for you." She followed her cousin down the steps.

Penny's deep scowl met them at the bottom of the staircase. "What on earth have you done to your hair, Millicent? And what are you wearing?" She turned Millie around. "Do you think I'll let you out of the house looking like that vixen, Tawny Lamour? Of course I won't."

Her mother's cruel words were all it took for Millie's

fragile demeanor to wilt.

Angry words formed in Carol's throat. Her fingernails dug into her palms as she swallowed choice words. However, she refused to plummet to Aunt Penny's level.

"Come on, Mills." Carol grabbed her arm and pulled her to the door. "We'll be late."

"What are you doing to my little girl?" Penny pivoted and yelled into the living room. "Stuart, get in here and talk some sense into your daughter. Carol has her looking like a tramp." She put her hands on her hips. "And look at Carol in that cheap, flouncy blue dress."

Stuart joined the women at the front door. "Stop it, Penny." He looked at Carol and Millie. "If my opinion counts, which I seriously doubt, I think they're stunning. You have a wonderful time tonight, ladies. Happy New Year!" He kissed them both on the cheek.

"Thank you, Daddy. I love you." Millie dabbed her eyes. "Ready, Carol?"

They hurried to the pink Floral Scent-sations van sitting in the driveway.

"Don't worry about getting dirty." Carol called across the front seat. "I had Andy sweep the flower petals and glitter from the seats. No shiny heinies for us."

The short drive to the church was quiet as Carol struggled to tame her mounting rage at Aunt Penny mortifying her own daughter. How many bricks had to fall on Millie's head to make her stand up for herself once and for all? It was past time for the poor girl to move out.

A relationship with Lou could be the ticket to love and acceptance for Mills. But according to Frank, the couple was so timid, cupid reinforcements may have to be called in to clinch the deal.

"Here we are." Carol turned off the van's engine and pointed to the cheerfully lit fellowship hall. "Let's join all those New Year's revelers."

When they approached the door, Millie grabbed Carol's arm. "Wait. Do I look okay? Mother made me self-conscious about this scooped neckline. Does it reveal too much?"

"Don't let your drama mama's snarky attitude ruin the evening. You're smashing in that dress. It's perfect for your complexion and dark hair." Carol hugged her for encouragement and opened the glass door. "Come on, your prince is waiting. It's now or never."

Millie gasped as Carol nudged her inside the brightly decorated hall. Dark blue and silver balloons bobbed above candle-lit tables where adults laughed and chatted. Young people stood in small clusters while children scampered around the perimeter of the room.

A current of warmth surged through Carol as Frank greeted them with a formal bow. "Ladies, I'm so glad you came." He eyed Millie and gave a soft whistle. "Miss Drake, get a load of you! Very nice."

"Thank you, Pastor Frank." Millie giggled and pushed her red-rimmed glasses higher on the bridge of her nose.

Frank's brick-red shirt enhanced his dark hair and tanned complexion. Carol swallowed. If being handsome was against the law, this man would be on the Ten Most Wanted List.

His dark brown eyes twinkled as he reached for Carol's hand. "And here's another beautiful lady. How are you this evening?"

Her face warmed. "Fine. Nice to see you again." She hadn't expected the flutters to hit. After all, they were only friends.

Frank offered both elbows. "May I have the honor of ushering you beauties to a table? Lou Blythe saved one up front by the window." He led them to the round table sprinkled with glittery star confetti. "Well, what do you know? Here he comes now."

A gold blazer complimented Lou's black dress pants and shirt. His gaze never left Millie as he neared the table. "Hi, Miss Drake." He cracked his knuckles. "You're pretty tonight. I've never seen you in red before."

"Thank you." She lowered her eyes. "I'd like you to meet my cousin, Carol Mason. Carol, this is Lou Blythe. He works on the office machines here at the church."

"Nice to meet you." Carol shook his hand and smiled at Millie. Why was she standing there like a bump on a pickle? The anticipation of dating Lou had her downright giddy at home.

"Pleased to make your acquaintance, Carol." His eyes brightened as he turned to Millie.

He was obviously smitten with her shy cousin, but Carol wondered if the feeling was mutual. Millie could do a lot worse than Lou Blythe. Once the introductions ended, a strange, awkward silence descended on their table.

Frank gave Lou's shoulder a little shake. "C'mon. We'll get punch for the ladies while they check out the snacks."

The cousins went to a long table spread with a variety of finger foods while the men headed for the beverages.

Carol met Andy there. Pigs-in-a-Blanket were piled high on his plate next to dill pickles and baked beans. "Are you having a good time?" She continued to fill her plate with a modest selection of vegetables, cheese and crackers.

The boy nodded and reached for a handful of potato chips. "I met a girl named Heather." He wiggled his eyebrows and produced a debonair smile. "I think she likes me. I gotta go."

The band played lighthearted pop music as Andy strutted to his new friends gathered around the stage.

Her maternal curiosity was piqued. Since people were

blocking her view, she stood on tiptoe and stretched her neck to get a gander at the femme-fatale in question. Not bad. She had to hand it to Andy, the girl was on the cute side.

Millie came up beside her. "You wouldn't believe how many people complimented me on my outfit and new haircut. Even a few of the guys said I looked nice." She blinked away tears. "No one but family has ever told me that."

"No surprise to me. I knew you'd be a hit." Carol patted Millie's shoulder. "Are you ready to head for the table?"

"Sure. Frank and Lou are waiting."

"By the way, Mills, Lou's a nice-looking man, don't you think?"

"I'm glad you like him." Millie's mouth split into a satisfied smile. "I knew the two of you would connect."

Carol nodded. Apparently Millie still needed approval for her first date with Lou. At least the poor soul made a little progress in the area of self-confidence. Hopefully, Frank had similar success encouraging Lou. Carol sighed and hurried to keep up with her cousin's swift gait.

The men sat across from each other with empty chairs between them. Frank smiled and stood as they approached.

"We wondered where you got to. Let me take your plate, Carol." He set it on the table and pulled a chair out for her. Then, he motioned for Lou to do the same for Millie.

Millie huffed, pursed her mouth, and abruptly set the paper plate on the table.

"Oh, yeah. Let me help you, Miss Drake." Lou took her elbow and pulled out the chair.

Once seated, she frowned and shifted her gaze from

Carol to Frank, then back to Carol.

Her cool stare caught Carol off guard. Millie had been so excited a few minutes ago, now she was brooding. What happened between the serving table and their chairs? A twinge tugged at her eyelid. Maybe the reality of an actual date was too much for her to handle.

"So, Lou." Frank cleared his throat. "Last week you said your quartet was going on the road again. Do you have your schedule set?"

"Yeah."

Millie's hand went to her mouth to hide a yawn. She picked up her fork and drew circles in the avocado dip.

Carol sighed and drummed her fingers in time with the music. *Come on, Mills. Get your mojo goin'. At least act interested.* "Millie mentioned your group is singing tonight, Lou."

Lou nodded, then picked up his drink and took a sip.

The lull in their conversation lengthened.

Frank ran his finger around the rim of his empty cup. "Millie, I know this is a party, and I hate to talk shop, but Lou's found a new copier for us with all the bells and whistles. It might take a while to learn how to use it, but he's offered to help you."

"I can't wait to see it." Millie picked at her fingernails.

Carol watched Lou crack his knuckles at fifteen second intervals. If he was hurt by Millie's aloofness, he wasn't letting on.

"Hey, Lou." Frank rubbed his chin. "Since you have plenty of time before your quartet sings, why don't you show her the copier now?" He reached into his pants pocket. "Here, take my office key."

Lou stood and touched the top of Millie's chair. "Is that all right with you, Miss Drake?"

"Miss Drake? Why so formal?" Frank chuckled. "Relax, this is a party. He can call you Millie, can't he?"

"Sure, that's fine." Millie scooted her chair away from the table. "Are you coming, too, Pastor?"

Frank shook his head and pointed to the door. "The Hamptons are here. I want to introduce your cousin to them before Howard goes into his usual political filibuster."

Frown lines scored Millie's forehead as Lou took her arm and maneuvered through the crowd. She stared over her shoulder and tossed a pleading look in Frank's direction.

Frank rested an elbow on the table and wiped his brow. "Don't know about you, Carol, but I'm spent. Looks like we need to add to our arsenal of cupid arrows."

༺✦༻

Twenty minutes before the midnight hour and the excitement of the crowd had picked up. Millie and Lou made their way to their empty table. Her heart sank as she peered around the room and saw the Hamptons laughing with another couple. Where was her date? And where was Carol?

Lou cleared his throat. "I'll bring you more punch before my group sings."

She sat alone while his tall figure hurried to get her drink. He returned, set the cup in front of her, and then rushed to the stage. She barely noticed the entertainment as her eyes once again darted across the room in search of Frank and Carol. Where could they be?

The noisy building was nearly filled to capacity. Small groups gathered along the walls, clapping their hands to Lou's gospel quartet. No one seemed to notice she sat alone at the table. The noise seemed to fade as Millie sipped punch and pulled deeper into herself. A blanket of self-consciousness threatened to smother her soul.

Movement out the window caught her attention. What were Frank and Carol doing in the courtyard? *Alone.* The empty plastic cup crumpled in her grip. One minute till midnight and her date was with another woman.

A warm arm came around Millie's shoulder, but her eyes never left the scene outside.

The crowd jumped to their feet. "Three. Two. One. HAPPY NEW YEAR!"

Millie's stomach clenched and an ache lodged in her throat. Frank kissed Carol.

"H-Happy New Year, Miss Millie."

Something soft brushed against her cheek.

"Yeah. Happy New Year." Millie felt her lower lip go into a pout. How would she pry Frank from Carol's clutches? A previous warning clearly rang in her memory. *'Mark my words, Carol's a conniving little flirt just like Tawny Lamour on Crest of Love. She'll leave you eating her dust.'* How she hated to admit Mother was right.

Millie almost felt sorry for them. When her mother found out she'd make their lives a living inferno. On the other hand, they deserved every smokin' minute.

Lou cracked his knuckles then picked up her crushed cup. "Want some more punch?"

"No, thank you. I've had quite enough." Millie closed her eyes and willed herself not to cry, lest anyone see tears of shame. She turned to Lou. "Will you take me home?"

"Sure. I have to tell the group. Be right back." He walked off, hitching up his pants.

She couldn't drop the idea of Frank ignoring her all evening. He practically pushed her on Lou. Maybe she'd find another job and show Frank how it felt to be dumped.

Lou returned, pulled keys from his pocket, and offered Millie his arm. He led her outside to his van.

Still fuming, Millie sat as still as a lawn gnome in the front seat of Lou's van. Why had she slipped and told her mother about their date? She would pounce and demand an exhilarating account of the long-awaited rendezvous with the Reverend Francis Bailey. She twisted in her seat, and the rest of the way home she scowled at her pathetic reflection in the window.

The porch light glared through the darkness as Lou's van pulled to a stop in front of her parents' home.

"Goodnight. Thanks. I'll see myself to the door." She reached for the handle.

"Wait. I have to open it from the outside." He jumped from the van, raced around to open her door, then gently touched her arm to help her out. "I'm sorry if I've done something to upset you."

"It wasn't you." Fighting tears, Millie pulled away from him. The last thing she wanted was to bare her soul to a *man*. She stomped to the front door, ready to write off the whole male species and torch every romance novel in the house.

The door opened, and her mother stepped out, eyes wide. The woman was *so* predictable.

"How did it go, Millicent? I want all the juicy details. Did he kiss you at midnight?" She followed her daughter into the kitchen. "When are you going out again?"

"I've got a headache, Mother. We'll talk in the morning." She turned. Her puffy eyes and splotchy face would be a dead give-away. "Where's the aspirin?"

"You can't hide those tears from your mother. Did he make a pass at you? Of course he did, with that tramp dress you're wearing. All men are beasts with only one thing on their mind."

Millie ripped a paper towel from the holder and blew her nose. "You were so, so right about Tawny Lamour." She smacked the kitchen counter, and her voice squeaked two octaves higher. "Frank . . . Carol . . . kissed—"

Angry thunderclouds darkened Penny's face. "That preacher's bacon is mine. And rest assured, Carol has just earned her way into a living H-E-double hockey sticks."

"I'm going to bed." Millie stormed out of the kitchen and ran up the stairs.

The misery of the party haunted Millie as she tossed and turned through the night. Pastor Frank specifically asked *her* to the party, and then openly ditched her for Carol. She grabbed a pillow and punched it a few times, then closed her eyes, resigned to a sleepless night.

Frank and Carol's horrific exhibition in the church's courtyard looped through her mind.

Without warning, another scene interrupted the replay. Millie's eyes popped open. She sat up in bed and put a hand to her cheek. Had Lou kissed her?

CHAPTER THIRTEEN

Carol grunted as she lifted a four-foot Greek column onto the platform of the Floral Scent-sations' front window. Thankfully, she'd stayed late the night before to clear the area and hang a white filigree curtain as a dramatic backdrop for the red velvet ribbons and other decorative objects.

A tap on the outside of the window caught her attention. She smiled and waved to her mom who headed for the door. With her help, the decorating would be done in no time.

Sylvia set her purse behind the counter and returned to the window. "It's January third and the hearts and cupids are finally taking center stage. Mammoth Mart started getting theirs out weeks ago."

"I know." Carol placed a vase of roses on a stand and adjusted them. "It's been so busy here with Uncle Stu gone. This is the first chance I've had to get everything out."

"So how are things with you and Millie?" Sylvia handed her a porcelain cupid.

Carol moaned. "I never thought life at Aunt Penny's could get any worse, but it sure did. She and Millie seem to have a nasty case of cold shoulder and selective laryngitis. The only words I hear are, 'Tawny Lamour.' Weird."

"Knowing those two, it probably has something to do with soap operas or sleazy novels."

Carol nodded and studied the window display. "I've

always had a wonderful relationship with Millie. Now any effort to speak to her ends with her walking away." She placed the figurine beside a bouquet of roses. "Uncle Stu's no help either because they've extended their cold shoulders to him, too. Personally, I think he's reveling in the peace and quiet."

"I don't blame him one iota." Sylvia sniffed. "Poor Stu rarely has a moment of harmony in his own home."

"I feel bad for him and Mills." Carol wiped her hands on her smock. "Why don't you see how the arrangement looks from the sidewalk?"

Sylvia went out the door, studied the display, and gave two thumbs-up.

Carol stepped out of the window while her mother came inside. "How about coffee, Mom? I made a fresh pot. I'll even share my unheated Toastee-Tortz."

"Coffee, yes, but I'll pass on the Toastee-thingies."

They linked arms and headed for the break room. Carol handed her a full cup and nodded to the table in the corner. "Thanks for letting me come over to your place in the evenings. I can't handle any more of Aunt Penny's emotional goose flesh. Millie isn't any better."

"Your dad and I have struggled with Penny's behavior for years. No matter how we pray, she still manages to push every button I own." Sylvia shook her head and sat at the small Formica table. "She came from an abusive childhood and insists on wallowing in it."

"I'm afraid if she isn't careful, she'll slip into a world of madness and pull Millie down with her." Carol touched her mom's arm. "Bob always said we need tolerance for others as they try to conquer the demons of their past. It's not always an easy thing to carry out."

"I'm glad you brought that up. Might help me keep things in perspective. Her nasty attacks make me forget she's a wounded soul." Sylvia sipped her coffee. "Bob did get along with her better than any of us."

"Mom, tomorrow is the first anniversary of Bob and Jake's death."

Sylvia nodded. "I wasn't going to mention it."

"I've been dreading it for weeks. A year ago Jake was bouncing around the house begging me to let him go on that youth outing with Andy. I said no until I knew Bob was going." She wiped her tears and took a deep breath. "Why did I give in and let him go, Mom?"

"Because you wanted him to have a good time with his dad and there's nothing wrong with that, honey."

"That's another thing. I broke my promise and volunteered Bob to take another chaperone's place. He wasn't supposed to be at that ski resort." She removed her torte from the microwave and joined her mother at the table.

Her mother reached for Carol's hand. "You volunteered Bob out of love for your church and the kids. Both of you served the Lord from your heart, and I'm very proud of you. It makes me sad to see you suffer and blame yourself for an accident you had no control over."

"It's great to have your support, Mom. I'm trying to be strong and not bring everyone down. Fortunately, making a big move and working here during the holidays have kept me so busy and exhausted I haven't had a chance to dwell on the date."

"That's good. I'm glad you're home. We're praying you find a place of your own soon." She took a sip of coffee. "Your father and I heard you and Pastor Frank have been visiting the elderly from church. He sure has been more chipper since you've been here."

"Tonight's our third time, so I won't be home for supper. We'll grab a snack when we're done." Carol's mouth eased into a smile. Since Frank had introduced her to Chug-a-Mug, it had become their place, but it might be best to keep that little morsel to herself. She couldn't afford to have Aunt Penny get wind of their growing friendship.

Visiting the elderly awakened Carol's dormant spirit. It was where she belonged. And going with Frank was the whipped cream on the latte.

※

With the workday finally over, Carol grabbed her jacket, turned off the lights, and ran out to Frank's car. "Boy, are you punctual. What's our destination for tonight?"

"Are you ever in for a treat." He chuckled. "I'm taking you to meet my favorite shut-in, Nola Nelson, otherwise known as the crazy craft lady."

The car followed a wandering lane and finally parked in front of a house adorned with enough lawn ornaments to rival any miniature golf course.

Carol turned to him and pulled off her sunglasses. "I can't wait to meet Nola."

"She's a creative soul. I think she made most of those decorations." He smiled, pocketed his car keys, and helped Carol from the car. "Be sure to watch your step. This has turned into a playground for stray kitties."

He slipped his arm around her as they strolled down the sidewalk lined with colorful whirligigs flipping in the wind. A flock of resin geese, sporting sunbonnets and matching ponchos, guarded the flowerbed. On both sides of the entrance were glistening gazing balls.

A munchkin-sized woman with silvery-white hair met them at the door. "Reverend Bailey! I haven't seen you in ages. Come in and have a seat on the couch." Her faded blue eyes widened as she grinned at Carol and pulled her inside. "Who's this lovely lady?"

"This is Sylvia Drake's daughter, Carol Mason. She and her son recently moved here from Vermont."

"The Drakes are nice people." Her rheumy eyes settled on Carol. "I sure hope you hang on to this one, Pastor."

Sitting on the sofa, Carol threw him a slip of a smile and wiggled into the sagging cushion. Would he consider this astute woman's keen insight?

Frank jumped when a tabby in a turtleneck sprang into his lap. "Hi, Banjo. Catch any good mice lately?"

Carol rubbed the cat's ears. "What a cute sweater."

"Why, thank you. I can crank two of those out in one day. Wait right here." Nola, in her crocheted slippers, shuffled from the room.

Frank lowered his voice. "I should've warned you. She'll expect you to buy something. FYI, the medium-size sweater will fit most Chihuahuas and the majority of pet iguanas. I know this from her past sales pitches."

While the elderly lady was out of the room, Carol took inventory of the living space. A Tabby cat cleaned herself on a stack of craft magazines in the corner while three tiny kittens tumbled from an empty oatmeal box like monkeys from a barrel.

"They're so cute." Giggles escaped Carol's throat as she leaned into Frank. An unexpected tingle ran up her arm.

Nola rounded the corner with an overflowing basket of crocheted items. "Banjo will be happy to model these for you. We'll start with the winter collection." Her knees cracked as she dropped into the avocado plaid recliner. "Ban-jo." She shook a bright red treat box.

An hour into the fashion show, Carol squirmed in her sunken seat, more than ready to escape. Nola's phone rang and Carol quickly locked eyes with Frank.

With an understanding nod, he snatched her hand and pulled her to her feet. He leaned close to whisper.

"Let's go before the next season of cat clothes come out." When they got to the door, he turned. "We'll catch you another time, Nola."

The older woman waved and continued to chitchat on the old rotary phone.

Once outside, Carol broke into a fit of giggles. "What a character. Who crochets cat clothes? And in Arizona?"

"It's good to hear you laugh." Frank led her to the car. "Nola was our only shut-in for the evening. Are you hungry?"

"Famished!"

"Me, too. Let's skip Chug-a-Mug and get something substantial." He opened the car door for her. "Do you like seafood?"

"Sounds wonderful." She slipped into the front seat and clicked her seatbelt.

"Let's go to Horatio's Halibut Haven." He got behind the wheel and smiled. "Thanks."

She brushed cat hair from her slacks. "For what?"

"For making it easy to visit the shut-ins again. You're a blessing."

Her face warmed, and she was relieved the darkness of the car hid her embarrassment. "I've totally enjoyed it." Her mind groped for something else to say. Should she compliment him in return? Maybe she'd let it go.

Frank turned the corner. "Have you been checking for apartments?"

She sighed. "I saw a duplex yesterday that might work. It's close to both Scent-sations and the high school."

"Sounds like a good fit, so what's the problem?"

"It's expensive for such a small place with only one bedroom. Everything else costs too much." She shrugged. "I've even considered selling a kidney, a spleen, or any other body part of black market value."

A sharp laugh pierced the air, and the car veered to the right. "You're a riot. Can I use that line for the next fundraiser?"

"It'll cost ya fifty bucks for my moving fund." She grinned. "Seriously, poor Andy's tired of sleeping on couches, and he needs privacy." She stared out the side window. "I'm tempted to grab the apartment, because Aunt Penny's been grouchier than a walrus with a toothache."

"I've been on the biting edge of her tusks." He snorted. "Only you know how much of her attitude you can handle. Even so, I hate to see you sign a lease for a place that isn't right." Frank glanced her way. "I've missed you at church."

"I've missed going, but you do understand it's about Aunt Penny, right?"

"Unfortunately, yes." Frank patted her hand. "Probably shouldn't say this, but between you and me, I think your aunt has a few knots in her yo-yo string. However, being a man of the cloth, I'll stop there."

"That's probably a good idea. Once we're out of Aunt Penny's domain, we'll go back to your church. Andy and I took your suggestion about going to Living Water Chapel."

"So I've heard." Frank pulled the car up to the restaurant and shut off the ignition. "If you're not going to Apache Pointe Community, then Living Water is second best." He flashed an irresistible grin and shrugged his shoulders. "Naturally, the pastor isn't quite as good looking."

Carol lightly smacked his arm. "You're a nut, Frank. I enjoyed his message."

He snapped his fingers. "Wait! I promised you and Andy a trip to Russ and JoAnna Foster's cabin up in the mountains." Frank reached into the backseat, retrieved his planner, then turned the overhead light on. His brow wrinkled as he flipped the pages. "I only have two weeks from Saturday open. Think you and Andy can make that work?"

Carol's thoughts swirled. The man certainly couldn't be accused of procrastination. She smiled. "I'll have to check with Dad and Andy, but I'm sure we can work something out. Go ahead and pencil it in."

"I'll give the Fosters a ring later." Frank got out and opened her door. "Let's go inside."

As they waited for a table, she focused on their upcoming trip. Her heart went into a topsy-turvy spin at the idea of spending personal time with him.

※

Frank lightly placed his hand on the small of Carol's back as they headed for their table. His arms ached to hold her close. How had his feelings evolved so quickly in the past few weeks? Maybe it was the balance she returned to his life.

Her natural compassion for working with shut-ins was commendable. They loved her. She seemed to be a perfect fit for his ministry . . . and his heart. He hoped the rest of the congregation would react as favorably to their pastor pursuing a new relationship.

CHAPTER FOURTEEN

On her way home from work, Millie pounded the steering wheel as shock gave way to outrage. How could Carol do this to her again? She had even looked forward to her cousin moving home because they'd always been as close as sisters, sticking together through melodrama and silly nonsense.

They hadn't spoken since the New Year's Eve Party three weeks ago—when the original back stabbing occurred. Now all the good memories were lost.

Millie shut the front door with a bang. "Mother!"

Penny emerged from the living room, romance novel in hand. "I've told you not to slam the door. Now what's so important?"

"I was in the office when Pastor Frank was on the phone. Guess what I overheard?"

"I suppose it has something to do with Carol?" She tossed her book to the couch.

"Yes. He's taking her up to the White Mountains. Today. Can you believe that?" Millie stomped her foot. "It gets worse. Andy was supposed to go with them, but something suddenly came up, so they're going alone. Unchaperoned."

"How convenient." Penny belligerently placed a hand on her ample hip and shook a finger. "Didn't I tell you she'd work her womanly wiles? Of course I did. You should be going with him, not that flirty little twit." Determination settled on her face. "That woman's got to go."

A black silence chilled the room.

Her mother's squinting eyes indicated she was plotting something sinister. Millie's stomach knotted. This could get ugly. "What kind of scheme are you working on?"

"Your dad and Max are delivering a huge wedding order, so we'll be alone for a while. Let's check her room for a journal or anything else that shows her true colors."

"We can't do that. It's her personal space."

"And why not, may I ask? She took your personal pastor. This is our home. It's up to us to protect our church from scandal." She gave Millie a push to the stairs. "C'mon, we need ammunition."

"Let's think this through before we do anything rash." Who was she kidding? A little revenge might soothe her frustrations. But it was Carol who'd always been in her corner. Millie crossed her arms. "I've changed my mind. I don't want any part of this."

"Didn't I give you more grit than that? We have to do this for your future. Come. *Now.*"

Like an obedient child, Millie trotted up the stairs. She'd go up, but she didn't have to be a part of her mother's malicious invasion of privacy.

Penny shoved the bedroom door open. "Now, you take that side and I'll check these drawers. The ones over there aren't worth another inspection."

A gasp escaped Millie's mouth. "You've snooped in here before?"

"This is my house, so I wouldn't call it snooping. I only wanted to make sure she was keeping her laundry done."

The phone let out a resounding ring. Millie yelped. It rang again.

"Are you going to answer it, Millicent?"

With a shaky hand, Millie reached for the phone beside Carol's bed. "Hello?"

"Is this Miss Drake?"

Her heart lurched at Lou's deep voice. She turned from her mother. "Yes, this is Millie."

He cleared his throat. "This is Lou Blythe, the copier repairman from church. Umm, I've been thinking about you since the party. I've never done this before, but I was wondering, umm, only if you want to, maybe we could sit together tomorrow morning during church. I mean, you know, in the balcony?"

He was thinking about her? All this time? Millie closed her eyes as the image of the strapping repairman, who might have kissed her, filled her inner vision. A quick glance at her mother's questioning stare warned her to act nonchalant. "Sure, we can probably do that." Now to keep the lid on her enthusiasm so Mother would be none the wiser. "Sounds good."

A resounding sigh came through the phone. "Great. I'll see you tomorrow. 'Bye."

She replaced the receiver and smiled. Lou was always a gentleman, a very sweet man. He'd been thinking about her for three whole weeks. She would show Pastor Frank, Carol, and Mother that she could catch a man on her own.

Penny's eyes narrowed. "Why are you grinning like a Cheshire cat?"

"It was something about morning worship." She cleared her throat. There, that wasn't a lie at all.

"Who was on the phone?"

"Just the copier repairman. He goes to our church once in a while, but I don't think you know him."

Penny's head jerked up from peering through Carol's underwear drawer. "Handsome? Married? Ask you out?"

"Mother. Enough. This isn't a big deal." Millie coughed. Okay, that was a fib. This was her first rendezvous . . . with a man who might've kissed her. She shivered. It was a big deal. A big, hairy deal. "He needs to talk to me at church."

"You will tell me if something does come up, right?" She returned to her snooping and pulled out an envelope. "O-o-oh, what have we here?"

"Is it from Frank?" Millie held her breath. *Please, don't be a love letter.*

"Shh, Millicent," Penny snapped. "Let me read." A satisfied smirk crossed her face. "Oh my word! Didn't I tell you there was a scandal? Look at this." She shoved the letter into her daughter's hand.

Millie's eyes quickly scanned the paper. "I can't believe Carol would break up a family."

"There it is in black and white. This Sue person ripped her to shreds because of it." Penny licked her lips and rubbed her hands together. "Sounds pretty incriminating to me. No wonder she came running home to mommy and daddy."

"Let's forget we ever saw this and put it where we found it. It can't be right, anyway."

Penny snatched the letter. "This is our chance to run that home wrecker out of town."

"So, what are you going to do with it?"

"Take it to the church board, of course."

"Mother! You can't do that."

"I can and I will." She straightened her shoulders. "We can't have a shepherd leading our flock when he's dating a wolf in sheep's clothing." She folded the envelope and stashed it in her cleavage. "You remember the last episode we saw of the *Darkest Night*? That dreamy Father MacLuring is doing the same thing, and he's dragging his congregation through the mud. I simply won't stand for it."

CHAPTER FIFTEEN

THE CAR SLOWED AS IT ROUNDED a snowy bend, and Carol couldn't take her eyes off the mountain view. Blue spruce gave way to a clearing where the sun peeked through clouds and sent its glare to the snowy mountaintops.

"It's beautiful, Frank. Feels like I'm home again."

"This is as close as I can get to winter in Vermont. I thought you'd like it."

Her smile broadened in approval. "Only the Swiss Alps could top this."

"Let's get out for a better view of the valley." He slammed the door, and cardinals flew from their evergreen perches and sent tufts of snow tumbling to the forest floor.

Carol stood beside him and filled her lungs with frigid air, released it, and watched her breath form a cloud. "This is a whole different world." She held on to his arm. "No pressure or worries, only peace."

He casually stepped behind her and rested his chin on her head. "I'm glad we have this special time together."

"Me, too." Feeling protected, she closed her eyes and relaxed, not wanting to move. "It's so beautiful up here, Frank."

"Yep. This is my favorite spot, but the Fosters are waiting so we'd better get going." He opened the door and helped her inside the warm car.

She gazed out the window. Majestic pines rested in their snowy blankets as they meandered along the steep incline of the White Mountains. Heavy branches bowed low, and the sun's rays kissed ice crystals, creating a wintry fairyland.

"Thank you for taking a day off to bring me up here. I know how difficult it is for a pastor to get away on Saturday."

"My pleasure. I've been looking forward to this trip since we planned it. The cabin isn't too far from here. I know you'll enjoy their friendship." He winked. "Russ said he'd fix his famous Moose Knuckle Stew for lunch."

Carol glanced at him with feigned delight. "Yum. My anticipation level is off the charts."

Frank took her hand and her heart fluttered. For nearly a year, her romantic feelings had been in cold storage—but an early spring thaw appeared to be in the forecast. She glanced at his strong profile. She'd underestimated this man's effect on her.

Carol stared out the window and tried to sort out her confused emotions. Was it time to start over? With Frank?

The faint scent of burning wood hovered over the snowy terrain. Her eyes noticed curling smoke from the chimneys of massive log cabins that peppered the area.

The car turned down a long, winding lane. "Here we are." He pulled to a stop. "Watch your step, it's a little icy in places."

They linked arms and carefully approached the Fosters' elaborate lodge.

The winter wreath hanging on the door shook as a pudgy, middle-aged man invited them inside. "It's about time. Get your tails in here before we all freeze."

A woman with auburn hair came up behind him and peeked over his shoulder. "I'm so glad you were able to come."

Frank allowed Carol to go in ahead of him. "Russ, JoAnna, this is Carol Mason."

"We've heard so much about you." JoAnna reached out and took her coat. "Why don't you put your boots on the rug? I love your sweater."

"Hey!" Frank tossed his jacket to Russ and pirouetted. "What about my sweater?"

She patted his shoulder. "Your sweater is lovely, too. That's the reason we gave it to you five Christmases ago."

Russ led Carol to the living room and motioned to the loveseat. "We noticed you and your son at Living Water. Unfortunately, the chapel has so many exits and hallways, it's impossible to shake hands with everyone. I'm sorry we haven't been able to formally greet you. We're glad you made the wise choice of worshipping with us instead of the snooze-fest at Frank's church." A whinny-like giggle followed and ended with a snort.

A sound like that should never come from a grown man. Carol's eyes watered as a throaty laugh burst through her lips. She covered her mouth and tried to regain composure.

"Snooze-fest, huh? Good one, buddy. If it wasn't for your in-laws, your amen corner would be on sabbatical." He took Carol's hand. "She has my blessing to attend your services for now. However, that will not always be the case."

JoAnna scooted to the edge of her seat. "She needs your blessing? No knots have been tied, right?" Her eyes popped. "Or did you jump the broom without benefit of witnesses?"

"Oh, my!" Carol's face grew hotter by the second, but she couldn't keep from snickering at Frank's dropped jaw.

Russ's high-pitched giggle returned, sans snort. "Maybe that's why they're here, m'love. I just happen to have a copy of my marryin' book on the shelf. Five minutes. Chop-chop."

"As nice as it sounds, I think we'll have to pass." Frank turned to Carol. "Although I've been told I'm quite the catch."

Russ nodded to the window. "You can ask any squirrel in the forest."

"I'm thinking we need to move on." Carol surveyed the room. "I heard you had a log cabin, but I wasn't expecting anything so open and extravagant."

"Pretty impressive, isn't it? It's been updated several times through the years." JoAnna smiled. "It's been such a blessing to our family. Russ and I think of it as our great escape. We come to unwind as often as possible."

"Thank goodness for our speaking schedule. We sure couldn't afford this on a preacher's salary." Russ pointed to an old portrait on the wall. "My great-grandfather, Sigmund Foster, was a lumber tycoon. Grandpa was an only child and my father was, too. I'm the last of the Fosters so it was left to me. My kids will have to share."

"Sigmund? So *that's* where you got your middle name." Frank smacked his knee and chuckled. "The Reverend Siggy Foster."

JoAnna shook her head. "Let's not get started on another battle of wits. It's time to eat." She stood and nodded to the kitchen. "Carol, would you help me serve?"

"I'd be glad to help." She followed her hostess into the modernized room.

"We decided to eat in the living room by the fireplace where it's warm and . . ." She pulled Carol close and lowered her voice, "romantic!"

Carol returned a whisper. "Sounds like a plan to me. Who do I get to sit by?"

"Hm-m-m, let me give that deep consideration."

Another whinnying laugh echoed from the living room.

JoAnna held up her hands in surrender and moaned. "I know, I know. I'm still saddled with Trigger, right?"

"Yup." Carol patted her arm. "Frank's lookin' better all the time."

The soup bowls were filled with a generous portion of hearty stew, and JoAnna placed them on a tray. She headed to the living room and called over her shoulder, "Would you bring the tray with the cheese and crackers?"

After placing the tray on the coffee table, Carol sat next to Frank on the loveseat, amazed at how comfortable she felt with the Fosters. It was just like the Lord to mend her broken heart by sending bubbly JoAnna to replace Sue's lost friendship. And Russ, even with his strange laugh, was light-years away from Grady the Groper.

As they ate, their light conversation hopscotched from Carol's boys to Nola Nelson's crocheted get-ups for cats.

Frank scraped his bowl clean. "By the way Russ, Nola is now taking Easter orders."

"Thanks, but I'll pass." Russ waved him off. "The tutu you gave Igor ruined his reputation. He still can't show his face outside without other cats heckling him."

"Gettin' tea party invitations, is he?" Frank yawned and draped his arm on the back of the loveseat. "I'm ready for a nap."

"Don't get too comfortable, Frankie, m' boy. The boss put me in charge of activities, so I decided we're going to have a snowman building contest."

Frank stood and rubbed his hands together. "You're on."

Russ shrugged into his coat and tossed Frank's to him. "Winner gets a batch of cookies from the local Rising Doe Bakery."

"A dozen Chocolate Grizzly Bars are on the line." JoAnna winked. "Trust me, they're fabulous! Okay men, we're the judges, and we'll watch from the window."

While Frank was busy rolling the largest portion of his

snowman, a snowball plastered his face, followed by Russ's cackle.

JoAnna turned from watching the snowball melee. "You know what? I haven't seen Frank this happy in a long time. It broke our hearts to see him so lost after Barb died. You've helped him."

"He's done a lot for me, too." Carol looked up. Her new friend made her feel at ease. "Andy and I were struggling in a lot of ways before we moved here."

JoAnna gave her a quick hug. "I'm glad you found each other. We'd better head for the kitchen and get our snacks ready." She led the way and called over her shoulder. "I hid the Grizzly Bars in the freezer so Russ couldn't find them. I'll pop them in the microwave to thaw. Then we'll taste test while our abominable snowmen are acting like kids."

"You hide your goodies in the freezer, too? We're kindred spirits. I personally use frozen vegetable bags."

"I hope the two of us can become close enough to share whatever we need to." JoAnna washed her hands and handed Carol a Grizzly Bar. "Just to ease your mind, I'm not here to push the two of you together."

"Thanks. We have enough people pushing us one way or the other. Honestly, I do feel a connection with him, but I'm hesitant to fall in love again. I mean, how do you tell your heart you're no longer married?" She rubbed her temple.

JoAnna shook her head. "That's a difficult question. My advice would be to let the Lord guide you when the time is right."

"At times I feel ready to move on, but something reminds me of Bob and I panic."

"Remember it's been a full year, so it's all right to fall in love."

"I appreciate that. There aren't many I can confide in."

Carol bit into the dark morsel and closed her eyes as flaky coconut joined smooth chocolate. "Mmm, these are the best. Where did you say you got them?"

"The Rising Doe Bakery." JoAnna cut a quarter inch from each three-inch bar. "Now, the small ones are ours to test. We need to make sure they're all fresh. The guys will never know the difference." She popped a sliver into her mouth. "This one passes."

A snowball hit the kitchen window, and a second later, two red faces peered through the frosty panes.

"Hurry, they're comin' in." JoAnna's eyes were as big as soccer balls as she went to the cabinet, pulled out a brown dessert platter, then slapped a paper doily on it. She quickly stacked the abridged Grizzly Bars. "I'll get the coffee; you get the cups."

The backdoor slammed when the men entered the cabin's mudroom.

JoAnna blocked them from going into the kitchen. "Not so fast, boys. Dry clothes are in the bathroom." She cleared her throat and motioned for Carol to swipe her mouth. "Would you guys put your wet things in the dryer?"

Oversized mugs were filled with steaming coffee. Carol and JoAnna shared a smile as the men joined them.

Russ eyeballed the plate. "Hey! They're making these things smaller. What gives?"

"Maybe I should speak to the bakery owner." JoAnna hummed, took the platter of gooey bars, and sashayed to the fireplace. Her husband followed with a tray of hot coffee.

For the next half hour, the foursome enjoyed dessert while the men told stories of sharing a room during their seminary days.

"What's that noise?" Carol turned to JoAnna then lowered her mug to the table.

Russ grinned. "Might be a bear. What's it sound like?"

"Bells. I hear sleigh bells." Carol turned to the window. "It stopped. Are they out front?"

"Could be." JoAnna hurried to the coat rack. "You can't truly enjoy our mountains without a sleigh ride." Her voice grew excited. "We made arrangements with the sleigh driver to take the two of you on an hour ride."

Carol's face warmed. A little embarrassing, but she was flexible enough to comply with their request. "What a wonderful surprise." She hugged her hostess and whispered, "I'm kinda glad Andy didn't get to come, now."

JoAnna grabbed her cell from the coffee table. "I want a video of you two in the sleigh."

Frank held Carol's coat as she slipped into it. He took her hand before they followed Russ and JoAnna out the door.

A shiny red sleigh with silver bells sat in front of the Fosters' cabin. Two brown horses shifted nervously, and their muscles rippled beneath glistening coats as they pawed the ground. Their snorts sent puffs of wispy vapors into the air.

The driver was in Victorian attire and offered a full-toothed smile as he tipped his top hat.

"It's icy here." Frank's arm went around Carol's waist. "Let me help you into the sleigh." As he lifted her, his body jerked left. "Whoops!" He staggered and then, took a sharp right.

Without warning, she dropped from his arms and landed onto the sleigh's floor with a thud. As she pulled herself into the seat, Russ's whinny-laugh ricocheted through the frigid air.

The horses spooked, eyes wide with fright. The darker bay reared and the lighter one bolted and tossed the sleigh in an odd angle. The team took off at top speed, clomping their huge hooves through the snow.

"Whoa, Pansy! Whoa, Snuffy!" The driver yelled and pulled the reins. "Snuff-feee!"

Caught off guard, Carol toppled to one side. She clawed for something . . . anything to correct her position.

Even faster than before, the animals thundered down the winding road. Carol winced as trees flashed past them. The sleigh pitched to and fro, went airborne and almost capsized, causing Carol to unceremoniously tumble to the floor again.

Her mind raced as she clung to the back of the driver's seat and braced for the inevitable pain looming in her near future. So much for romantic excursions.

The sleigh stopped abruptly. Carol lost her grip on the seat and tumbled out. The world grew dark. Her chest tightened as if someone pulled the plug on her lungs. Air. She needed air.

A few seconds later, the eerie quiet surrounding her was interrupted by footsteps crunching in the snow. Frank's voice called out. "Carol! Are you all right?" He gently wiped the snow from her face. "Speak to me."

The sleigh driver stood behind him. "Is she gonna make it?" He leaned closer. "I'm so sorry. Snuffy and Pansy never spooked like that before."

Carol gasped and struggled to fill her depleted lungs. "C-Can't . . . breathe." She finally inhaled. "H-Help me up?"

Frank knelt on one knee and his arms went around her. She leaned against him for support and stood. As he brushed the snow from her coat, Russ and JoAnna ran to their side.

Carol breathed deeply and pointed a sore finger at Russ. "Don't you dare put this on YouTube."

The driver's face scrunched with worry. "You're not

gonna sue me, are ya?"

Carol shook her head. "Of course not. I'm fine." She sniffed and walked with forced dignity to the velvety blanket on the ground, shook it, then went to the sleigh. While the driver calmed the horses, she climbed in and gazed over her shoulder. "Coming, Frank?"

"Yes, ma'am." Frank joined her and laid the blanket across their laps. "Are you sure you still want to do this?"

She nodded with a teeth-chattering smile. "I was promised a sleigh ride for a full hour, and I intend to have one."

"If it's a sleigh ride you want, sweetie, a sleigh ride you'll get." Frank chuckled, held her close, and kissed her temple as Snuffy and Pansy lurched forward.

Horse hooves thumped as the sleigh's runners sliced through fresh snow. Her pulse quickened as she snuggled closer for warmth. Was it the higher altitude—or Frank's nearness?

Ponderosa Pines stood erect like steeples pointing heavenward. She relaxed as her head rested between his shoulder and neck. Her boldness came as a shock, but she couldn't pull away.

His lips brushed the top of her head. "We have something special, Carol. I think you feel it too, don't you?"

Cautiously, she searched his eyes. "Is it appropriate for us to feel this way? We've only known each other for two months." She glanced away.

"Sometimes you immediately know when it's right. Maybe it's because we've both experienced real love, so it's easy to recognize it again." Frank placed his hand under her chin and gently raised her face so she had to look at him. "How do you feel about going forward in our relationship?"

She swallowed. "Could we approach it slowly and let everyone get used to the idea?"

"Of course. I remember that first year without Barb. It was hard to think of ever being with anyone else."

They cuddled and chatted until a gust of wind lifted the lap blanket, allowing frosty air around their legs. He grabbed the plush fabric and tucked it tightly around them.

His breath was warm against her face, and Carol's heart raced. Her eyes fluttered shut while a caress as soft as a snowflake brushed her lips.

No doubt about it, one kiss wouldn't be enough. This was crazy. JoAnna's voice repeated in her mind, 'It's been a year. It's okay to fall in love again.'

Her eyes connected with Frank's. She tilted her head. The dreamy intimacy of his kiss generated a rush of desire. That kiss had rocked her world.

CHAPTER SIXTEEN

CAROL HUGGED HER NEW FRIEND AS they said good-bye at the door. "I've enjoyed getting to know you, JoAnna. Thanks for a wonderful day."

"I'm glad we finally met. Let's get together soon." She leaned closer and lowered her voice. "You and Frank make a great couple."

Heat rose on Carol's face. "We'll see what develops." How awkward. "Thanks for introducing me to Grizzly Bars. They're now on my 'must have' list."

"Any time you need a fix, let me know and I'll get a box for you."

Frank held Carol's coat while she eased an arm into a sleeve. "We'd better get a move on if we want to get home before midnight." He took her elbow as they walked to the car and lightly kissed her cheek before opening the door.

※

Lights were on in Aunt Penny's house. Carol's stomach recoiled when she noticed a shadow looming in the front window. If only her exciting day in the mountains didn't have to end in a gut-wrenching face-off. Her nails sunk into the armrest of the car door. She was always the target of her aunt's anger no matter what upset her.

"Looks like someone's lying in wait." Frank parked the car in front of a neighbor's house and reached for Carol's hand. "I should've brought you home earlier."

She pointed to the clock on the dashboard. "It's nearly midnight. No wonder Aunt Penny's pacing. Maybe I should shinny up the trellis to my bedroom and avoid the third degree."

"Need me to go inside for support?"

"No, but thanks. I'll get skewered either way." Carol shivered and squeezed his hand. "Might as well get this over with."

"Gotcha." Frank pulled into Drakes' driveway. As they walked to the house, he stopped and gathered Carol close. "I know we're under surveillance, but how about one more smooch?"

Not waiting for an answer, his lips softly pressed hers with a kiss she could melt into.

The front door opened, and Carol tensed at the expectation of flying monkeys coming to snatch her away. Her vitals returned to normal when Uncle Stu stepped out with his cane.

"There you are. We were getting worried." He gave Carol a bear hug.

"I'm sorry. I didn't mean to be out so late. We had such a great day with the Fosters."

"Your dad said you went to their cabin. I hear it's a pretty snazzy place."

"It's gorgeous, and the mountains were breathtaking. I didn't realize how much I missed a winter setting." Her smile widened. "The whole trip was wonderful."

"That's great. You needed a day away." Stuart winked at Frank. "I think the mountain air agreed with you, too."

Carol stood on tiptoe and kissed Frank's cheek. "Thanks for helping me relive a day in the snow. I loved it." She giggled. "Even the sleigh ride."

"My pleasure. I hope there's a next time."

Stuart opened the door for Carol. "I need to talk to Pastor Frank about the next board meeting. I'll be right in."

Time to deal with her aunt. Carol took a cleansing breath to mentally gird her loins and went inside to battle the fire-breathing dragon. The door quietly closed behind her, and she tiptoed to the stairs.

Penny stepped from around the corner, arms crossed, and nostrils at full flare. "I hope you're happy with yourself. You've succeeded in snatching Pastor Bailey from your broken-hearted cousin."

"What?"

The brassy woman poked Carol's shoulder. "They were getting serious before you showed up and turned his head with all that indecent body language. Do you think Millicent stood a chance with you around? No, she didn't."

Carol stood with her mouth agape. She'd been accused of flirting with Grady, then with Frank at Christmas dinner, and now she had indecent body language? Her animal magnetism must be off the charts. Oh, for a life without melodrama.

"Millicent and Pastor Frank have been inseparable since his wife's death. Together every single day."

As angry words flew in her direction, Carol inched closer to the stairs, her only possible route of escape.

Penny squinted and closed the space between them, wielding her dog-eared romance novel. "You made a mockery of poor Millicent. Shame on you for destroying her relationship."

"Relationship?" Carol's hand fisted in her coat pocket. "Oh, please. They work together."

"He specifically invited *her* to the New Year's Eve party. You do the math."

"There's been a huge misunderstanding. I need to talk to her." Carol hurried upstairs. No wonder it had been so cold around here. She tapped on her cousin's door. "It's me, Mills."

"I'm not in the mood to talk. Go away, Carol."

"I'm sorry. I can't do that." She opened the door and peeked inside. Crumpled tissues covered Millie's bed. "I need to apologize and clear things up. May I come in?"

"Suit yourself." Millie blew her nose.

Carol closed the door behind her. "Your mother said you're angry with me because of Frank." She paused and moved a step closer. "Mills, we had no idea."

"But he asked *me* to the New Year's Eve party, and I saw you kiss him. How could you? My heart nearly stopped when I saw your lips touch." She turned her face to the wall.

"What are you talking about? He kissed me on the forehead."

Millie's posture was stiff as she crossed her arms and huffed. "Even so, Frank invited me, not you." She pushed herself off the bed and stomped to the window. "I never thought you, of all people, would betray me."

Betray. That was the word Sue used in her letter. Two of the most important women in her life thought of her as a romantic Mata Hari. She couldn't lose Millie, too.

"Listen to me, Mills. It's not what you think. Let me explain."

"There's nothing you can say to change my mind." She sobbed into her tissue. "Mother said I didn't stand a chance with you here. You're so pretty and outgoing, and I'm frumpy."

"Please don't put yourself down like that. It hurts God when we think those things." Carol pulled Millie to the bed. "Your mother has drummed negative things into your head for so long you believe it. She uses hurtful words to control you."

"I know, but those thoughts haunt me all the time."

"Remember all the compliments at the New Year's Eve

party? Everyone thought you were beautiful. And you are." She put her hands on Millie's cheeks. "We all see you as kind, loving, patient, faithful, and gentle."

"Really?"

"Of course. Whenever those hurtful thoughts echo in your mind, try to replace them with how we see you."

Millie dabbed her eyes. "I'll try to remember that."

"There's something else you need to know." Carol closed her eyes and silently prayed for the right words. "Lou told Frank—"

"Lou? Shh." Millie turned the radio on and whispered. "Mother's probably listening at the door. Now, what about him?"

Carol nodded and started over. "Lou's had a big crush on you forever, but he's been too shy to ask for a date."

"No! A crush, on me?"

"Frank's plan was to encourage both of you to go to the New Year's party as a way to bring you together. At Christmas, you said someone asked you to go, so Frank and I naturally assumed it was Lou. It never occurred to me that your mystery date was Frank."

Millie half-cried and half-laughed into her tissue. "Would you believe I was trying to set you up with Lou?"

"Are you kidding? No wonder you were so upset."

"I need to share something with you." Millie wiped the last of her tears, turned the radio's volume up, and lowered her voice. "I feel so stupid now. After Pastor Frank's wife died, the single gals at church were vying for his attention. Mother insisted we were perfect for each other, and I had a better chance of winning his heart since I worked with him."

"Aunt Penny can be quite persuasive."

Millie's demeanor calmed. "Let's face it, Carol. I've been single way too long with no prospects in sight. Mother had me convinced Pastor Frank was my last chance. My destiny. He's handsome like the heroes in our stories, and I wanted to believe he loved me." She held up a novel. "I've never had a real-life romance, so these books have been a substitute for all the love and acceptance I've been denied."

"But, Mills, risqué books like those create unobtainable desires and make things worse. What we all want and need is genuine love." Carol took the novel and set it aside. "Why don't you try inspirational romance stories? They show sweet, lasting kinds of relationships."

Tears formed as Millie covered her face. "I've never had a man put his arm around me or even hold my hand."

"If God has someone for you, he'll be the right man to fill the empty void. Who knows? It might be Lou Blythe."

"You said he has a crush on *me*?" Millie's eyes narrowed. "Are you sure? I've known him for years, and the only thing he's ever said is hi and goodbye, Miss Drake. He's never even looked me straight in the eye."

"He's sure been baring his soul to Frank."

"I've always thought he was cute. Oh, my! This has never happened to me before." Millie fanned herself. "What'll I do?"

"If he asks you out, and Frank will make sure he does, just go and have fun. Let your relationship happen naturally."

Millie pointed to the door, put her index finger to her lips, then reached over and turned up the music. "Well, he did call this afternoon and asked me to sit with him in church tomorrow. Then he asked me out for next Saturday, but Mother doesn't know the details. I thought it was a pity date because he felt sorry for me. I didn't know there was a crush involved."

"I'm so happy for you." Carol hugged her cousin. "Please don't listen to your mother. You have a hunk on the hook, girl. Enjoy! You deserve a sweet gentleman like Lou." She grinned. "Doesn't his beautiful deep voice make you shiver all over?"

"Down to my toes." Millie giggled.

Carol scooted closer. "I'm sorry for the misunderstanding on New Year's. I wouldn't hurt you for the world. Forgive me?"

"Sure. You and Pastor Frank have my blessing." A shy grin spread across Millie's face. "If we do start dating, I'll need a new outfit—nay—a whole new wardrobe. Will you help me?"

"I'd love to." Carol stood to leave. "This is going to be so much fun."

"I have one more favor to ask. I'm terribly nervous about tomorrow morning. Would you go to church with me? I don't want folks, especially mine, to think Lou and I are an item. At least not yet."

"I'd love to, as long as you don't plant me between you." Carol waved goodnight and walked from the room with a smile. Frank wasn't expecting her to be at his church, and she couldn't wait to see his reaction.

CHAPTER SEVENTEEN

CAROL ENTERED THE CHURCH VESTIBULE AND glanced around for Millie.

The smiling greeter was a tall man, almost cadaverously thin with a shock of white hair. He broke away from his companions and hurried to greet her with an outstretched hand. "Good morning, welcome to Apache Pointe Community Church."

She returned the smile and took the bulletin he offered. "Thank you, it's nice to be here."

"You look familiar." His keen, pale eyes squinted. "Do I know you?"

It was impossible not to like the old gent. Carol pointed to her parents talking to another couple. "I'm Carol Mason, Max and Sylvia Drake's daughter."

"Now I remember. It's good to see you again." He gave her a bear hug and then pulled out a bulging envelope of snapshots. "Our kids came in from Poughkeepsie for the holidays. I've got some great pictures of the grandbabies."

Who was he? Carol cheated and peeked at his name tag. "Good to see you, too, Mr. Kerrigan." She glanced at glowing red eyes in each photo. "Looks like you had a nice time."

From the side, Carol could see her dad winding his way through small clusters of people.

"Carol! Millie told us you were coming. Better hurry, she's waiting for you in the balcony. The stairs are right behind you."

"Thanks, Dad." Carol kissed his cheek, overjoyed for the timely reprieve. She waved to Mr. Kerrigan and hurried up the steps as her father valiantly took her place viewing the photos.

The balcony door squeaked open, and Carol cringed as it slammed shut behind her.

Millie nervously tapped her watch and whispered. "You're late, I thought you changed your mind."

"Would I do that to you? Mr. Kerrigan recognized me."

"Say no more." Millie motioned to the man beside her. "You remember Lou?"

Carol wiggled her fingers at him as she scooted next to her cousin. "Hi, Lou."

"Mother's in the second pew, organ side." Millie pointed. "Let's hope she doesn't gawk up here and see us."

The piano and organ prelude began. A warm tingle flowed through Carol when she saw Frank sitting on the platform. Her eyes gravitated to his lips, and she recalled their tenderness against hers. Would the events of yesterday's sleigh ride make it difficult for him if he saw her? She turned her focus away and swallowed. This was going to be a long service.

The music faded as Frank walked to the pulpit. "It's nice to see everyone here this morning. Most of the announcements are in the bulletin, however, I'd like to draw your attention to—" Frank spotted her, and his mouth stretched into a toothy grin. "Carol, you're here!"

A murmur rose as the entire congregation twisted in their pews to gawk at the upper tier.

Great. What should she do? Give a queen's wave? Blow a kiss?

Frank cleared his throat. "Uhh, where was I? That's right, the bulletin. I was going somewhere with that, I promise." He turned to the praise band leader. "It seems

I've had a memory glitch, Darren. Now's a good time to sing, don't you think?" Frank returned to his seat and on the way, sheepishly smiled into the balcony.

"Yikes!" Millie slumped in her seat and whined. "Mother saw us."

Carol's gaze immediately went to second row, organ side. Penny's arm lingered on the back of the pew. She lowered her red-framed glasses to the end of her nose and stared into the upper level, her forehead scrunched into accordion pleats.

The familiar refrain of "Here I Am to Worship" came from the praise band, and the song director raised his arms. "Let's all stand and sing it out."

The music swelled and beautiful harmony lifted heavenward. Lou's deep voice reverberated in their confined quarters as he closed his eyes and lifted his arm.

Carol nudged Millie and mouthed, "Wow!"

A vigorous nod came from her cousin, who then feverishly fanned her bulletin. A set of bright yellow inserts flew from her fan and wafted over the ledge to the crowd below.

Carol pinched her nose to keep the snorts at bay. Too little, too late. She grabbed her clutch purse and pulled out tissues for both her and Millie. Embarrassment kicked in, which only fueled the giggling. Had Frank witnessed her awkward lapse into adolescence? No way was she going to look at him now.

When the congregation sat, Lou moved a little closer to Millie. A sense of satisfaction filled Carol. Had her sweet cousin finally captured a man's heart? She grinned. To think, Aunt Penny sat below, totally clueless to the couple's growing attraction.

Carol's attention was consumed by the couple's budding relationship. Where would it all lead? She envisioned her cousin puckering for her first kiss. With Millie's luck, her mother would glance into the balcony at the moment their lips locked.

Applause from the congregation brought Carol out of her impromptu musings. Her face warmed as the soloist stepped off the platform. How had she missed the special music? Frustration settled in. Why wouldn't her mind stay on spiritual things today? Hopefully, the rest of the service would keep her attention where it belonged.

Frank walked to the pulpit, glanced in her direction and smiled.

That's all it took. Visions of their sleigh ride dashed through her mind. No doubt about it, she'd fallen in love, which was absolutely ludicrous. They'd only known each other since Thanksgiving. Carol grabbed her purse and found a small notebook and pen. Taking sermon notes would help keep her thoughts from ricocheting to the day before.

With pen on paper, she licked her lips, determined to stay focused. She could do this. However, somewhere between her pen scratching Roman numeral one and Frank's first word, memories of his tender kisses flooded her mind. *Please Lord, help me concentrate on the message.*

Roman numeral two. Her pen traced and retraced it.

Scripture appeared on the screen behind Frank. Determined to write it down, she sat up straight and sighed.

The pitch of his voice deepened with emotion. "In Psalm 30:5, we read, 'Weeping may endure for a night, but joy comes in the morning.' This verse has helped me since my wife passed away over two years ago."

Carol reread the verse, then pulled Bob's pressed flower bookmark from her Bible. *To everything there is a season, and a time to every purpose under the heaven.*

This was her new morning and new season. The words from both verses seemed to confirm God's blessing on a new future.

After the service, she followed the lovebirds down the stairs and rejoiced at the onset of their relationship. Lou took possession of Millie's hand. Carol grinned. A little power flirting never hurt, and if things stayed on course, the couple would get married and Millie would be free from her mother's tyranny.

Carol purposely waited to be last in line to greet Frank.

His face reddened as he shook her hand. "Sorry I made you uncomfortable at the beginning of the service."

"It wasn't just you." Her hand tingled within his grip. "I behaved like a giddy schoolgirl all morning. I've never acted that way in church before."

His smile turned up a notch. "Would you like to discuss it over Sunday dinner?"

"Are you kidding? I'd like to forget my embarrassing behavior, thank you very much." She giggled. "Andy and I were planning to go out for hamburgers. You're welcome to join us."

"Do you think Andy will mind?"

"Of course not. He likes you. As long as there's food involved, he won't care." She nodded to her son. "He's a bottomless pit."

"I remember being a voracious teen. We'd better go to the Hollow Coyote Buffet."

Her heart skipped a beat. What a great opportunity for the three of them to bond.

∞

The weekend had gone so well that Frank couldn't wait

to call his daughters to tell them about Carol. He wasn't worried about his youngest, Gwen. Being a nurse, she had accepted her mother's death and even encouraged him to find love again. Lisa, however, had been devoted to her mom. She'd need more time to accept another woman in his life.

CHAPTER EIGHTEEN

February started with record low temperatures for the area. Carol stepped from the delivery van and shivered as she headed for the church office, treasurer's report in hand.

There was a gleam in Uncle Stu's eyes when he asked her to personally deliver his papers to Frank. Bless his heart. Was it his cunning way of nurturing their romance?

She closed the office door behind her and was greeted by chamber music softly playing in the background. A cinnamon candle flickered in the window as Millie sorted the church mail.

"Hi, Mills. I have your dad's board report." Carol pointed to Frank's office. "Is he free?"

Millie nodded and put the envelopes down. "Oh, Carol, I'm so nervous. Lou finally asked me out for dinner tomorrow night."

"Now aren't you glad we got that new dress? You'll look great." Carol leaned on the desk and lowered her voice. "Has your mother found out, yet?"

Millie shook her head. "I knew you had a date, so I told her we'd *both* be out Saturday night." She covered her mouth with her hand. "I didn't bother to mention you and I wouldn't be out together. And since Mother didn't ask, it isn't technically a lie, is it?"

"Millicent Drake! My inner preacher's wife is absolutely shocked, but as your cousin, I understand. How will you explain Lou picking you up?"

"I've got it all figured out. I'm taking one article of clothing to work each day. I'll change my clothes here, and he'll stop by to get me."

"The things we do to save Lou from the initial face-to-face with your mother." Carol giggled. "Be sure to let me know how your date goes."

"You'll be the first and only one I'll tell." Millie answered the office phone.

Carol waved to her and hurried down the short hall to Frank's office. Her pulse skipped with expectation as she tapped on the door and peeked inside.

He rolled his chair away from the desk and stood, arms outstretched. "Hi, pretty lady. Come in."

"Here's Uncle Stu's report." Carol put the papers down and hurried into his embrace. "I needed to see my favorite pastor while I'm here."

His face reflected pleasure as he leaned in for a kiss. "Can you get away for lunch?"

"I could, but I'm going to look at an apartment." She grinned and playfully batted her eyes. "Would you go with me? I'd like you to check for things that need fixed and help me consider the cost. If it's at all livable, I want to grab it and move in as soon as possible."

"Sure, I can give you a couple of hours. Let me clean off my desk and we'll leave now."

She sat in a chair to wait. "If the flower shop wasn't going to be so busy next week, I'd wait until then to see it."

"That's right." He tapped his filled planner. "Valentine's Day. You'll be swamped. Andy told me he gets to help Grandpa with deliveries."

"He's looking forward to it. He also mentioned how much fun you had together last night. I'd like to hear your side of the story."

"I plead the Fifth. Andy's a great kid. I didn't know

what I missed by not having a son." Frank took her by the arm and led the way to the outer office. "We're going for an extended lunch, Millie. I'll be here around 1:30-ish" He turned to Carol while opening the door. "Did you know Andy taught me how to burp the alphabet?"

She groaned. "That's Bob's legacy to his sons, and the reason I wanted girls."

"You wanted him to teach your sweet daughters how to burp their ABCs?"

With a playful smack to his shoulder, she got into the car.

Frank buckled his seatbelt. "Andy's desire to be a missionary to Native Americans really impressed me. But then he mentioned he'd also like to be a race car driver." He shook his head. "Your boy's quite diverse in his career choices, isn't he?"

"He takes after his dad. Bob wanted to be a preacher or a jockey. Fortunately, he was too tall for his second choice."

"Compared to those two, I'm pretty boring. I've always wanted to be a preacher. Are you sure you're ready to deal with a man without a backup profession?"

Carol smiled. Only for the rest of their lives. She grabbed his hand and squeezed it. "A little predictability never hurt anyone. Turn left at the corner. The house number is 1507."

"I think it's the yellow house on the right." Frank pulled to a stop and took her hand. "Maybe this one will be fit for human habitation."

A gray-haired lady introduced herself at the door. "Hi. I'm Kay, the duplex manager. Please come in and look around. Your neighbor's adjoining walls are soundproof. If you have any questions, feel free to ask."

Carol stepped into the vacant unit where the smell of fresh paint greeted her. Sunlight spilled through the large picture window as Frank checked under the kitchen sink.

"I really like the open floor plan." She turned to Kay. "How many bedrooms?"

"You have two." She pointed down the hall. "I'll stay here. Take your time."

Frank was first to walk into a small bedroom. "This isn't a bad size for Andy."

"He'll be thrilled to have a room to himself." Carol shut the closet door and crossed her arms. "It'll be a tight squeeze, but I think his furniture will fit in here."

As they inspected the other rooms, her pent-up tension slowly dissipated. "We've searched for over three weeks, and now here's a nice clean one in my price range. I'm going for it." She grabbed his arm. "Just think, Frank, we'll be out from Aunt Penny's stranglehold in no time. I don't think I've ever been so excited and relieved."

"Good for you, sweetie. I'm pretty stoked, myself." He pulled her close and gently brushed his lips on her forehead. "So, you'll be coming to my church permanently?"

"We'll see."

He whispered in her ear. "There's another plus to this duplex. The parsonage is only a block away."

Carol's eyes widened. "Aunt Penny will have a field day with that news. How long until the rumors fly?"

"She'll have juicy stories airborne before you unpack that first box. But be strong. You have the Almighty and little ol' me to lean on."

"How sweet." Carol stood on tiptoes and kissed his cheek. "Let's get the papers signed and see how quickly Andy and I can move in."

CHAPTER NINETEEN

Two days before Valentine's Day, the moving process began. Carol hauled a few boxes and the sweeper from her storage unit, and then rushed to meet Frank and Andy at the apartment.

"My bedroom's ready to move in, Mom." Andy wiped the sweat from his brow. "This is the first time I've ever been excited about housework."

Frank set a bucket on the floor. "I told your mother I have an extra couch for you." He ducked as a wet sponge flew past his head. Then after chasing Andy into his room, he tackled the teen to the carpet, and their wrestling match began.

Carol stood in the hallway, arms crossed. "If you two are doing this to get out of cleaning, I've got news for you. It's not gonna work. Get busy."

"Nice try, Sport." Frank laughed as he helped the boy to his feet.

"It was worth a shot."

"Apparently the two of you can't be trusted to work together." She pointed to a box of folded bath towels and washcloths. "Put these in the linen closet, Andy, and then I'll have something else for you to do." She turned to Frank. "And you, mister, can assemble the beds."

Andy kicked the box down the hall and opened the closet door. His voice squawked from the bathroom. "Aww, Mom, it smells like Grandpa Drake's Wintergreen Joint Gel." He paused. "Yuck! A Dr. Boone's Bunion Buster box, and a buster's stuck to the door."

"Just rip it off, Andy. Think of it as being one step closer to manhood." She laughed and sprayed cleaner into a kitchen cabinet. "Where's the "Home on the Range" song coming from?"

"It's your phone, Mom."

"Great. I told you it's not funny anymore." She followed the sound until the singing phone was in sight.

"Hello. Hello?"

"Hi, Sweetheart. It's Mom. How's the new apartment?"

"It's great. Nearly move-in ready." The doorbell rang. "I'll have to call later, Mom. Love you, bye." She opened the door. "Mills! What brings you here?"

"I came to offer support and elbow grease. Besides I was curious about your new place." Millie stepped inside and removed her jacket. "Mind if I look around?"

The door was almost closed when Carol noticed another car pulling into the drive. "Hey, Frank, JoAnna Foster's here." She waved and waited for her friend. "Come on in."

JoAnna gave her a hug and offered a bakery bag. "I brought you a housewarming gift. Fresh from my freezer to yours."

"Could it be the infamous Grizzly Bars?" Carol placed the gift on the kitchen counter and peeked inside the bag.

Frank entered the living room. "Hi, JoAnna. Is Russ hiding in the car?"

"I have to pick him up at the church in a few minutes."

Carol wiped chocolate from her lips as she joined them. "Let me introduce you to my cousin, Millie Drake. Millie, this is JoAnna Foster. Her husband, Russ, is the pastor at Living Water Chapel."

"So good to meet you, Millie."

"Thank you. Nice to meet you, too. I've talked to your

husband on the phone when he calls Pastor Frank at the office." Millie grinned. "I thought he had a wrong number when he asked for Reverend Puddintane."

"That would be my man." JoAnna surveyed the room. "What a cheery apartment. Wish I could stay and help you settle in, but Russ and I are on our way to the airport."

"Oh, yes. You guys are the guest speakers at the More Amour Marriage Retreat this week."

JoAnna turned to leave. "I'll call when we get home, Carol. Nice to meet you, Millie."

"I know you've worked hard on your presentations. We'll be praying for you." Carol and Frank gave her one last hug before she left.

"I have Andy's bed together." He kissed Carol's cheek. "Yours is next."

She gave him a fist bump, then pulled her cousin into the kitchen and slowly reached into the bakery bag. "Wait until you wrap your gums around a Grizzly Bar."

"I've heard about them but thought it was an urban legend." Millie closed her eyes and bit off a mouthful of the chocolate delicacy. A few chews later, she smacked her hand on the table. "These could be addictive. Where have they been all my life, Carol?"

"There's a place in the mountains called the Rising Doe Bakery. We'll have JoAnna be our mule."

Millie giggled, wiped her mouth on a napkin, and reached for another bar. "Your kitchen looks like it's been remodeled. Everything is clean and beautiful. Mother's house is cluttered with ruffles, tassels, and floral wallpaper." She took a deep breath and closed her eyes. "Now I have a question. Would you mind if Lou picked me up here for our next date?"

"That's fine. Why?" Carol pulled glasses from a box and handed them to Millie.

"Mother doesn't know we're dating, yet, and I'm not ready to tell her until I'm sure the relationship is going to last."

"I don't blame you." Carol took a pitcher from the refrigerator. "How about a glass of tea?"

A loud, youthful voice came from the hall. "Me and Frank want some, Mom."

"Not in your room, young man. That's new carpet." She looked at Millie. "How did he hear me from the other room?"

Millie's eyes squinted. "I wonder what else he heard."

A deeper voice boomed. "Nothin'!"

Carol hugged her. "We're all on your side. Don't worry about it. I doubt Andy or Frank have plans to confide in Aunt Penny."

Millie lowered her voice. "Lou is my first boyfriend, and I'm afraid Mother will open her trap and ruin everything. I think it's best to hold off the introductions."

"Absolutely, but your folks need to know before your golden anniversary." She patted Millie's back.

Millie nodded. "Thanks, Cuz. You've helped me understand I need to pray more about these situations. I'm even reading my Bible at bedtime instead of Mother's novels."

"That's good, Mills. I'm proud of you. Keep at it and your days will go better."

"Seeing Lou more often would make my days better, too." She leaned forward and whispered. "We've been dating a couple of weeks now, and he hasn't even tried to kiss me. What am I doing wrong?"

"Frank says he's overly shy and may be afraid of rejection. You might have to make the first move, like touching his hand and gazing deep into his eyes while talking to him."

"I'm not sure I can do that."

"Sure you can. Find an opportunity and seize the moment. Or better yet, create an opportunity." Carol gave her a sly smile. "Give him a call and see if he can help us move."

"Sounds like a plan. I'll go on the porch for privacy." A few minutes later Millie poked her head in the front door. "Lou wants to know if you'd like him to bring sandwiches."

Andy walked into the living room. "Did I hear something about sandwiches?"

Millie laughed. "Lou offered to bring hamburgers."

"Tell him I'd appreciate that." Carol continued to wipe the cupboard shelves.

Her cousin joined her a few minutes later. "He said it might be a half hour before he gets here."

"That's good, it'll give us time to get more done." She stepped down from the stool. "We'll be flooded with orders at the flower shop the rest of this week. Are you helping on Valentine's Day?"

"Only until three o'clock, if I can get past Mother's eagle eye. Lou's taking me out, and I need time to get ready." She giggled, picked up the window cleaner, and headed for the living room. "Thanks to you, I now have an agenda."

Carol turned away and smiled. Millie was growing a spine. Time to ramp up prayers for Aunt Penny's control issues.

CHAPTER TWENTY

CAROL PLACED A BAG OF POTATO chips on the table in front of Frank. "I can't believe it's March and we've lived here for two weeks already. After all the hassle with Aunt Penny, it feels good to have a home of our own."

"You deserve that sense of accomplishment." He snitched a chip.

"Andrew Mason! This is the third time I've called you for supper." She shook her head. "He must be on the phone. I don't want to make you late for your board meeting, so let's start without him."

Seconds before Frank offered thanks for the food, Andy dashed into the kitchen and slid into his seat as if it were home plate. "Yum. Sloppy Joes and chips." The boy scooted his chair up to the table and slapped a slice of cheese on his sandwich.

Frank gave her a wink and bowed his head. "Dear Heavenly Father, we thank You for this day, the food, and the hands that prepared it. In Jesus' precious name, amen." He ruffled Andy's hair. "Now you can eat. I brought Armadillo Ripple ice cream for dessert."

"Are you kidding me?" Carol shuddered. "That sounds disgusting."

He laughed. "It's from the new Jen and Berry's limited edition of Desert Desserts."

"Hey, great. That's my favorite." Andy took a double bite of Sloppy Joe, causing his cheeks to expand.

Much to Carol's horror, the boy nearly swallowed it whole. "Slow down, son. Savor the flavor, why don't ya?"

He washed it down with a gulp of milk and offered a toothy grin. "Tyson's mom asked me if you guys were gonna get married. What should I say, Mom? Are you?" He stuffed a handful of potato chips into his mouth.

Carol nearly choked on her drink and threw an S.O.S. Frank's way.

He laughed and playfully punched Andy's arm. "Umm, good question. What do you think, Sport?"

"Mom and I've talked about it a few times. I'm good with it." Andy looked at Carol and wiggled his eyebrows. "Grandpa says you'll be hitched before Thanksgiving, and Uncle Stu says Christmas at the latest." He licked his fingers. "Wanna know what Aunt Penny says?"

"No!" Carol and Frank replied in unison.

"According to Uncle Stu, she said it'll be a cold day you-know-where before she allows that to happen."

"On that sour note, I need to get to the board meeting. Carol, let's talk about this marriage thing tomorrow." He kissed her cheek and rushed out the door.

Millie's office phone rang as she passed the March board packets to the members. "Excuse me, I need to answer that." She returned to the boardroom a few minutes later. "Cassandra's husband called from the hospital. She's in premature labor."

"We'll remember her in prayer in a minute." Frank cleared his throat and scanned the table. "Looks like we're without a secretary. Any volunteers? How about you, Harold?"

"Nope. I'll pass, thank you."

"Stuart, Leland, either of you men interested?"

Leland smacked the table. "You kidding?" He pointed

to the woman entering the room. "Let Marvel Ann do it, her handwriting's better than mine."

"What have you volunteered me for now?" She took her seat.

A scuffle from the outside office drew everyone's attention. Penny barged into the boardroom unannounced, her frown firmly in place. "Stop the meeting!" She slammed her purse on the table.

Millie grimaced as her dad jumped to his feet, his face stark white. "What are you doing here, Penny?"

"Hush. Sit, Stuart." She waited until he complied, then waved an envelope over her head. "I have an issue with our esteemed pastor."

Millie's eyes were riveted to the flapping object. Oh, no. Carol's letter. Her throat went dry, and every fiber in her body signaled impending doom.

Several board members mumbled, and others shifted in their seats as if sitting on blisters.

Her mother's eyes held a vicious glint as she stared at Frank. "*You've* been carrying on with my husband's niece these past couple months."

Stuart's hands shook. "Penny, don't do this."

"Quiet, I'm going to have my say." She faced the pastor. "Carol isn't as innocent as you think she is. I have proof you might all be interested in." She straightened her shoulders, cleared her throat with great importance, then read the letter aloud.

"*Carol, what have you done? Grady confessed your growing attraction to each other, but I couldn't believe it. Now I find you're the one who's been having an affair with him. I understand you're still mourning the loss of Bob, but how could you betray me? You've ruined my marriage . . . and shaken my faith in God . . . I never want to see or hear from you again.*"

Stuart's chair hit the wall as he sprung to his feet.

"That's enough, Penelope Joy."

Millie shot a look at her easygoing father, his face now contorted with anger. He never interrupted Mother in public, and knew better than to use her given name. But then, he hadn't been pushed this far before. Millie closed her eyes and silently pleaded for the Rapture.

"I said sit, Stuart." Penny pointed to his chair. "The truth needs to come out."

Board members appeared to be in shock as Stuart's eyes narrowed and his neck veins bulged. He stomped to his wife, grabbed her arm, and yanked her to the door. "You're getting help."

Penny jerked loose, and with her usual theatrical flair, threw the letter in Frank's direction. "Our shepherd has taken up with a wolf in sheep's clothing."

Millie wept into her hands as her father forced his wife from the room. She never dreamed Mother would actually go through with her threats. The woman was out of control. Poor Carol. Poor Frank. Millie's thoughts reached for the heavens. *Please make this nightmare go away.*

Penny's voice shrieked from the hallway. "I'm doing this for you, Millicent."

With a pale face, Frank retrieved the letter. "Out of respect for Stuart and Millie, let's keep this to ourselves. Meeting's adjourned." He left the room without another word.

Chairs scooted and the remaining board members escaped with reckless abandon.

A tumble of confused thoughts and pain assailed Millie. Would her parents' marriage survive? Hot tears clouded her vision. Her mother could be forever banished from the church. Who'd blame them if they expelled the whole family? She wept aloud in the empty boardroom.

A few minutes later, Millie's head ached with a

throbbing pulse, so she went into the bathroom to rinse her face with cool water. The first thing she needed to do was apologize to Pastor Frank. She walked to his office and tapped on the door.

"May I come in, Pastor?" When no answer came, she peeked inside. The back of his chair was all she could see. "I'm so sorry Mother barged into the meeting. She had no right to say those things, especially in front of the board."

He slowly swiveled his chair around to face her, the letter crumpled in his grip. "Why didn't she simply come to me privately like a rational person?"

"Rational is *not* Mother's style."

"I can't believe this letter." Frank shook his head, eyes filled with sorrow. "Are these accusations true?"

"All I know for sure is my cousin is the most kindhearted woman I've ever met. There has to be more to this story."

"I don't know what to think." Frank smoothed out the wrinkled letter on his desk and read a portion of it aloud. ". . . You're having an affair with him. I understand you're still mourning the loss of Bob, but how could you betray me? You've ruined my marriage, compromised the relationship of our children, and shaken my faith in God." He refolded the paper, stuffed it into the envelope, and narrowed his eyes. "I realize there are two sides to every story, and I want to believe in Carol, but on the surface, this letter appears pretty condemning, don't you think?"

CHAPTER TWENTY-ONE

Carol wiped plant debris from the glass counter in the showroom and then dusted various knickknacks, vases, and planters. She yawned. Another typical, slow Thursday morning at the flower shop and far too nice to be stuck inside. She'd rather be with Frank.

Things were getting serious between them and marriage seemed imminent. Carol picked up a sample bridal bouquet and took a few halting bride-steps. Did she really want another big wedding or something more private and romantic? Apache Pointe was his stomping ground; she'd let him decide.

Her dad came from the workroom. "Hey, Carol, your purse is chirping back there."

"Thanks, I'll get it." Her phone had fallen silent by the time she got to the workroom.

The tone of Frank's short voice mail set her antenna quivering. "Carol, we need to talk."

Oooh, he sounded perturbed. Bob always appreciated her support, and now she had a chance to be there for Frank. She poured a cup of coffee, said a quick prayer, then called the church office. "Hi, Mills. I know it's early, but is this a good time to talk to Frank?"

"Umm." Her voice wavered. "I'm sorry, he's in an impromptu meeting on the phone right now, but you're supposed to meet him at the Hot Dog Hacienda around noon."

Carol wrinkled her nose. Hot dogs weren't her favorite. "Sounds unique. Where is it?"

"Next to Discount Doohickeys on the south side of town." Millie blew her nose. "Oh, Carol." She sniffed. "I can't apologize enough for Mother's actions at the board meeting last night." A click indicated the conversation was over.

Carol stared at the phone. What was she talking about? Everyone knew Penny Drake's name meant trouble, but why did she go to the board meeting? And what did Penny's meddling have to do with her? She shrugged. No wonder Frank's voice mail sounded strange, he probably needed to unload. Her stomach wrenched into tight coil-mode.

The lack of customers left too much time to dwell on Millie's puzzling comment. Only a half hour until she met with Frank. Maybe her dad could tell her how to get to the hot dog place.

She found him watering plants in the hothouse. "Do you care if I leave a little early to have lunch with Frank?"

He glanced at her and smiled. "Hey, I can handle things here. Why don't you take the rest of the day off?"

She hurried to him, raised the bill of his cap, and kissed his creased brow. "You're the best, Dad. By the way, how do I get to the Hot Dog Hacienda?"

The lines on his forehead deepened. "Why do you want to know?"

"Frank wants to have lunch there."

"I can think of healthier places." Max took his work gloves off. "Remember where your elementary school was?"

Carol nodded. "Didn't it close years ago?"

"Yep. Go past it and you'll see an old laundromat, a More-Bang-For-Your-Buck store, and a park. The Hacienda is right across the street from the park entrance. Don't expect much."

"Got it. Dad, did Uncle Stu call you about last night's board meeting? Millie said Aunt Penny made an appearance."

He groaned. "Can't be good if ol' Penelope's involved. Might be why Stu hasn't come in yet. I'd better give that brother o' mine a call."

"Be sure to fill me in later." Carol went to the delivery van and opened the door. Scorching heat blasted her face. She hesitated, then climbed in and set out for Frank's strange choice of restaurant.

Her brain meandered to the brief conversation with Millie. Why did she feel the need to apologize for the board meeting, and what poor soul had been Aunt Penny's target this time? Since she upset the meeting so much, it could've been Frank in her crosshairs. Penny remained convinced that he jilted Millie, and it would be just like her to call for his resignation out of spite.

Carol parked in front of the Hot Dog Hacienda only five minutes late. She glanced up and down the street. No Frank yet. She turned the radio on, and waited. Even the golden oldies station couldn't keep her thoughts from jumping to Penny. She rubbed her forehead. At least everyone knew not to take the aggravating woman's tirades seriously. Carol's fingers went to her left eye to calm the nervous twitch.

By half-past twelve, she clenched her jaw. If Frank wasn't coming, why hadn't he called by now? Maybe the meeting went longer and held him up. Millie would know. She found the church number and hit speed dial.

"You've reached Apache Pointe Community Church. Your call is important to us, so please leave your name and number, and we'll get with you as soon as possible. *Be-e-ep.*"

Frank must be on his way. Carol grumbled and got out of the delivery van to stretch and take in the surroundings. Her gaze fell on the small park her dad had mentioned. As she turned to get in the air conditioned van, Frank's sedan pulled in next to her.

He merely sat and stared straight ahead. Why didn't he get out? She lightly tapped the window and smiled.

With a stern face and slumped shoulders, he finally got out and walked around his car.

Carol's left eye tic resurfaced, and her stomach wound tighter as he slowly approached. He didn't kiss her. Something wasn't right.

"Let's order our dogs and go to the park to talk."

She cleared her throat. "What's going on?" Maybe ignorance truly was bliss.

The mixed aroma of aging raw onions, sauerkraut, and chili sauce permeated the air as Frank opened the door for her, and they headed for the counter.

A number of gut-wrenching possibilities were illustrated on the faded menu overhead. Deutsche Dogge? Eww, that had to be with kraut. She swallowed and searched the list for the least offensive item. All had the makings of a digestive disaster.

"I'll take a Mellow Mutt with mustard." She forced a smile. "And a bottle of water."

Three minutes after Frank paid for their order, the clerk shoved a grease-stained food bag over the counter. Frank and Carol strolled to his sedan. She waited for him to open the door.

He pointed to teenagers roosting on the hood of a car outside the Sudsy-Wudsy Laundromat. "You don't want to leave the van parked here. Why don't you follow me?"

They pulled into the small neighborhood park across the street. He led her around the bend near a horseshoe pit where two older men in Bermuda shorts bickered over the last toss.

She waited in the van while Frank grabbed the lunch

bag and headed to the nearest table. After a short hesitation, she frowned, climbed out, and joined him. He usually opened her door. It was a bit too early in their relationship for chivalry to be taken out of the equation.

Once she was seated at the picnic table, Frank bowed his head. Her sense of abandonment intensified when he broke their usual custom of holding hands while saying grace.

The clinking of horseshoes in the nearby pit made his clipped words barely audible. Without looking up, he handed her the Mellow Mutt oozing with bright yellow mustard, then tossed his wrapped chili dog to the table.

Carol pushed her hair behind her ears and reached for his hand. "Want to talk about it?"

A muscle worked in his jaw as he pulled away.

The stinging rejection caused her hopes to tumble. Poor guy. Aunt Penny must've seriously crushed his spirit. Would he feel the need to leave Apache Pointe?

Frank wiped his red-rimmed eyes and spoke in a hushed tone. "This is very difficult for me. I just had the most grueling phone conversation with the elders at headquarters." He took a deep breath and released it slowly as if holding in raw emotion. "This whole mess began when Penny took it upon herself to drop a bomb at the board meeting last night."

Clink . . . clink.

They turned toward the sound of metal against metal. One of the horseshoe pitchers, apparently the victorious clinker, danced with his arms over his snowy-white head.

Carol held her hot dog mid-air and stared at Frank. "Penny's always dropping bombs. Can you tell me what happened?"

His eyes held disappointment as they bored into hers. "She brought a letter from Sue North."

"S-Sue?" Carol's face grew hot and her stomach pitched. Warning bells clanged in her head as she crushed the waxed paper that once covered the crusty Mellow Mutt. She'd hidden the condemning letter in her room. Did Aunt Penny steal it from the dresser, or had a new letter arrived? Either way, the woman had no business with it. Under Frank's pained stare, Carol stiffened and gripped the edge of the picnic table.

"Since the letter was addressed to you, I assume you know the woman."

She swallowed the acid rising in her throat and pushed the uneaten hot dog away. "Sue North was my best friend for over twenty years."

He squinted. "So, were you going to tell me about her claim that you broke up her marriage?"

Clink.

A pause followed as his smug mug intensified her irritation. *Self-control, Carol.* She searched for the right words. "May I explain, or are you in a hurry to burn me at the stake?"

Clink.

"Of course I want you to explain. That's why we're here." Frank's tall figure leaned forward as he placed his hands on the table. "All I know is Sue accused you of having an affair with her husband. She also said you ruined her marriage, and shook her faith in God." He rubbed his neck. "That seems pretty clear."

Carol breathed in shallow, quick gasps. Was this the *real* Frank? Cold and judgmental? How could he believe those accusations without getting her side of the story? "And you brought me here to condemn me?"

His voice softened. "Look, honey. I know the anguish you went through when you lost your husband. Sometimes loneliness can bring on temptation, but we have to be strong enough to fight it off."

She stood and crossed her arms. "And what makes you think I succumbed to *that?*"

"I have to remind you any sin can be forgiven, including adultery."

Clink.

His words cut her heart like shards of glass and heat rose in her face. She drew a breath between clenched teeth and took a step forward to meet his disturbing stare. "Adul—I cannot believe you just said that. You're the most arrogant, self-righteous—" Despite a warning within, she continued to rail. "Why did I ever want to marry you?" By now, her right index finger hurt from repeatedly poking his chest.

Clink.

Wrapping one of those horseshoes around Frank's scrawny neck would be the perfect ending. Too bad Sue wasn't in her life to help dispose of the body. An image of an unflattering prison jumpsuit popped into her thoughts. She grimaced. Lucky for him, orange wasn't her color.

With a resounding huff, she stomped to the van, slammed the door, and strangled the steering wheel. The delivery van's tires spun, spewing dirt and stone in all directions.

A blanket of silence covered the small park while Frank stood with his mouth open. Even the horseshoe pitchers ceased their match to gawk in his direction.

Cold dignity formed as he snatched their untouched hot dogs. Who would've guessed sweet Carol could react with such a nasty temper when faced with constructive criticism? He slam-dunked the food into the trash barrel and headed for his car amid the pitchers' heckling.

"You sure bungled that one, dummy."

"That beauty slipped right through your fingers."

Frank grumbled, gave the gravel a hard kick, then settled into the driver's seat. The scene didn't go as planned, but he had to confront Carol and remind her that forgiveness was only a prayer away. If she'd only come clean earlier, he wouldn't have been blindsided in front of the board, district office, and his own congregation. He started the engine and put the car in gear.

Thoughts of taking her and Andy to Sky Harbor Airport in November came to mind. She didn't appear to be a blatant man hunter. Her purse was wedged between them on the car seat, apparently to give the impression of keeping things proper. Could she really be that good of an actress?

Driving home he thought of Carol and this Grady character. Could it be they'd been an item for a long time? Maybe even before Bob died? His conscience clawed at his gut. No, that just wasn't possible. Carol loved her family, she wouldn't have done that. But how could he find the truth behind the lurid accusations?

Her biting words rang in his ears. 'What makes you think I succumbed to that?' What if she was innocent? Would he be able to undo today's damage?

CHAPTER TWENTY-TWO

THE HIGH-PITCHED RING OF MILLIE'S office phone startled her. She glanced at Pastor Frank before lifting the receiver. "I hope this isn't another angry call about the board meeting. We had a dozen complaints yesterday. It's made me a nervous wreck."

"Let it go to voice mail again. We both need a break." Pastor Frank pointed to his office. "I need to get a little work done." He frowned when the front door opened.

Andy stomped in and dropped his school books on Millie's desk.

Frank patted the lanky teen's back. "Hi, Buddy. Shouldn't you be in school?"

"I'm on my way." He took a deep breath. His voice was firm. "I need to talk to you first, Reverend Bailey."

"I see. Sounds serious." Frank's forehead creased. "Let's go to my office."

Andy straightened his shoulders and followed the preacher.

As the door closed behind them, Millie's curiosity piqued. Was Carol all right? They hadn't even discussed the ill-fated church board meeting. Her conscience pricked at the thought of being mixed-up in Mother's search of Carol's bedroom. She hurried to the office door in order to catch every word. Eavesdropping was something Mother would do, but Millie didn't care. Her concern for Carol was more important.

"Mom's mad at the world and won't even let me talk about you." With a rankled voice the teen added, "What did you do?"

"It's complicated, Andy. I'm not sure it's proper for us to discuss it."

"This is about my mom. She's been through a lot this last year."

Pastor Frank cleared his throat. "Do you know Grady North?"

Holding her breath, Millie inched closer to the door.

Andy groaned. "Yeah, I know the bum. What about him?"

"What was his relationship with your mom?"

"Relationship?" His voice intensified. "Don't make me puke. Grady and Sue North were Mom and Dad's friends. After the accident, Grady took over our lives like a howitzer."

Millie bit her thumbnail. She didn't know what a howitzer was, but it didn't sound good.

Finally, Andy spoke again. "He let us live in their dinky garage apartment when we had to move from the parsonage. He's the main reason we moved here."

"Do you know what happened?"

"Grady was making all the decisions for us, me especially. He came to fix the furnace, and I got mad when he pushed my buttons. I locked myself in the bathroom. Then Mom got home. When I came out, he was holding her and kissing her. I pounded him and ran out of the house. Later, Mom showed me the reason why he was holding her."

With her ear suction-cupped to the door, Millie envisioned Pastor Frank on the edge of his seat.

"Finish your story, Andy. I need to hear it all."

"Did you know Mom hates mice?"

Mice? Silence followed. Millie couldn't get closer to the door. *Come on, Andy. Speak up.*

"See, Mom was fixing supper and found a dead mouse

in the can of beans. I was in the bathroom and heard her scream. I came into the room when Grady had his fat mouth on hers. I was so mad I jumped on his back, hit him, then ran off. Later, she said the mouse scared her so much she fainted and Grady caught her. Anyway, he lied to Sue, she got mad, and here we are."

"So there was really nothing between her and Grady?"

"Mom *never* liked him, but he's married to her best friend. We've even talked about that creep always gawking at women."

Millie's hand went to her throat as she slowly tiptoed from the door. Mother had definitely done it this time and made her an unwilling accomplice. A sudden coldness surged through her. Would Carol ever forgive her for being a part of the scandal?

Tears fell as she scribbled a sticky note: "Feeling ill. Had to leave." She slapped the note on the computer monitor and fled to her car. She knew of only one peaceful place to go—the river walkway across town.

Sunbeams glistened across the rippling water as she rested on a bench, but the tranquil reprieve from the office didn't offer the needed peace of mind. She'd always been ashamed of Mother's overbearing personality. Her meddling caused a lot of pain and grief to so many people, and now Carol's reputation was shattered.

Millie bowed her head and saturated her Snuffs tissue. Insufficient income prevented her from getting her own place. Now, even if it meant living in a room at the YWCA, she was determined to move.

"Millie?"

With a quick swipe at her nose, she peeked up at the sound of a familiar voice. Of all the times for Lou to show up, and no way to hide her puffy, red-splotched face.

"I didn't expect to see you here." He sat beside her and frowned. "What's wrong?"

Millie looked away and drew in a deep breath. What could she say? The first man to show any interest in her, and the truth would surely scare him off.

Lou cleared his throat and held up a bakery bag. "I love to come here in the morning to have breakfast while the day is still fresh and clean."

She covered her face with a wad of soggy Snuffs. "I've been a part of something awful and possibly destroyed the life of my cousin and Andy." Millie crammed the used tissues into her purse and gathered a handful of fresh ones. "She'll never forgive me, and I don't blame her." A blubbering-induced headache pounded through her skull.

"People say I'm a good listener." He set the bag aside and rested his elbows on his knees.

Like it or not, now was the time to expose their family's dirty laundry . . . but, should she even mention Mother's personality disorder? If Lou left over this, she vowed to sign her mother's commitment papers at the most remote nuthouse available.

"Remember the first time you called me? I was trying to stop Mother from searching Carol's room. She found an accusatory letter and took it to the church board this week. Now there's gossip all over town." Her voice squeaked. "I just found out it was all circumstantial. Carol's innocent of all those accusations."

He put his arm tightly around her. "You need to tell Carol right away. If she's as loving as you say, there's no need to worry. Give her time to think about it, but everything will be fine."

She stared at him through her tears. "I will *never* be like my mother."

Stabbed with guilt, Frank stood by his office window and watched Andy cross the street. How could he have ever doubted Carol's character? "You're so stupid, Bailey!"

A sincere apology, followed by much groveling, was definitely in his future. He reached for his cell phone.

CHAPTER TWENTY-THREE

CAROL BREATHED IN THE AROMA OF freshly brewed coffee and rushed to pour her first cup of the morning while Andy showered. Surely by now he'd heard the cruel gossip insensitive people were spreading about her.

From the bathroom came Andy's rendition of the "Rubber Ducky" song in pitch-perfect Muppet voice. She laughed in spite of her dismal mood. It was just like him to try to pick up her spirits. She loved that kid.

Her thoughts returned to Aunt Penny trumpeting an inflated version of the scandal all over town. A knot tightened in Carol's stomach. Now all of Apache Pointe deliberately avoided eye contact with her. The dreaded fishbowl effect had returned.

At least her parents offered the needed support. She grabbed the strawberry preserves, slathered a thick layer on her toast, and dunked it in the hot coffee. After taking a healthy bite, she gagged. What on earth? The jar's label boldly proclaimed "Hot Salsa." As she spat the spicy bite into a napkin, the phone rang. Caller ID indicated it was Frank. Again.

She laid the phone face down. There was no reason to bow at Frank's big feet, or explain any relationship with Grady. Didn't his mother teach him not to believe everything in print? Her teeth clenched. Hopefully, the big galoot took notice of her absence from his fancy-shmancy church yesterday. Although throwing eye daggers at him from the front pew might have been more therapeutic than church hopping.

A knock at the front door brought her out of defense mode. Her slippers scuffled across the kitchen floor. Better not be Frank. She closed her eyes. Or Aunt Penny.

Before Carol reached the living room, Andy zipped past her, notebook in hand. He gave her a quick kiss on the cheek and opened the door.

"Millie's here. 'Bye, Mom. See ya after school." He ran to meet his friends.

"Hi, Mills." She scrutinized the pinched look on her cousin's face. "Come on in."

Millie stepped inside and hung her head. "Can we talk?"

Great. Another lecture on family values. Carol led her to the kitchen and motioned to the table. "I wasn't expecting company this morning. I'm not in the best of moods."

"Neither is Pastor Frank." Millie frowned and took a seat. "There's been a definite icy ambiance at the church office since Tuesday's board meeting."

Ugh. That meeting brought on the infamous hot dog picnic where Frank flip-flopped from a hotty to haughty when he lambasted her with false accusations. "Want a cup of coffee?"

"Yes, please." Millie tapped her fingers on the table. "I'm so sick about what happened."

Carol placed a steaming mug in front of her cousin and sat down. "It wasn't your fault."

Millie's chin quivered, and she took a deep breath. "I've been too embarrassed to show my face since Dad hauled Mother from the board meeting."

"Were you there?"

"I had to work late on the board packets, and a call came. Cassandra was in labor at the hospital. As the group was choosing a fill-in secretary, Mother bolted into the room."

Carol groaned, sipped her coffee, and nodded. "Go on."

"I'm afraid you're going to hate me." Millie shifted in the chair. "But you need to know the whole story."

"I could never hate you. What happened?"

"The way Mother found your letter was so wrong." Millie took a deep breath. "It happened the day Pastor Frank took you to the mountains. She was furious, and if you remember, I wasn't too happy with you, myself."

Carol frowned. "And . . .?"

Millie hesitated and nibbled her pinkie nail. "Mother got the notion to ransack your room, hunting for ammunition to turn Pastor Frank and the entire church against you."

"I gotta hand it to her. The plan worked like a charm."

"Mother said she'd share it with the church board, but I never thought she'd go that far. She's sicker than we thought." Pieces of Millie's shredded napkin drifted to the tabletop. "We got to your room when Lou called and asked for a date. I sure didn't want Mother to know about it, so while my brain went into spin cycle, she had free reign over your things." Her voice choked. "Mother did all the snooping, but I didn't stop her. It's my fault. So, I'm here to beg your forgiveness."

Carol patted her cousin's slumped shoulders. "How can this be your fault? No one can stop Aunt Penny when she sets her mind to something."

"Dad and I decided she needs professional help. Her first appointment is Monday." Millie rubbed her temples. "Do you think they'll put her away for good?"

"I'm sorry you have to go through this, Mills. We'll pray she gets the proper help."

Millie looked away. "When Mother found Sue's letter, she read it to me, but I knew the affair couldn't be true."

"Thanks for having faith in me." Carol shifted to face her squarely. "It was stupid to keep that letter, but I never dreamed it would go public. If I'd only confided in you, we might have avoided this disaster."

"At least we've cleared the air. Thanks for not hating me."

"We have to be here for each other. Now it's your turn to give me advice." Carol swirled the last bit of coffee in her cup and sighed. "You've been around Frank for a long time. What should I do about him? He instantly condemned me and said, and I quote, 'Any sin can be forgiven, including adultery.'"

"Wow!"

"Can you believe he had the nerve to say that to my face?"

Millie's expression grew serious. "He's not usually that blunt, but his pride was trampled for all to see."

"My pride took a major hit, too." Carol waved her hands dismissively. "Frank Bailey hasn't cornered the market for humiliation."

"He's hurt, but you know he still loves you."

"Oh, yeah? He didn't call after our hot dog lunch, and I was happy with that." Carol threw up her hands. "But, since yesterday he's been calling every hour."

"What does he say?"

"I'm not answering him, Mills. Who wants to be preached to?"

"I think he probably feels pretty stupid by now." Millie smiled and scooted to the edge of her seat. "Andy stopped by the office on the way to school yesterday and explained the situation with you, Grady, and the canned mouse."

Carol sat straighter. "Andy did that? He never said a word. Bless his heart." She'd have to show her appreciation right away. But as for Frank, he could stew in his own judgmental juices a little longer.

The next two weeks passed slowly, and the Arizona temps continued to rise. Carol wiped perspiration from her neck, then scrutinized her appearance in the bathroom mirror. She pulled her damp hair into a haphazard ponytail.

In the time it took to drop Andy off at school and make it across town to Floral Scent-sations the temperature had climbed another five degrees. After twenty years in the cool mountains of Vermont, every molecule in her body joined in protest of the stifling desert heat.

The business phone rang as she entered the flower shop workroom. They wouldn't be open for another hour. Only Aunt Penny and Frank called this early. It couldn't be her aunt who was happily sedated at home, and Carol certainly didn't want to speak with Frank. However, she missed his embrace.

She shrugged her tight shoulders to relax them. "Good morning, Floral Scent-sations."

"This is Dolores Garcia. I'm sorry to call so early."

Carol's tension eased at the stranger's voice. "That's fine. How may I help you?"

"My husband placed an order for an urn arrangement and a red carnation rosary yesterday, and I'm calling to verify delivery time to the Boxwell and Berriham Funeral Home."

"Let me check, Mrs. Garcia." Carol referred to the work calendar and changed the page to April. "Yes, the items will be delivered shortly after noon tomorrow, April second, as he requested. If there's anything else we can do for you, please let us know."

"I will. Thank you very much. Goodbye."

"Goodbye." Carol replaced the receiver and stared at

the calendar, relieved March was over. April was going to be 'corral your morale' month, even if it killed her.

The phone rang again. Carol glanced at her watch. Still fifteen minutes before her dad was due to come in and take over phone duty.

She struggled to maintain a pleasant voice. "Good morning, Floral Scent-sations."

"This is the health department," a man's sing-song voice warbled. "We've been notified your roses have an aphid epidemic. We're going to have to quarantine your shop." A familiar high-pitched laugh blasted Carol's ear. "April Fools!"

"Pastor Russ, I'm adding your church to my blacklist."

A woman's voice cut in. "This is JoAnna. I had nothing to do with his tomfoolery. I'm coming to the shop's front door waving a white hanky. Will you let me in?"

Carol rushed to greet her friend with a hug. "Hey, JoAnna. How are you?"

"I'm fine. I locked Russ in the car for your sake. Can you chat a minute?"

"Sure, I can spare more than a minute since we haven't opened, yet. What's on your mind?" As if she didn't know.

"I came about Frank." She pointed to the door. "Now, do you want me to leave?"

"Of course not. You've earned the right to plead his case, not that it'll help."

JoAnna linked arms with Carol. "I know letting go of anger is hard when we've been deeply hurt, but maybe he's suffered long enough."

"Listen, some people can pop off and be over it in a minute. Others like me are slow to anger and equally slow to cool off." Carol turned to hide the heat rising in her face. "Call it a character flaw, but that's the way I am."

"Fair enough." JoAnna leaned closer and lowered her voice. "Don't tell Frank I said this, but the poor clod's downright pathetic without you. When Russ suggested he might be jealous of Grady, Frank's preacher brain went into full denial."

Carol stifled a giggle. "Good."

"If you love Frank, don't give up. You're responsible for the light returning to his eyes after Barb's death. Admit it, you need each other."

"What I *need* is a man who has confidence in me."

"Frank wants the same from you. He was looking forward to sharing his pastorate with you. Now, he's on sabbatical in Canada asking the Lord if the door to his ministry is closed." JoAnna's hand went to Carol's shoulder. "Would you simply talk to him before he does something crazy like buying a used camel and moving to the Empty Quarter of Abu Dhabi?"

CHAPTER TWENTY-FOUR

Early morning sunlight drenched Carol's living room. She sat by the window, sipped her coffee, and searched her devotional list for the day's scripture.

Romans 12:20. *Therefore if thine enemy hunger, feed him; if he thirst, give him drink: for in so doing thou shalt heap coals of fire on his head.*

Heaping coals. Hmmm. She knew of a couple heads she'd like to heap coals upon.

It was easy enough to forgive Frank for his doubts, but Reverend Know-It-All didn't have the Christian fortitude to listen to her side of the story. She huffed. Great. Now she'd become unforgiving and judgmental like him.

Heaviness filled her chest, and she bowed her head in shame. "I stand corrected, Father. That wasn't a kind thought, and I know it grieved You. Please help me to genuinely forgive Frank and Aunt Penny as You have forgiven me." An image of the bearded lawyer flashed in her mind. She clenched her jaw. "Dear Jesus, I need special help to forgive Grady."

For two weeks she'd considered JoAnna's advice to call Frank when he returned from sabbatical. She stared out the window. Was it possible to release the anger for the man who had abruptly turned condescending? Shame gripped her heart. Forgiveness was needed, not to rekindle the relationship with Frank, but because of God's command.

A car horn honked outside. "Andy, your friends are

here."

"I'm coming."

"Come on, Andy. Hurry. Your grandpa took the day off, so I have to get to the shop early. Be home before supper."

Another blare of the car's horn, and Andy flew out the door. "I will. 'Bye, Mom."

Carol glanced at the living room clock. She had enough time to buy coffee and snacks for the employee's break room. She grabbed her purse and rushed to the van.

The parking lot at Kolonial Kubby was relatively empty this time of morning, making it easy to find a spot close to the door. She nodded to Herb, the smiling greeter, who offered a cart. It took her all of three feet down the main aisle to realize the front wheel had locked sideways, and a rear wheel sported a wad of pink bubble gum.

A frown creased her brow as she returned to Herb. "I need a different cart. You might want to take this one to a body shop."

The yellow-vested greeter's smile faded. "Whatever you say, ma'am."

Carol sighed when her fingers stuck to the second cart's tacky handle. Should she tempt the wrath of Herb again? Not a chance. She ripped a sanitizer wipe from the nearby dispenser and attacked the goo on her hands and cart. What else could go wrong today?

A few minutes later, she was sorry she'd asked. After putting a can of coffee in her cart, she rounded the next corner where an angry woman loudly complained to the butcher. The cross voice reminded her of Aunt Penny. She winced, made an abrupt U-turn, and bumped into an older lady passing out samples. Barbecue sauce splattered the frail woman's tan smock and white hair as faux meat links peppered the floor.

Carol reached to rescue the lady as she did a herky-jerky side step but missed the saucy hand by an inch. The poor old gal went into a double reverse spin and landed headfirst into the boxed display of veggie sausages and bottles of Uncle Bernie's BBQ Sauce.

A man in a white apron rushed from the nearby produce section, kumquats still in hand. "You okay, Erma?"

A giggle emanated from under the pile of small boxes. The poor dear answered with a wave of her barbecue-coated latex glove.

An agitated voice boomed above their heads, "CLEAN UP ON AISLE SEVEN."

The phone in Carol's purse vibrated. A canine choir woofed the tune, "Who Let the Dogs Out?" She dug through her bag until the barking cell was found. "Hello?"

"Is this Carol Mason?"

She turned from the commotion. "Yes, it is."

"This is Apache Pointe Memorial Hospital. There's been an accident, and this was the contact number. We don't want to alarm you, but Max and Sylvia Drake have been admitted, and we need you to come right away."

"What?" Her heart nearly stopped. "I mean, how bad are they?"

"All I can tell you is Mr. Drake's in surgery, and the doctors are still with Mrs. Drake."

"I'm leaving now." She dropped the phone in her purse. How she missed Bob's strong arms around her in times of crisis.

She leaned over the saucy lady still sprawled and marinating in Uncle Bernie's BBQ sauce. "I'm so sorry. I have an emergency." She left her cart with the five pounds of coffee and snacks, and then raced to the delivery van.

Her jumbled brain attempted to sort through the situation. Quick, call Frank. Her eye twitched. No, *not* Frank. The hospital could do that. She had to call someone. Maybe Russ and JoAnna. No, Uncle Stu needed to know first. She hit speed dial for his cell phone.

Uncle Stu gave simple directions to the nearby hospital and promised to get in touch with Andy. He reminded her that God was faithful. She could trust Him.

Scrambled memories of family gatherings flashed in her mind as she nervously turned onto the busy street. They surprised Mom on her sixtieth birthday, and the boys showered her with sixty kisses. On Christmas Dad made a great Santa to Bob's homely Mrs. Claus.

In a few minutes, Apache Pointe Memorial came into view. The closest parking spot to the main entrance was in row D, so she haphazardly pulled in and shut off the engine.

She half-walked, half-ran to the entrance. Her parents could be at death's door for all she knew. The gruesome memory of her husband and son's bodies haunted her as she raced down the hall to the welcome center. "I'm Carol Mason. Could you give me information about my parents, Max and Sylvia Drake?"

A few clicks on the computer brought up the needed information. The woman nodded. "Here we are. It appears Mr. Drake's still in surgery, and nothing's changed with Mrs. Drake. Go to the third floor and ask for a pager at the desk. They'll contact you as soon as possible."

The noisy cafeteria across from the elevators reeked of sausage and onions, which didn't sit well with her nervous stomach. The ride to the third floor offered a welcomed escape.

Two middle-aged nurses sat at the desk. The older one

looked up from her chart.

Carol introduced herself and added, "My parents, Max and Sylvia Drake, had an accident and were brought here." Her throat tightened. "I was told to get a pager from you so the doctors could notify me." She leaned against the desk and waited for the nurse to verify the information.

"Here you go, hon." The woman handed her the heavy device. "As soon as it beeps, you can bring it back here."

"Thanks. Where's the chapel?"

The nurse pointed. "If you stay on the red line, it will lead you there."

"Thanks again." The black box warmed her hand as she followed the directions.

Silence filled the empty chapel. A beautiful stained glass window offered the only light for the small sanctuary. She hurried to the front, knelt at the carved altar, and placed her purse and pager on the floor beside her. With head bowed, she pleaded for her parents' lives.

"Heavenly Father, I know You were with me when I lost Bob and Jake, but please don't take Mom and Dad, too." Thoughts of another double funeral made her tremble. What would she do without their love and support?

Her brain groped to process thoughts. She ripped a tissue from a nearby box, wiped her tears, and leaned harder against the altar. Several deep breaths lessened the tug of queasiness. She turned her attention to the cross above the altar. "I can only get through this with Your help."

She was about to stand when the chapel door opened and softly closed. Footsteps approached the altar. She peeked as someone knelt beside her.

Frank. His serious countenance caught her unprepared. Did he still carry any doubts of the supposed adulterous affair? She pursed her lips. Now was the time to forgive and douse the still-smoldering embers.

His husky voice cracked. "Heavenly Father, we come humbly to Your throne to lay our request at Your feet." He took her hand, squeezed gently, and continued his earnest petition for the Drakes. "Your will be done. Please give Carol and the boys peace during this difficult time. We'll give You all the honor and glory, in the precious name of Jesus."

The small chapel grew quiet as she focused on the ornate cross above the altar. *Yes, Your will be done.* Submitting to God wasn't always the easy thing to do, but she'd learned with Bob and Jake's death, there wouldn't be peace any other way. If He wanted to take her parents, was she ready to let them go?

Tears fell as she grasped the wooden railing and in full surrender confessed her weakness. "Lord Jesus, I *will* trust You." The weight gradually lifted from her shoulders.

"Amen." Frank's voice quivered as he patted down his unkempt hair. "You're not going through this alone, Carol. Let's go over here and sit down."

Stubble decorated his jowls, and his blue suit was unusually wrinkled as he helped her stand. She held on to his arm, thankful the blood returned to her tingling limbs. His disheveled appearance caught her unprepared. Did their breakup rattle him that much?

Sitting on a nearby pew, he kissed her hand before releasing it. His understanding gaze held no judgment.

Her face warmed as she struggled to still the thrill brought on by the touch of his lips. Maybe he'd broken her heart, but the man continued to have more sway over her than she'd like to admit. "Thanks for coming."

"I need to say something, Carol." His forehead

crinkled. "I've been a jerk."

"Let's not discuss it now. I'm upset about Mom and Dad so it's hard to think about anything else."

"You're right." He leaned closer and wiped a tear from her cheek. "I'm here to help."

The woody scent of his cologne was nearly her undoing. So much better than Bob's Wild Moose Musk, but she resolved to fight the urge to fly into his embrace.

The pager vibrated on the pew. Saved by the beep!

"There's your call." The muscles in his jaw clenched. "Let's go to the nurses' station."

Her skin tingled when he took her arm. Crud. Betrayed by her own flesh. She tried to pull away, but he held tight as they walked down the hall.

"The doctor will be with you shortly to explain your father's surgery." The nurse directed them to a nearby waiting room.

"What about my mother?"

"We don't have her information here, but I'll see what I can find out for you." She leaned forward at the desk. "Be assured both your parents are in good hands."

Nearly a half hour of sterile silence ticked by before a brawny woman burst through the waiting room door. Perspiration soaked her green scrubs, and a chart was positioned under her arm like a football. "I'm Dr. Ramsey. Are you Carol Mason?"

Carol nodded and clutched Frank's elbow.

"Mr. Drake's in recovery." The doctor referred to her chart. "He had a compound fracture of the radius in his left forearm. We put in two titanium plates. The procedure went well, and we expect him to regain full use of his arm." She looked up. "You can see him once he gets settled in his room. The nurse will contact you."

"What a relief. Thank you, Dr. Ramsey." Carol blinked her tears away. They shook hands before the surgeon left the room with all the grace of a linebacker on a mission.

"Thank you, Lord. Please continue to keep Max and Sylvia in Your care." Frank stepped closer and drew Carol into a hug. His gaze held concern as he searched her eyes. "I love you."

The warmth of his embrace flirted with her resolve. She pushed away and reached for the last dry tissue in her purse. "Not now, Frank."

"This misunderstanding has lasted too long." He shortened the gap between them. "Reading Sue's letter was like a knife in my heart. It was foolish of me not to hear your side. I've wanted to apologize, but you've refused my phone calls all this time." His eyes closed for a second. "Look, I admit her letter flipped me out, but a wise young man talked sense into my thick head. So will you please forgive my judgmental attitude?"

"Yes, I forgive you, but I don't want to get hurt again." Her throat constricted. She turned away from him, trying to regain composure.

He touched her shoulder.

She spun to face him. "Can you even fathom what it's like to be falsely accused of adultery by someone you love?"

"I'm truly sorry." He tenderly kissed her cheek and lowered his voice. "Can't we mend our relationship? My love hasn't changed, and I distinctly heard you say you loved me."

"A huge part of loving someone is trust."

"Touché. *And* a huge part of trusting someone is total forgiveness." He leaned forward and cupped her face in his hands. "What can I do to prove my sincerity?"

She closed her eyes, unable to look at him.

He wiped her tears with his thumbs and then kissed her again, their lips barely touching.

"Frank, I-I—" She wrapped her arms around his waist

and released a sigh of contentment and then returned his kiss, a little more urgently than she intended.

He continued to hold her tightly, dropping soft kisses at her temple. Tiny shivers ran up and down her spine as his warm breath tickled the tip of her ear.

Tears streamed down her face as she leaned into his hug and drew on his strength. "I forgive you, and I never stopped loving you."

A nurse escorted Carol and Frank to a consultation room. They took their seats at the highly-polished oak table. Pale green walls seemed to close in on her as they waited for news of her mother's condition.

"I'm scared, Frank." She dabbed her eyes. "What would we do without Mom?"

The door opened, and a weary looking man walked in. "I'm Dr. Perkins, Mrs. Drake's physician." A smile eased the tension on his face. "Carol Mason?"

Her heart labored to keep a steady rhythm. "Yes, and this is Pastor Frank Bailey."

The doctor shook their hands. "Mrs. Drake has a severe head injury. She's in an induced coma to help her brain heal and heart rest, but she's stable. We'll keep her unconscious for a while and then evaluate her progress. Do you have any questions?"

Frank took Carol's hand. "Would you explain the induced coma?"

"With a head injury, the metabolism of the brain is significantly altered. There might be sections without adequate blood flow. We want to reduce the amount of energy in those places, so as the brain heals and the swelling goes down, those at-risk areas need to be protected."

She sat up straight. "How long will Mom have to be in the coma?"

"It's difficult to say. It depends on how she progresses. We'll try to have her awake as soon as possible." Dr. Perkins cleared his throat. "This option is only used as long as it's needed. Once the swelling recedes, we'll lighten the meds to see what her level of function is. Nurses will monitor her around the clock."

Her mom was still alive, but would what about her quality of life? She thought of her dad lying unconscious two floors below. How would she break the news to him?

"I'll check in on her periodically." Perkins rubbed his neck and checked the clipboard. "If there's anything else we can do, please let us know."

"We appreciate all you're doing for Mrs. Drake." Frank shook his hand.

The doctor's eyes revealed compassion. "You may look in on your mother, but please stay only a minute."

She finally found her voice. "Thank you, Dr. Perkins."

He nodded and left.

Frank placed his arm securely around her shoulders. They walked down the hall and into the darkness of her mother's hospital room.

Several tubes and hoses trailed from machines, and the repetitious beeps of monitors unnerved Carol as she approached the bed. Her mom's face was partially bandaged, and the exposed tissue bruised and swollen.

"I'm here, Mom. I love you." She lightly kissed the wrapped forehead.

Frank passed her a tissue box from the nightstand, and then reached for Sylvia's hand. "Our gracious Heavenly Father . . ."

A sob caught in Carol's throat. She talked with her a few hours ago, and they laughed about a new hiding place for chocolate. This couldn't be happening.

". . . and again we ask for Your healing touch on Max and Sylvia." Frank paused. "Give the doctors wisdom as . . ."

She tried to focus on his words, but her mind was a whirl of unanswered questions. What caused the accident, and where did it happen?

He placed a hand on her shoulder. "Please comfort Carol and her boys during this difficult time. We ask all these things in the precious name of Jesus." Frank pulled her close. "Let's check on your dad now."

She gave her mom one more kiss before they headed to the elevator.

"What should I say when Dad asks about her?" Carol's voice quivered. She focused on the opening metal door and stepped inside the empty compartment.

He pushed the third floor button and stepped back as the door whooshed shut. "We'll say she's resting for now."

She nodded and gripped his hand even tighter.

A young nurse stood by her dad's bed, checking the IV bags. "It's still going to be a while before he wakes. Why don't you folks get something to eat?"

"Good idea." Frank stretched his arms over his head. "I think both of us could use coffee and a sandwich. What do you think, Carol?"

She released a heavy sigh. "Sounds great to me. I need to update Uncle Stu and have him tell Andy. Then I'll get in touch with Ethan."

He went to the door. "I'll get a pager and meet you at the elevator."

Carol kissed her father's cheek. "We'll be back in a while, Daddy."

A long week later, Carol climbed into Frank's sedan, and once again the two of them headed for Apache Pointe Memorial.

"I'm relieved that Dad's coming home today." She took a deep breath. "Asking Mrs. Clark to stay with him was a good idea. Thank you. She'll come mid-morning and stay until Andy gets home."

"Alma's been frantically seeking opportunities to use her nursing skills since she retired."

Carol nodded. "Dad said they made arrangements for Mom to stay at Comfy Care Convalescent Complex. Her recovery process has been so slow."

"But at least there's been steady improvement."

She nodded. "That's true." Improvement was good, but would her mom's head injury heal enough for her to function normally? Would she ever be the same?

CHAPTER TWENTY-FIVE

Six weeks later

CAROL BUTTONED HER PINK SMOCK, RELIEVED she'd weathered the cruel gossip of her supposed affair. Friends and sympathizers stopped by Floral Scentsations, and their support more than doubled last year's Mother's Day sales. She helped Uncle Stu and a team of designers fill orders while her dad greeted customers and answered the phone with his one good arm.

She made her way to the shop's front window and flipped the sign to say open. Before unlocking the door, a pudgy, unshaven man pressed his oily nose to the glass. She flinched, offered a weak smile and let him in.

"May I help you?"

"The name's Skeeter Swakhammer, and I'm in sanitation and waste control." His voice sounded like he regularly gargled with thumbtacks. He wiped his fingers on his stained coveralls before offering to shake hands. "You must be Max's purdy daughter from back East."

Her dad came from the workroom and sat on a stool at the counter. "Hey there, Skeeter."

"Hey, Max! I see you're still babyin' that gimpy wing o' yours. How's the wife doin'?"

"She's at Comfy Care and doing great. Can't wait to get her home." He pulled an order sheet out. "Need Mother's Day flowers for Mom?"

Skeeter's scalp reddened beneath his thinning, white crew cut. "Yeah, Mama said not to come home without 'em. I never heard the end of it last year."

Stuart poked his head out from the workroom. "I remember last Christmas you went overboard to make up for your lapse of memory." He chuckled and snapped his multi-colored suspenders. "The mistletoe wreath was a first for our shop."

"Not everyone gives their mother mistletoe." Max leaned over the counter and winked. "By the way, how'd that work for ya?"

"Aw, the old bat said it was a waste o' money." The burning color of Skeeter's face intensified. "At her request, I need two dozen, long-stemmed, ruby red roses." He walked behind a display.

Carol was sure her uncle would trade old bats with him in a heartbeat. "How about a nice card to go with your roses?"

A deep, guttural groan came from Skeeter's general direction. "Guess I could write: Roses are red, violets are blue. Ain't no hope with a mama like you."

She gasped. "Mr. Skeeter, are you serious?"

"Aw, I'm just kiddin' 'round. Let me take a gander at 'em cards. You got any that ain't too sticky sweet? I don't wanna have to resuscitate the ol' gal."

Frank walked in as laughter filled the shop. "Did I miss something?"

"Skeeter's ordering for his mama again." Max pushed his glasses on top of his bald head.

"Let me guess, a leftover mistletoe cupid?" Frank grinned and smiled at Carol. "Speaking of cupids, I came to see my favorite florist."

Skeeter cleared his gravelly voice and sidled up to Frank. "Did ya want the one in poky-dot suspenders or the one in a sling?"

Frank playfully shook his finger. "That, folks, is how nasty rumors get started. I meant the pretty one."

"Guess he means me. Sorry, Max." Stuart batted his eyes and pulled on his suspenders. "What did you have in mind, Pastor Buttercup?"

"Paws off, Uncle Stu. Buttercup is mine." Carol linked her arm in Frank's and led him out the back door to the small hothouse.

He gathered her into his arms and held her snugly. "I want you to know Stuart was never in the running." Frank's kiss was short and sweet as they stood among the succulents.

"You came early today." She gazed into his dark brown eyes. "What's up?"

"An idea came to me this morning, and I couldn't wait to run it past you." He planted a longer kiss on her neck.

She leaned closer. "I like your ideas. Have any more?"

"Yes, but they'll have to wait." He winked and gently tapped her chin. "I still have my daughters' old VW gathering dust in the garage."

"I'm so glad you rushed over here with that news flash." Her mouth twitched with amusement as she leaned in for another kiss. "But I liked your other idea better."

He turned his head and lifted his nose. "Listen, Miss Smarty-pants, I was going somewhere with this, but you ruined my flow."

"I'm sorry." She hooked her arm in his. "Resume your flow."

"What I wanted to tell you, and this will make you feel horrible for being such a smart aleck, is that Andy can have the car. I even planned to take him out to practice his driving. It'll give us a chance to bond."

She squeezed his arm. "Really? What a blessing. Poor kid's had to practice with the pink posy van since we gave our car to Ethan."

"The VW needs major work before I give Andy the good

news."

"By the way, Bob's insurance check finally came. Want to help find a car for me?"

"Finally! Of course I'll help."

She wrapped her arms around his neck. "You're a good man, Buttercup Bailey."

CHAPTER TWENTY-SIX

THE RADIO ANNOUNCER'S VOICE WOKE CAROL from a light sleep.

"The weather forecast for this eighth day of June—"

She turned the radio off and groaned. June eighth. Her second wedding anniversary without Bob. The only way to keep her mind from the inevitable memories was to keep busy, so she'd better get moving. She flung the sheet aside and hauled her weary bones out of bed.

After a warm shower, which did nothing for her mounting headache, she plugged in the curling iron. While it heated, she dried her wooly mane.

"Mom, mail came." Andy knocked on the door. "You got something from Sue."

"Sue North?" More accusations? "Is it ticking?"

"Naw, it's only a letter. Want me to open it?"

"No, thanks. I'll read it later." Her hand emerged from the bathroom, snatched the envelope, and laid it on the counter. She rear-ended the door shut and worked to tame her curls into a decent style.

The familiar handwriting on the letter attracted her eyes like a magnet. What would Sue gain from sending another hurtful message and aggravating an old wound? Today already started on an off-note. Could she wait until after work to read it? One thing for sure, Aunt Penny would *never* get her sticky fingers on this one.

Carol slipped the letter into the pocket of her jeans and headed for the kitchen. "Do you want your Toastee-Tortz warmed or fresh from the pack?"

"Warmed." Andy sat at the table and poured a glass of milk. "I have an idea about driving."

"This is not a good day to bring up that topic, Son. I'm doing the best I can for you."

"But—but—listen. Maybe someone has a car we can borrow."

"That might work. Why don't you go ahead and ask around." She bit her lip to keep quiet about Frank's offer of the VW and practice sessions. Only a few more weeks until the car would be ready.

"I'll be glad when I don't have to drive a pink flower van, with 1-800-4 Posies on it."

"I can't help the color or the telephone number. And even if we do get a car, I don't know when I'll have time to take you out." She glanced at the clock and put her coffee cup in the sink. "Our work calendar is completely booked with June weddings and graduations. And on my free time, I have to visit your grandma at the convalescent center. Speaking of work, we have to leave right now." She tossed the keys to her grumbling son on the way out of the apartment.

He jumped into the driver's seat, slammed the door, and backed the van a couple of feet before she got in.

She clicked her seatbelt as they took off down the street. "Please slow down, and if you don't straighten that attitude, I'll have you chauffeur Aunt Penny around town." She looked out the windshield, braced herself, and screamed, "Andy! Stop sign!"

He slammed on the brakes with both feet and Carol's head flopped like a ragdoll. The older Scent-sations van wobbled and came to rest in the middle of the intersection.

She closed her eyes and leaned her throbbing head on the headrest. The day had to get better, right?

A flashing light and two short "woops" from a siren

confirmed they were not alone. This was all she needed to complete her perfect morning. The shiny squad car pulled to the side of the road. The officer took his time getting out of his cruiser, and slowly approached the vehicle.

"Want to pull over to the side of the road?"

Andy's hands shook as he turned the key. Nothing happened. His face turned the color of oatmeal as he stared at the officer. "It won't start. What'll I do, now?"

Carol moaned.

"Relax, kid. That's fine." The officer leaned his forearm against the van door as his partner directed traffic. "Do you have your license, registration, and proof of insurance?"

"I have my permit. Do I have that other stuff, Mom?"

Thankful for the man's understanding, she searched the glove compartment for the needed documents. Oh yeah, this kid was ready for his license.

A broad smile came to the young policeman as the boy struggled to pull his wallet from his back pocket. The officer took the papers and returned to his cruiser.

Several cars passed them, and then came a black mini-van filled with giggling girls leaving a chorus of "Hi, Annn-deee!" in their wake.

The boy's forehead dropped to the steering wheel.

"It'll be all right, son." Carol patted his arm and retrieved her phone.

Her uncle's groggy voice answered. "Hello?"

"Uncle Stu, the van needs a jump, so I'm going to be late. Can you hurry and open the shop for me? Dad has a doctor's appointment so he won't be in until later."

"Uhh, I'm not in the position to come right now. I'll have to send Penny to do it." He groaned. "Just hurry, for everyone's sake."

"I'll get there as soon as possible, but could you slip

her a couple of pills?" She rubbed her aching forehead. Her stomach churned at the thought of being ambushed by Aunt Penny. The day kept getting better and better.

※

Carol mentally practiced her litany of excuses, reminding herself to avoid conflict at all costs. They drove past the shop where Aunt Penny stood at the front window, arms crossed.

With a loud moan, Andy pulled into the rear parking lot and cut the ignition.

"Listen, son. There's no need to go into detail about this morning. We'll simply tell Aunt Penny we had van trouble."

"Thanks, Mom."

A wall of fragrance smacked Carol in the face as she joined her aunt in the showroom. The woman's overpowering perfume masked the usual scent of the shop.

"We had a little trouble with the van on the way here, but we made it." She buttoned her smock. "I appreciate your willingness to fill in for me."

Penny tapped her foot. "You think you'll get paid for coming in at noon, Carol? Of course you won't." She sipped from her Java Joe's cup and set it on the counter.

"It's only nine-thirty." Carol walked to the refrigerated case. "I'll take it from here. Thanks again." Kill her with kindness. Kill her with kindness. Even with six weeks of medication and therapy, Aunt Penny's disposition hadn't improved one iota.

Penny's turkey neck wiggled. "Don't let it happen again. Where did you put the catalog? I need an arrangement for Millicent's birthday. And mind you, I don't want a bunch of that fern filler, understand? It looks so cheap."

"What kind of arrangement do you have in mind?" She placed the book on the counter as her eyelid arrhythmia kicked in.

Penny jerked the sales book closer and knocked over her cup. Brown liquid quickly puddled and warped the slick photos. The rest of the coffee splashed onto Carol's smock, down the front of the display case, and dribbled onto the floor.

"Can't you do anything right? Millicent always had catalogs where customers could reach them. Stuart will hear about this."

Kindness, kindness, kindness. She took a deep breath to regroup, then wheezed on the perfume overload. She handed the irritable woman another catalog. "Don't worry about the mess, Aunt Penny. I'll clean it up and then write your order so Uncle Stu can fill it."

"And get a fresh smock. You look disgraceful. It's not how we want Floral Scent-sations represented." The older woman licked her finger then flipped a page. "This is what I want. I'll write the form out myself so there will be no more mistakes." She quickly scribbled her order and stomped out the door.

Carol was a step behind her, braced the door open to air out the room, and then hurried to the counter. She reached for the window cleaner and paper towels. The smell of ammonia heightened her headache as she took out her frustration on the glass. There was no pleasing the miserable woman. "Thank you, Lord, for helping me hold my tongue." Her tone raised another few notches. "And please give me a gentle spirit."

In that instant, strong arms went around her and squeezed. She gasped for air, elbowed her attacker, and then spritzed him with the window cleaner.

Sunglasses fell to the floor. With hands covering his face, the man spluttered and snorted.

"Frank! What were you thinking?"

"What were *you* thinking, spraying me with ammonia, Miss Gentle Spirit?" He tore a paper towel from the nearly empty roll. "Good thing I had my shades on."

"I'm sorry, but you scared me. I didn't hear you come in."

He wiped the dripping cleaner from his chin and retrieved his sunglasses. "I saw your aunt leave and figured it was safe to come in. Boy, was I wrong."

She giggled and kissed his freshly disinfected cheek. "This hasn't been a good day at all."

"It's only morning. What happened?" He tossed the paper towel into the trash and reached for her hand.

"First of all, this is my wedding anniversary, and I miss Bob."

"I cope with that same occasional wave of emptiness. Losing Barb still hurts." He gathered her close. "What else happened?"

"I got a letter from Sue North. Does that name ring a bell?"

"Sure does. What did she have to say?"

"Who knows? It's smoldering unopened in my pocket." She searched his eyes. "Then Andy got a ticket on the way to work for running a stop sign, which made both of us late. Of course, Aunt Penny was waiting to pounce the minute I walked in the door."

He lightly touched her elbow. "I'm sorry your day has been so bad. How about I take you out for a nice supper?"

"Thanks for the offer, but why don't you join Andy and me for pizza and movie tonight?"

"Sounds great. Around six as usual?"

How did his mere presence ease her stress? She

nodded and smiled. "See you then."

"Let me bring the soft drinks." He kissed her cheek. "I'll pray your day gets better."

She watched his tall figure go out the door. The Lord knew she needed Frank's encouragement this morning. She changed into a clean smock before working on the next day's bridal order.

For the next two hours, she became immersed in a world of Chopin, baby's breath, and roses while Uncle Stu manned the showroom.

Andy tapped on her shoulder. "Mom, it's lunchtime."

"Already?"

"Yeah. Uncle Stu gave me money to go to Rick Shaw's Imperial Emporium for take-out. What would you like?"

"Moo Goo Gai Pan and an egg roll, please. Hurry, my headache's gone and I'm starved."

A half-hour later, she put the finishing touches on the last bridesmaid bouquet, and then searched for a spool of ribbon behind the work table. A mock Asian voice interrupted her.

"Moo Goo Gai Pan for honorable mama."

Carol peeked over the table. "Ethan Maxwell Mason! What are you doing here?"

"I was in the neighborhood and thought you'd like to see your favorite son."

"You silly kid, come here." She opened her arms wide. "I'm so happy to see you."

"C'mon, Mom. Don't maul the poor guy." Andy took his take-out bags to the break room table.

She held her oldest son at arms' length. "It's so good to see you, even with that unshaved face. Does Rikki like it? Is she with you?"

"She couldn't come, and the five o'clock shadow was her idea." Ethan rubbed it with his finger and thumb. "She thinks I'm manly, but boy, does it ever itch."

Andy pulled the food cartons from the bag. "Come on, Mom. I thought you were starving. We can talk while we eat."

After saying grace, Carol passed the napkins and watched her boys eat from the containers. Both had inherited the Mason good looks. Maybe their baby blue eyes were from her, but the thick, dark lashes and strong chins were definitely Bob's. Her heart warmed. She felt her husband's presence every time they smiled. Exactly what she needed on their anniversary.

The changes in Ethan were striking since he'd been away. He'd sprouted to nearly six feet and towered four inches over his younger brother. It wouldn't be long until Andy caught up with him and his cherub face took on the same chiseled appearance.

Stuart walked into the break room, sniffing the air. "I knew I smelled my Kung Pao Chicken." His eyes widened. "Who's this big, good-lookin' stranger?"

"Hey, my favorite uncle." Ethan gave him a hug. "You haven't changed a bit."

"You mean I looked this bad fifteen years ago?" He chuckled. "I'll man the showroom while you three eat and catch up. We can talk later." Stuart took his meal and left.

"Thanks, Uncle Stu." Carol turned to Ethan. "How long can you stay?"

"My flight leaves on Sunday. I have to be back for work and my sweetheart." He took his mother's hand. "How's Grandma?"

"I'm worried. She's still weak and tires easily, but she'll be thrilled to see you."

"Maybe Andy and I can go to the convalescent center and cheer her up."

"Good." She pulled him into another hug. "Are there wedding bells in your near future?"

"That's one reason I'm here. We want to get married

next spring after graduation, but we're concerned about the broken friendship between our moms."

"Honey, I promise not to make a scene. I'll stay as far away from the Norths as possible."

He frowned. "Didn't you get Sue's letter?"

"It came this morning. To be honest, I've put off opening it all day."

"You should read it now, Mom. Trust me, it's important."

Carol pushed her food aside and took the letter from her pocket. A knot formed in her throat as she opened the envelope and read the letter aloud.

"Dear Carol, last week Grady had a massive heart attack in another woman's home."

She lowered the letter, searched her son's eyes, and then continued to read.

"Considering the circumstances, I can only assume he died without getting right with the Lord. Grady always said tithing, going to church, and praying before meals was all God expected. He insisted he was ready for the 'big Courtroom in the Sky.' I've written off and on, but never heard from you."

The letter grew heavy in her sweaty palms. "I never got any letters, Ethan."

"I'm guessing Grady pitched them before they were mailed. Keep reading, Mom."

Her eyes went to the paper. "I promise not to keep bothering you, but I wanted to be the one to tell you about Grady. I miss you. As I said in previous letters, renewing our friendship would be wonderful, even though it can't be like before. None of this mess was your fault. It was all Grady and me, and for that, I deeply apologize. Sincerely, Sue."

Carol swallowed to squelch the ache in her throat. Tonight she'd write a long overdue letter to her old friend, Sue.

CHAPTER TWENTY-SEVEN

With less than an hour to get home and put groceries away, Carol pulled from Kolonial Kubby's parking lot into the late afternoon traffic. Frank would finally meet Ethan tonight. Would her eldest son accept him as a possible stepfather?

Peanut butter cookies from the bakery would surprise the boys, and if she got them into a warm oven, they'd never suspect they weren't homemade. JoAnna guaranteed this would end all jokes about her lack of kitchen competence.

Turning into her drive, she came to a stop as Andy ran to relieve her of the grocery bags.

"We noticed your frozen pea bag was empty, Mom." He raced ahead of her to the door. "I hope you bought refills."

She followed him to the kitchen. "Thanks for your help, Mr. Snoop. Now, go away while I put cookies in the oven. I have JoAnna's secret recipe."

"This I gotta see." He pulled out a chair.

"What part of secret recipe don't you understand?" A distraction was needed, and quick. "Why don't you call Ciao Down Pizza and order one veggie and two Macho-meat pizzas? And ask how much it'll be with delivery." She hustled the teen from her kitchen before he discovered the telltale bakery bag.

Once the coast was clear, she crammed all three dozen cookies onto a baking sheet. After shoving them into the warming oven, she scurried to put the groceries away.

A half hour later, the Ciao Down delivery boy rang the doorbell. She paid him, took the pizzas, and noticed Frank coming up the walk cradling three two-liter bottles.

"I hope you like macho-meat pizza. The boys' favorite. I managed to get one with veggies." She kissed his cheek. "Come on inside. I want you to meet Ethan."

As he followed her to the living room, the young man stood and offered his hand. "You must be the Pastor Frank I've heard so much about."

"Pleased to meet you. Your mom says you have a wedding in the future. Congrats."

Ethan's eyes brightened. "Thanks. Rikki's one special girl." He pointed to the sofa. "Let's have a seat."

Frank sat next to Andy, who leaned over and opened a pizza box on the coffee table.

"Close the box, son. We want them to stay warm." She could relax now that the initial meet and greet was over. Their male bonding rituals would have to come in small increments throughout the evening. Maybe Frank and Ethan could connect better with Andy out of the room. "Andy, wash your hands and help with the paper plates and napkins."

A whiff of peanut butter cookies caught Carol's attention on her way to the kitchen. She needed to rescue them from the oven. However, when Ethan scooted next to Frank, curiosity fused her feet to the floor. She stepped out of sight.

"What are your intentions toward my mother?"

"Purely honorable, sir." Frank chuckled. "I'd like to talk to you and Andy about it."

Carol jumped at Ethan's booming voice. "Hey, squirt! Get in here."

"What?" Andy bounded from the hallway and plopped

onto the couch.

"I want to discuss something with you." Frank's tone was calm. "First of all, I want you to know I love your mom very much."

"Mom and Andy told me you two were getting serious. I'm glad you've been there to help them through these rough times."

"I struggled after losing my wife, so I understood the changes they were going through. They've been here for me, too. I'd gotten used to being single, then your amazing mom showed up. She even helped me regain parts of my ministry that fell through the cracks. We've weathered a lot of adjustments together, and I'd like your permission to marry her." He took a deep breath and released it slowly. "What do you say, men?"

Carol couldn't stand it any longer. She had to peek around the corner to catch the reaction of her sons.

Andy raised his hand. "You got my vote."

Silence followed. Ethan rested his elbows on his knees. He was a deep thinker like his father, who had often over-analyzed situations. Carol leaned against the wall and held her breath. If he didn't give his consent, what would they do? This warranted another peek. C'mon, son.

"I appreciate your honesty. That couldn't have been easy." Ethan's voice was compassionate. "Andy, Rikki, and I have discussed her remarriage for a long time. There's no doubt you're the answer to our prayers." He stood and offered his hand to Frank.

Frank got to his feet, pulled him close, and patted his back.

"Group hug!" Andy jumped into the mix.

Carol's first instinct was to waltz into the room and plant a kiss on Frank's lips. Instead, she smiled demurely and took her place beside her almost fiancé.

"Men, mind if your mother and I eat in the kitchen while you watch the movie?"

"Fine with us." Ethan winked and nudged his brother. "Let's watch the one I brought from home."

"I have a better idea." She handed them a pizza, their soft drinks, and pointed down the hall. "Here. Enjoy it in Andy's room."

"You mean we can eat in there?"

"Just this once and don't make a mess. Please close the door."

Like a flash, she lit two candles, dimmed the lights, set the radio to soft music, and went to the sofa. She fluttered her eyes and patted the cushion. "Any questions for me?"

With a hearty laugh, Frank settled beside her. He clasped her hands and kissed them. "Before we move into this next phase, let's remove the symbols of our previous commitments. I loved Barb and no one can replace her. I was truly blessed to have her as my wife." His eyes pooled as he placed his ring on the table.

That single unselfish act of leaving his past behind fueled her love for him. Tears trickled down her cheeks. Did she have the same courage to release Bob?

A deep breath escaped as she gazed into his eyes. The confidence she witnessed offered the assurance needed to loosen her wedding band and place it beside his.

"I promised to love, honor, and cherish Bob until death parted us." Her heart ached at the finality of those words. Their life together seemed so long ago. "He was a wonderful husband, and I thank God for the twenty-three years we had together."

"He's brought us a long way since you moved here." Frank pulled her into his arms.

She felt the rapid beating of his heart against her temple. "We've had an amazing relationship so far, sweetheart, and with His help, we can do this together."

"I promise to always respect your memories." His voice rumbled in his chest, as he tenderly smoothed her hair. "But now we're ready to take the next step and make new ones." He reached into his pocket, pulled out a small velvet box, and opened it.

She gasped at the princess-cut diamond ring nestled inside. "It's beautiful."

He scooted off the couch, dropped to one knee, and took her left hand. "My life was empty for two years. Then you came along, and I discovered the Lord had prepared a special place in my heart specifically for you. Will you marry me?"

"I don't even have to think about it. Absolutely." She smiled through tears. "I love you, Frank Bailey." A fiery tingle ran up her spine as he slipped the ring on her finger and kissed it.

He stood, pulled her into the circle of his arms, and held her snugly. The softness of his lips covered hers, and she was filled with a sense of security.

The living room lights came on, and Andy's voice broke the enchanting moment. "Mom, is it safe to come out?"

"Yes, it's fine." She held out her left hand. "Look what Frank gave me."

"Very nice. Congratulations!" Ethan stood behind his brother and sniffed the air. "Do I smell burning peanut butter?"

CHAPTER TWENTY-EIGHT

Last week of July

AFTER A LONG DAY OF DEALING with a cheapskate father-of-the-bride and his weeping daughter, excitement grew as Carol shut down the flower shop's cash register. She was more than ready to leave town with Frank and Andy. Two glorious weeks in California with Frank's daughters lay ahead of them. A great way to end the month.

Carol locked the shop door and hurried to Frank's car. She settled into the seat beside him, buckled the seatbelt, and released a deep sigh. "I had lunch with Mom at the nursing home. She said you went to see her this morning."

"I did. She's really looking good." Frank kissed her hand. "I was happy to see how much stronger she is."

"The doctor said if she keeps improving she could be home by October." Her purse resonated with a wolf whistle. She rolled her eyes at him. "Probably another text from Andy. This has been one crazy day."

As she pulled the phone out, Frank put the car in gear and headed into traffic.

"Andy said he and Dad are delivering a huge wedding order on the other side of town. It's taking a bit longer, so Dad will drop him off at the house when they're done. They'll call when they get there." She glanced his way. "At least our bags are packed, and we're ready to see your family."

"I guess we have time to kill." He winked and steered

the sedan into a nearby park. "How about ice cream while we wait?"

"Sounds good." She climbed from the car, stretched, and breathed in fresh air.

A scrub jay took flight into the stirring air current. Its flapping azure wings seemed to represent her own freedom from work and pressure.

She followed Frank to the ice cream truck sitting at the park entrance. The list of frozen treats was enticing. Her mouth watered as she narrowed the choices down to one. "I'd like a Pudgy Fudgy Bar, please."

The ice cream man nodded. "What would you like, sir?"

"Let's make it two Pudgies." Frank paid the man, put the change in his pocket, and turned to Carol. "Wanna walk along the river?"

"I'd love to." She took her ice cream and grabbed a handful of napkins. "I'm going to enjoy the ride to Desert Hot Springs. How long will it take to get to your daughter's place?"

"About four hours unless you want a break. We'll see a lot of interesting things along the way." He pulled a napkin from her hand. "Lisa wants to take us to Cabot's Pueblo Museum next week."

"That'll be interesting." She squeezed his arm. "I can't wait to see little Shea in person. Those dimples and blonde ringlets are adorable. I loved the picture of her in a bubble bath wearing a tiara."

"I gave her that sparkly crown on her second birthday last winter. She's quite the princess like her mother was." His eyes crinkled with amusement. "It won't take long for her to summon Sir Andrew to slay fire-breathing dragons."

"I'll have to get a video of his derring-do." The thought brought a giggle. "I'm used to rough and tumble boys, so it'll be fun to have tea parties for a change."

"I guarantee you won't be disappointed with my granddaughter." He slowed his pace and waved as they passed a picnic table where a family of six was eating. "That's JoAnna Foster's nephew and his family."

Tops of mesquite trees gently swayed in the warm breeze as they continued their walk. A roadrunner skittered from the scrub ahead of them and disappeared just as quickly.

"Hope there's no coyote in pursuit." He laughed and released a hearty, "Meep-meep."

"Still into cartoons, I see." Carol's purse whistled. She licked chocolate ooze from her thumb and checked the message. "Andy's on his way to the house. I'll tell him we'll be there soon." She nudged him and pointed to a park bench. "Look. Isn't that Lou with his dog?"

"I think you're right." He lowered his ice cream and dabbed fudge from his mouth. "He doesn't seem too happy, either."

"He's supposed to be at Millie's. Today's her birthday." Something inside her sent a warning signal. "She was going to introduce him to Aunt Penny."

"Uh-oh. Wonder what happened?" Frank pointed with his Pudgy bar. "Let's go talk him off the ledge." He picked up his pace and yelled, "Hey, Lou!"

"Hi." Lou wiped his eyes with the heel of his hand, and then scooted over to make room for the couple. "What are you guys doing here?"

Frank motioned for her to sit beside Lou. "We're enjoying a nice afternoon together." He took a bite of ice cream and scooted next to her. "What's wrong? Weren't you going to be with Millie today?"

"Farfel and I were there." He scowled and scratched his basset's ears.

She narrowed her eyes and her insides quivered. Was

he serious? "You took your dog?"

He nodded. "Big mistake. Then we left."

"You bore the brunt of Aunt Penny's finely tuned social graces, didn't you?"

"Sure did, and that daughter of hers came in a close second in the war of the banshees."

Frank's eyebrows nearly met his hairline. "Whoa, wait a minute. Millie's been my secretary for years, and she's always been very soft spoken."

"My cousin is nothing like her mother. She has her dad's kind and loving spirit. If she raised her voice, Aunt Penny must've really pushed her over the brink."

"You know the old saying about the daughter taking after the mother? I believe it." Lou cracked his knuckles. "Who wants to be tethered to someone that harsh and controlling?"

"Uncle Stuart's been too laid-back. He should've reined Penny in a long time ago, but he lets her get away with things just to keep peace. She's even crashed a church board meeting with her anger and false accusations."

"Millie told me about that meeting."

A pathetic groan came from Frank's direction.

"The board meeting and today's party are examples of Aunt Penny's personality disorder. She's an oppressive tyrant and provoked Millie for years. If I saw a hint of my cousin morphing into her mother, I'd warn you *and* the world."

"We'll help you pray about it." Frank handed his business card to Lou. "Carol, Andy, and I are leaving this afternoon to visit my daughters for two weeks, but you can still call or text."

"Thanks, but my quartet is leaving tonight for a six-week cruise. I might not be able to contact anyone." Lou took the card, hunched over, and stared at his basset hound. "I was beginning to think Millie cared for me."

Carol placed her hand on his shoulder. "Your relationship is more important to her than anything else. She's standing up to her mother and fighting for you."

Desert Hot Springs, California

Deep twilight hugged the horizon as Carol relaxed by the pool in Lisa's backyard. Who knew little girls were insatiable when it came to tea parties? Seven long days of pouring tea and passing crumpets and they still had another full week to go.

Frank came from the house, sat on the end of her chaise lounge, and rubbed Carol's bare feet. "Lady Shea can't go to sleep. She loves wearing Aunt Gwen's purple nail polish with sparkles and keeps explaining how she made crumpets with you today."

"We only frosted animal crackers." She folded her arms behind her head. "Do you realize it's been a whole week since we saw Lou in the park? Millie hasn't texted me once. I'm dying to know if the two have patched things up."

"Remember, he'll be gone for six weeks and wasn't sure he'd be able to contact anyone."

"Oh, that's right." She took in the gathering of stars overhead.

"It took me two long years to get him to ask her out. To be honest, I'm not sure he can work through his insecurities and step up to the plate again." Frank raked his hand across his jaw, then glanced her way and chuckled. "The poor guy's gonna be as helpless as a rubber-nosed woodpecker in a petrified forest."

"Stop it." She giggled and playfully smacked his shoulder. "This isn't a laughing matter. They're perfect for each other."

"Sometimes it's best not to stir the pot."

"You're right, Frank. We need to let them work it out on their own."

"God has everything under control. We'll find out when we get home next week."

CHAPTER TWENTY-NINE

August

Carol brought her hand to her mouth and yawned. Next time she'd factor in a day to rest from a trip before returning to work.

She called into the back room of the flower shop. "Dad, you have a hospital delivery."

"I remember. Be right with ya."

After removing the pink and white arrangement from the cooler, she placed it on the glass counter. Her fingers grasped a shiny Mylar balloon and filled it with helium. Then she snipped and curled several lengths of ribbon, and attached them to the 'It's a Girl' balloon.

The flurry of corkscrew ribbons reminded her of Frank's curly headed granddaughter. Carol's heart warmed at the thought of her impending grandma status. She pulled the phone from her pocket and viewed a photo of Shea dressed for a tea party.

She noticed the time on the phone and stepped to the door. "Dad? Are you coming?"

"I'm on my way." Max was nearly out of breath as he entered the showroom. "Thanks for getting this ready." He snatched the arrangement from the countertop then hurried off to make his delivery. The door slammed behind him.

The bell on the front door jingled. Millie waved. "I'm so glad you're here. This has been the longest two weeks of my life." Her face reddened. "I'm sorry. How was your trip to Desert Hot Springs?"

"It was great. Frank's daughters are as sweet in person as they are on the phone. His little granddaughter stole my heart. She's two and a half now." Carol came from behind the counter and hugged her cousin. "Have I missed anything?"

"Remember how excited I was for my birthday cookout? Someone ruined it. I'll give you one guess who it was."

"I don't even have to guess. I'm sorry, Mills." She was dying to ask about Lou, but kept quiet and hoped her cousin would be forthcoming.

"Mother put Lou down and I finally stood up to her." She wiped her nose.

Carol tapped her foot and waited for more information. Time for a little prodding. "Good for you. And then what happened?"

"She scorned and besmirched Lou. I've had it up to my eyeballs, Carol. I was so mad I said we should've had her committed right after that board meeting." Millie rubbed her forehead. "My mouth just erupted like Mt. Vesuvius. I don't know what came over me."

"I know. You crossed swords with your mother in order to protect the relationship with Lou. You love him."

"Yes, I do." Millie's face flushed. "However, Lou witnessed the whole ugly scene." She closed her eyes. "I'll never forget the horror on his face as he walked out and slammed the door. I haven't heard from him since."

"I'm so sorry. Carol pulled her into a hug. "Have you called him to apologize?"

"He's still on that cruise with his quartet, and I'm afraid I'll call at the wrong time." Millie's eyes saddened. "Besides, Mother always said proper ladies never chase a man."

"Calling Lou isn't chasing him, it's damage control. It's

perfectly acceptable for a lady to call her sweetheart." She smiled. "Especially when their relationship needs mending."

With a sigh, Millie nodded. "I'm not sure he thinks it's a relationship worth repairing."

The aroma of garlic filtered through the house as Carol stirred the bubbling spaghetti sauce. She turned the heat down and covered the pan before joining Andy in the living room.

After rearranging the sofa's throw pillows, she knocked his feet off the coffee table and sat beside him. "Frank's on his way over to have supper with us."

Andy sniffed the air. "Are we having spaghetti *again*? Have you told him that's all you can cook?"

"He'll find out soon enough. Besides, I can fix a few other things, too." As she took the remote from his hand, a car pulled into the drive. "There he is. I need to get things going in the kitchen. Will you let him in?" She stood to watch her son's reaction to Frank's belated birthday gift.

Andy hurried to answer the door. "Hey, Frank."

"Hi, kiddo." Their personalized handshake ended in a man hug. He put an arm around Andy, and led him to the couch. "I wanted to give you something for your birthday, but we were in Hot Springs." He handed him two keys on a ring. "It comes with a few conditions."

Andy's mouth dropped open as he dangled it from his finger. "You gonna let me drive?"

"Better yet, those are your car keys. Lisa and Gwen shared a VW when they were in high school, but now it's been collecting dust in the garage. I thought you'd like to drive it instead of the delivery van."

Andy looked from Frank to his mom and back again. "For real?" He broke into his own version of a happy dance, then stopped and jiggled the keys. "Let's burn rubber!"

"Whoa. Slow down." Frank put his hand on the boy's shoulder. "You haven't heard my conditions. First of all, no burning rubber, use your seatbelt every time, no texting or calls without pulling over, and obey all traffic rules. Can you promise?"

"Yeah." His face brightened as he tossed the keys in the air and caught them. "Wow! Thanks, man." Another man hug ensued. "Where is it? Can I try it now?"

"It's in the driveway." He took Carol's hand as they followed the boy to the car. "Do we have time for a quick ride before we eat?"

"Go ahead. I'll have supper ready in twenty minutes." She turned to Andy. "Have your permit with you?"

He nodded, plopped into the driver's seat, and revved the engine. "Look, Mom. It's black instead of pink, and no flowers. C'mon, Frank. Let's go."

"Use your seatbelts." Their camaraderie warmed her heart. What a blessing to have a man like Frank taking on the role of father.

Two masculine voices chimed. "Yes, Mom."

The grating sound of stripped gears echoed from the drive. Once, then a second time. On Andy's third exasperating attempt, Frank jumped out and changed places with the boy. "We'll be at the church parking lot for a quick lesson in gear shifting."

The VW backed from the drive. A lump formed in her throat as she watched the car disappear down the street. Her son was growing up, and she had to fight the urge of being an over-protective mother, especially after the loss of Bob and Jake.

She went inside and stood at the door. The solitude was overpowering and seemed to shout empty nest.

Was she ready for it?

CHAPTER THIRTY

September

CAROL WAS BLESSED WITH AN UNEXPECTED day off after a hectic weekend. She vowed nobody but nobody would interfere with it. Even her phone was exiled to the living room.

Tub filled, candles lit, daisy pillow inflated and in position. A mound of luxurious bubbles beckoned like a shoe sale at Tootsie's Footwear.

She eased into the aromatic bath and indulged in her quiet haven with a mug of steaming coffee and a fifteen-ounce bag of chocolates, fresh from the freezer.

Many bonbons later, the phone rang. Too bad—she'd reached a level of chocolate euphoria where no telemarketer, domestic or foreign, was permitted. The call went to voice mail. She'd deal with it later. Maybe.

A long, hot soak left her an emotionally rejuvenated human prune. Dissipating bubbles and cooling water motivated her to relinquish any further wallowing in luxury. She wrapped her towel securely and tiptoed to the bedroom.

Her jeans refused to zip. The chocolate hadn't had time to reach her hips, so it must be bathwater retention. Didn't matter, she was in a stretchy pantsuit kind of mood, anyway.

She went to the kitchen, refilled her cup, and then listened to the voice mail message.

"Hi Carol. I'm melting on your porch swing. I hope

there's a pea bag in your freezer."

She squealed all the way to the door. "Sue North, what are you doing in Arizona?"

Following a hug, she held her friend at arm's length. The sallow complexion and wrinkles around Sue's eyes made her look as though she'd aged five years in the last nine months.

"I crossed the continent specially to see you." She grinned. "That, and to attend the National Flour Power Expo in Scottsdale. I never dreamed it would be this hot in September."

"Welcome to my world." Carol nodded to the front door. "Let's go in where it's cool. How long can you stay?"

"I have to get the rental car to Hertz at the Phoenix Airport by four." Sue grabbed her purse on the swing. "I was encouraged by your sweet letter, and since Scottsdale is less than an hour from here, I jumped at the chance to see you."

"I'm so glad you did."

Tears trickled down Sue's face. "I've missed you so much, Carol, and I'm sorry for all those nasty things in my letter."

"It's forgotten." Carol led her friend to the kitchen and poured a glass of iced tea. She opened the freezer and then tossed a backup frozen pea bag. "Catch!"

Sue caught the bag mid-flight. "I knew you'd have a stash handy."

"Enjoy, I've had more than my share of sweets this morning." Carol pulled an extra glass from the cupboard.

"Yum. Reminds me of the good ol' days." Sue nibbled on a peanut cluster and then set it down. "I can't apologize enough for that horrible letter and for what Grady did to you. With his ability to put a spin on the truth, I momentarily believed him, and I was afraid of his volatile temper."

"The only way to deal with the past is to forgive everyone involved and then allow the Lord to heal our hearts."

"I've been working on that." Sue added sugar to her drink and stirred. "My life has changed a lot since you moved. I miss you."

"Leaving Vermont was tough for Andy and me. I'll admit at first I resented you and Grady for putting me in that position." Carol lifted her gaze to Sue. "But God has shown me this is where He wants us."

"It's so good to hear that. When you didn't answer my letters, I thought we'd never get back together."

"Ethan told me you wrote, but he thinks Grady must've confiscated the letters."

"Wouldn't surprise me." Sue nodded. "Thanks for accepting my apology."

"I'm glad we have closure from that dark time, Sooze." Carol patted her hand, thankful for their restored friendship.

"How's your mom? Ethan's tried to keep us updated on her progress."

"She's getting better with her walker. Barring any more problems, she should be home the middle of next month. Thanks for asking."

"That's great news. I'm happy to hear it." Sue sipped her tea. "I remember how much she loved my double fudge brownies. Wish I had some to take to her."

Carol jumped from her chair. "Stay right there. I have something you need to try." She revisited the freezer, retrieved a white paper package, and placed the goodies on a saucer. "Tell me what you think."

"You labeled it chopped liver? Nice decoy since you only make spaghetti." Sue giggled and took a nibble. "Carol Mason, don't tell me you made these."

She shook her head. "Do you like them?"

"You betcha. What are they called and where do you get 'em?"

Carol laughed. "Grizzly Bars from the Rising Doe Bakery."

"I've got to recreate these with my own special twist and serve them at the next church dinner." Sue finished the treat and licked her fingers. "By the way, Ethan told us something else. Tell me if it's true. He said you're getting married in December. To another preacher." She wiped her lips with a napkin. "I thought you were happy to get out of the stained-glass fishbowl."

"Ethan talks too much." Carol laughed. "As for the stained-glass fishbowl, you know what Proverbs 16:9 says." She raised her eyes heavenward. "A man's heart plans his way, but the Lord directs his steps." She raised her hands. "Works with women, too."

"He also talks highly of your intended. How does Andy feel?"

"Frank and Andy love their pranks so they clicked immediately." Carol pushed the Grizzly Bar plate closer to Sue. "Andy misses his dad, and Frank only had girls, so they're enjoying male camaraderie. Their bond was cemented when he gave Andy his daughters' car."

"No kidding. How many daughters does he have?"

"Two. Lisa and Gwen. And a gorgeous granddaughter named Shea, whom I adore."

"How sweet. I'm glad you finally get a little girl to pamper." Her hands shook as she wiped the moisture from her iced tea glass. "Is it possible to meet Frank today?"

"I think it could be arranged." Carol glanced at her watch. "It's almost eleven. I'll call him now and see if he can meet us for lunch around noon." She needed to prepare Frank before introducing him to the author of the scorching letter that nearly ended their relationship.

"Let's take your car to the local Hertz Rental. I'll see to it you get to the airport on time."

Sue stood and pushed her chair under the table. "I'll freshen up while you call Frank."

"The bathroom's down the hall." She all but skipped to her bedroom to tell Frank about her unexpected visitor. Closing the door, she dialed his number and waited for an answer.

"Hi, Frank. You're not going to believe this, but Sue's here for a quick visit."

"Your poison pen pal?"

"One and the same, but we're buddies again. It's like nothing ever happened."

"I'm happy for you. Is this your way of telling me we'll be living in Vermont?"

"Whither thou goest, I will go." She laughed. "I need a favor from you."

"I'll bite. What is it?"

"Ethan told Sue about our wedding plans, and she wants to meet you. We're taking her rental back to Hertz. Could you pick us up there, take us to lunch, and then give us a ride to Sky Harbor Airport? I'm not comfortable driving in all that Phoenix traffic."

"Turns out I planned to leave early anyway. I can be at the car rental in an hour."

"Perfect. What a relief. Thanks honey." She hung up. Was Frank kidding about moving to Vermont? She grinned and entered the kitchen.

Sue tossed the pea bag and liver package into the freezer. "What are you smiling about?"

"I love that man." Carol put their dirty dishes into the sink. "Frank's looking forward to meeting you. He'll be at the rental place in an hour to take us to lunch."

"We won't have to say anything about our misunderstanding, will we?"

"Only if you bring it up." Carol shrugged. "As far as I'm concerned the past is behind us. It doesn't have to be mentioned." Sue didn't need to know Aunt Penny shared that awful letter with Frank and the entire church board.

Any doubts Carol had of Frank accepting her friend had been put to rest as they reminisced over a leisurely meal at the airport. She glanced at her watch and then at Sue.

"I know it's time for my flight." Sue scooted her chair away from the table. "The afternoon went too fast."

"Are you sure you have to go home now?" Carol linked her arm with Sue's as they left the restaurant. "I'd love to have you stay a few more days."

"I've been gone four days and a bakery can't run without the baker." She grinned. "I could be persuaded to come in December for your wedding. By then I'll have a larger staff to carry the load."

"That would make my wedding that much more special. I hope you can work it out. Then I'll be in Vermont for Ethan and Rikki's wedding." Carol took Frank's hand as they walked through the busy terminal.

"There's my flight number." She walked into Carol's embrace.

Carol was hesitant to let her go. She reached into her tote bag. "Here. Take the rest of these Grizzly Bars. Let's stay in touch, Sooze. Do you have a Facebook account on the internet?"

"I do. Ethan set it up as Sue's Pie Hole. Send me a friend request." She glanced at the screen. "Oh, no. My flight's boarding. I gotta run." Sue went through airport security, turned, and waved.

After using her last tissue, Carol accepted Frank's

handkerchief as the plane accelerated down the runway and disappeared. She squelched the sob that rose in her throat. "For two decades Sue and I were inseparable. We went through everything together." She took a quick gulp of air and wiped her eyes.

Frank's hand rested on her waist and drew her near. "It took a lot of courage for Sue to come here and beg your forgiveness. You've shown compassion by accepting her apology unconditionally. I'm proud of you."

Was it only a year ago she had been a woman at the end of her rope—broken, weary, and close to a breakdown? Thank God she had moved from death to life. Her head rested against the soothing beat of Frank's heart.

CHAPTER THIRTY-ONE

October

CAROL'S HANDS SHOOK AS SHE RUMMAGED through her jewelry box for the elusive necklace that matched her turquoise blouse. As she reached for it, the doorbell chimed. Her head shot up. Frank was early. She dashed to the door, almost losing a slipper.

Millie stood on the porch, tears trickling down her cheeks.

"Let me guess. Your mother?" Carol stepped aside to let her cousin in.

With a vigorous nod, Millie walked in and fell into her arms. "Mother's furious that she hasn't been able to break you and Frank apart." She sniffed. "I think the family's Thanksgiving dinner is going to be a major disaster."

"Why worry about that now? It's a whole month away."

"Think, Carol. That gives her four whole weeks to plot and scheme." She bit her lip and turned away. "Mother wants to sit Andy between the two of you and I'll be on his other side."

"Frank's going to pick me up to get our marriage license." Carol took Millie by the elbow and led her to the bedroom. "You can tell me about her plan while I finish getting ready."

"The date she set up for me last summer didn't work out so she wants me to snatch Frank from your arms." Millie sighed until her lungs were nearly depleted.

"According to her, until a ring is snug on his finger, he's available and I still have a chance. Those romance novels have warped her psychotic brain."

Carol shook her head and buckled the strap on her sandal. Months of therapy for Aunt Penny had been a total waste of time and money. But she'd keep that thought to herself. "I'm sorry, Mills. Maybe we can think of an early escape from Thanksgiving dinner." She rubbed Millie's shoulder. "Don't worry, we'll work something out to lessen the drama."

<hr>

With their marriage license securely in her purse, Carol and Frank wandered through Beddy Buys furniture store checking out bedroom sets. She flipped a page of her notepad. "My favorite is the pecan suite. Let's look at it again."

"Wait." He rubbed his hand over the coarse surface of a massive bedpost. "What about this one? Check out the sturdy craftsmanship. You can't go wrong with good, solid cedar logs."

"Are you serious?" How could she tactfully talk him out of a bedroom suite riddled with woodpecker holes? "The Paul Bunyan collection is a bit too rustic to suit me. The old railroad ties might fit in the Fosters' cabin, but it's way too big for our new house."

"But it's manly, honey. Remember, I've lived in a house filled with feminine gee-gaws and frillary for way too long. My testosterone level is hanging in the balance."

"C'mon Frank, I lived with four, count 'em, *four* men, so I think my pain trumps your endangered man card." She rubbed her forehead and managed a smile. "It's the end of October. Our wedding is only six weeks away, so we'd better find a compromise. Let's discuss it over lunch."

"Sure. A nice restaurant is only two blocks down the street. Wanna walk and discuss furniture on our way? After I humbly give in to your wishes, we can enjoy the meal."

"Give and take, that's what it's all about." She threw him a playful wink as they left the store. "Thanks, honey. You made a wise choice by agreeing with me."

"Remember, I've been married before. I know the ropes." He winked and synchronized their steps. "Besides your Uncle Stu's been mentoring me in the fine art of husbandry."

"Wait. Are you comparing me to Aunt Penny?" Her eyes narrowed. "Of course you are." She covered her mouth to stifle giggles. "Don't cross me, Francis Bailey. You're not the only one who knows the ropes."

He threw his head back and laughed.

For nearly a block they walked in silence, until Millie's situation came to mind. She slowed their pace. "I heard Aunt Penny might try to drive a wedge between us during Thanksgiving dinner. Apparently counseling hasn't helped."

"Did you think it would?" He led her across the street. "It seems she thrives on the attention complaining gives her. Maybe it makes her feel important and irreplaceable."

"What a miserable way to live."

"She needs to surrender her life to the Lord before there can be a change."

Carol tightened her hold on his arm. "Absolutely."

"I appreciate you telling me about this. We need to ask the Holy Spirit to protect our relationship and Millie's from Penny's spiteful shenanigans."

"I did mention to her that if we put our brains together

we could surely come up with a clever scheme to leave the dinner early."

"Sounds good to me." He grinned and rubbed his hands together. "Count me in. Let's get to work on it."

CHAPTER THIRTY-TWO

Thanksgiving Day

WHEN THE GRIZZLY BARS WERE ARTFULLY stacked on a glass plate, Carol covered them with plastic wrap and placed them in the freezer. She made sure Andy hadn't eaten the other snacks she'd stashed away for their post-dinner retreat with Millie.

Frank's game plan for an early escape from Aunt Penny's was brilliant. Everyone would take their designated positions immediately after eating. Team Carol would snatch the dishes from the table, while Team Millie transported leftovers to the kitchen. If they worked like a well-oiled machine, Aunt Penny would be hard at work refrigerating containers to her own specifications.

They would say their good-byes, and while Andy went to a friend's house to watch football, they would retreat to Carol's house for dessert and coffee. Her folks and Uncle Stu supported the plan and promised to be on the sidelines cheering them on.

A peaceful ending to a stressful day.

Where were Frank and Carol? Millie put her cell phone away and fidgeted by the front door. They hadn't arrived for the Drake Thanksgiving dinner yet, and Mother detested tardiness.

Penny marched into the living room. "You do know they're almost half an hour late." She tapped her watch. "Our dinner was scheduled for precisely twelve-thirty. We don't want dry turkey and shriveled yams, do we? Of course we don't."

"Carol called and said they're on their way, Mother." Millie's stomach churned. They had already fumbled their game plan.

"I have a notion to start the meal without them." She stomped to her kitchen.

Squealing brakes caught Millie's attention. "There they are now." She ran to the porch and waved her hands.

Carol jumped from the car and rushed to her side. "I'm sorry we're running late. We've been serving Thanksgiving dinners at the homeless shelter, and my replacement was behind schedule."

"You're only twelve minutes late, so ignore Mother's ranting. We'll try to get through this meal unscathed." Millie took a deep breath, and they headed for the dining room.

Although Max lovingly steadied Sylvia, she took slow, deliberate steps to the table.

"Sit beside me, Mom." Carol pulled out a chair. "Are you feeling all right?"

The older woman offered a slight nod. "I'll feel better after I eat."

Penny placed the turkey platter on the table and seated herself. "We could've eaten a lot sooner if everyone had come on time." She gave Carol 'the look.'

"Hey, Frank." Andy filled in the silence. "This is your last holiday as a bachelor. By Christmas, you and Mom will be on your honeymoon."

Millie noticed her mother's puckered face glaring at Carol. How long would she hang on to her vendetta?

"Let's not take all day. We're behind as it is." Penny

shook her linen napkin open with one quick snap, and then smoothed it on her knees. "Stuart, as the man of the house, you can return thanks for the bountiful feast provided for our sustenance."

The dinner guests sat stiffly around the table scrunched together like sardine mannequins. They all joined hands and bowed their heads. Following the short prayer, Andy was the first to grab a serving bowl and pass it.

"Andrew Mason." Penny's saccharine voice cooed from the other end of the table. Her eyes glanced at Pastor Frank. "Food is to be passed *counter*-clockwise. I'm sure your mother taught you proper dining etiquette, dear. This is the time to use it."

Sylvia winked at Andy. Her hand wobbled as she picked up her fork. "I can't wait to try your new yam casserole, Penny. Is this your own recipe?" She returned the fork to her plate without taking a bite.

"Yes. I enhanced one of Emeril's award winning favorites."

"It's quite good." Max wiped his mouth. "I'll save room for seconds."

Millie tried a bite of gravy laden turkey. She was proud of her family as they tried to keep the atmosphere civil. Still, she couldn't wait to get to Carol's and away from the stress.

When the room grew quiet, Stuart spoke up. "Carol, how are the wedding plans going?"

"Mom has a lot of great ideas to make it beautiful." She toyed with her napkin. "I still have to get my old, new, borrowed, and blue things."

Sylvia offered a weak smile to her daughter. "I ran across my mother's pearl necklace and earrings yesterday. I'd be honored if you'd use them for your something borrowed."

"Thank you, Mom. I'd forgotten about Grandma's pearls. It's perfect."

"I wasn't born with a silver spoon in my mouth like you, Syl." Penny's double chin nearly touched her chest as she wiped a tear. "I don't have any precious heirlooms to pass down to my one and only daughter." She pushed her plate away.

Sylvia heaved a sigh. "I didn't mean—"

"Of course you did. You know very well all I have left is my faded blue garter with stretched out elastic." In an instant, a full-blown sob erupted.

And there it was. Mother's typical all-about-me performance. Millie rose from the table and headed for the bathroom. She needed time alone before her silent scream became audible.

Why did Mother insist on baiting poor Aunt Syl? Millie reached for the toilet paper to wipe her runny nose and jerked a little too hard. In quick response, the remaining Royal Flush Tissue zigzagged into a pile on the ceramic floor, leaving the empty cardboard tube spinning.

She sat on the edge of the tub, held one end of the paper with quilted crowns, and attempted to rewind the roll. Her vexation grew as the spool formed an asymmetrical mess.

Her mother's shrieking voice reached a crescendo. "You're always trying to show me up, Syl! I'll not have disrespect in my house."

A knock on the bathroom door jarred Millie. Her dad's stern voice called, "Bring your mother's sedatives when you come out, princess."

Mother's meds weren't alleviating the problem. Millie gave her hands a quick lather and rinse, then returned to the dining room with the tranquilizers.

Carol was kneeling beside her mom's chair. "Mom?"

"What's wrong with Aunt Sylvia?"

At that moment, the older woman's complexion paled as she slumped over on Carol.

"Syl?" Max gently smacked her hand. His eyes searched the room. "Quick. Somebody call 9-1-1."

Andy made the call. "Please send an ambulance right away. My grandma had a stroke or heart attack. She's sixty something. Huh? Oh, Grandpa said she's sixty-four. The address is—"

"Hang in there, Mom." Carol held her limp wrist and felt for a pulse. "Help's coming."

Frank raised his hands. "Let's give her air. Andy, watch for the ambulance."

A lump formed in Millie's throat. She leaned into her dad's strong embrace as he guided her away from the table. "Did Mother's remarks bring on Aunt Syl's attack? How could she be so insensitive?"

Within minutes the EMTs arrived and wheeled Aunt Sylvia out on a stretcher. They lifted her into the ambulance and sped off, sirens blaring. Frank drove Carol, Andy, and Uncle Max to the hospital.

Millie hugged herself and cried. "We should be there with them, Dad."

"She's going to be fine, honey. If it was a stroke, they caught it early. I'll get your coat and we'll follow them." He kissed the top of her head then headed for the hall closet.

"Get in here, Millicent." Penny grabbed Millie's arm and pulled her into the kitchen. "Our Thanksgiving is ruined and my stomach is upset. Help me clear the table."

"Aunt Syl might die." Millie clenched her teeth. "Have some compassion."

"Oh, Millicent, you're such a drama queen. Sylvia's not going to die. She always does something to get attention. It's all about her."

"Stop it." The veins in Millie's neck began to throb. She purposely lowered her voice to gain control. "You know she didn't do this on purpose."

With gravy boat in hand, Penny stomped to the kitchen. "Whatever."

"Let's help your mom clean up real quick." Her dad laid the coats on the back of a chair. "We'll go straight to the hospital after that."

She swallowed her anger, mustered a half-smile, and picked up a stack of plates.

Her mother came from the kitchen. "I spent two long days on my feet to make this day special. The very least you two can do is get this house cleaned up. I'm going to bed and read."

CHAPTER THIRTY-THREE

Monday morning following Thanksgiving, Carol left her mom's hospital room and headed for work. The doctor said normal recovery time for a moderate stroke was three months. One thing for sure, any contact with Aunt Penny would be strictly forbidden.

The Chug-a-Mug sign lured her to the drive-up window. Time to splurge. Had it honestly been almost a year since Frank introduced her to that wonderful eggnog-flavored coffee?

She lowered her car window and smiled at the drive-thru barista. "I'd like a half-caf, double grande, whipped Chug-a-Nog, please."

"Thank you." The lady nodded. "You want a Mug-a-Muffin with that?"

"Just the coffee."

"That'll be four-ninety-eight."

Carol's phone resonated with a Woody Woodpecker laugh. She handed the grinning woman a five-dollar bill and put the phone to her ear. "Hello?"

"Hi, Carol, it's Millie. People are calling the church office about Aunt Sylvia, so I'm updating the prayer chain. What's the latest news on her recovery?"

"Simply say Mom had a moderate stroke. She's pretty weak but is getting rest and physical therapy. The doctor's confident she'll be able to go to rehab soon." Carol cleared her throat. "We think it's best to hold off visits for a while since she's going through lots of evaluations and needs rest. Please add a thank you from all of us for the continued prayers and encouragement!"

"That's wonderful." Millie released a long sigh. "I still feel like it's Mother's fault."

"Don't go there, Mills. It was probably brought on by her head injury last spring." Carol took a deep breath. "Last night Frank and I agreed to postpone our wedding until Mom's healthy enough to be there." She cleared her throat. Verbalizing the delay for the first time was painful.

"Oh, no. What a shame." Millie paused. "Someone came into the office. We can talk later. 'Bye."

Blinking tears away, Carol took her coffee from the gal at the drive-thru window, and thanked her. She drove to the flower shop hoping holiday shoppers would keep her mind from her mom's illness and the disappointment of postponed nuptials.

Upon entering the shop, she went through her morning ritual of turning on lights and flipping the sign on the door to open. She braced herself for the next few weeks of long days filled with hospital visits and dealing with the Christmas rush at work.

December 28th

Carol hurried down the rehab corridor. A familiar figure stepped out of the elevator and came her way. "JoAnna! I'm so glad to see you."

"It's been ages." JoAnna gave her a hug. "Frank's kept us updated on your mom's progress. He said your candle's burning at both ends. I hoped to see you here or at the shop."

"It's been an exhausting December. We celebrated

Christmas with Mom here in rehab. I've been filling in for Dad at the shop a lot and then coming here most evenings." She rubbed her neck. "I came before work today to bring her favorite devotional book."

"What a difficult holiday for your family, especially you and Frank." JoAnna rested her shoulder against the wall. "Sorry the wedding had to be postponed. How are you holding up?"

"I'm doing better since Mom's making huge strides. Unfortunately, she'll have to be here for several weeks yet." Carol brushed a wisp of hair from her face. "Her occupational, speech, and physical therapy is intense, but she fed herself an entire meal yesterday."

"That's good news."

"I'm not asking for sympathy, but instead of taking a romantic honeymoon, I'll be stuck taking inventory and rearranging the stockroom with Andy all week."

"No pity, huh?" JoAnna laughed, reached in her purse, and drew out a small, white bag. "My sympathy comes in chocolate."

"Grizzly Bars! Thank you. I'll take this kind of pity any day." Carol drew her friend into a sideways hug. "I'd better get to work before Andy thinks he has a day off."

As she drove to Floral Scent-sations, a smile pulled at her lips. Sometimes just talking to a friend relieved tension. Grizzly Bars were a bonus.

She parked behind the flower shop, finished JoAnna's rejuvenating treat, and headed for the stockroom.

"What took you so long, Mom?" Andy's arms were loaded with boxes of holiday decorations. An animated Christmas tree wobbled on top.

"I ran into JoAnna at rehab." She flipped the light switch and gaped at the disarray of their seasonal storage area. Time had come to have a serious talk with the men about their lack of organizational skills.

The musical Christmas tree toppled from the boxes

and hit the concrete floor. It came to life and began to squawk "On the first day of Christmas . . ." Its bulging ornamental eyes blinked in time to the melody. She turned it off, quickly removed the batteries, and put them in the pocket of her smock. "This creepy thing's got to go."

"Uncle Stu said we have to get his approval before we toss anything. He's not in a very good mood today."

"Sorry, Andy." Her arm went to his shoulder. "Aunt Penny's medicine and counseling sessions still aren't helping, and he's dealing with disappointment. Let's try to brighten his day."

"This isn't what I had in mind for Christmas break."

"I know. I don't want to be here, either. We'd best get busy so Aunt Penny doesn't feel compelled to supervise."

"'Nuff said."

With a heavy sigh and a furrowed brow, Carol overtly assessed the mess. "Dad and Uncle Stu must've squirreled away forty years' worth of tree ornaments and miscellaneous items." She pulled a storage bin close. "Remember to label everything."

For hours, muscleman Andy moved and stacked storage containers. Carol's back ached as she pitched worthless items, then carefully wrapped and boxed the viable.

She stood and stretched. "It's been a long day. I couldn't have done it without you, Andy. Are you ready to quit?"

"I've been ready since lunch. What time is it anyway?"

She brushed the cobwebs from his hair and checked her watch. "Six-thirty. Would you take those two trash bags on your way out? I have to pick up a prescription for your grandpa. Let me give you money for a pizza. I'll see you at home. Save me some."

Sweaty and grimy, Carol trudged to her car as the wintery dusk disappeared over Apache Pointe. She'd make her necessary stop and then it was bubble bath time.

One look at her sloppy appearance in the visor mirror made her shudder. She instinctively finger-combed her hair before mashing Andy's Phoenix Suns' cap on her head. Then, taking a tissue, she wiped smudges from her cheek, and took a deep breath. At least this wasn't her usual pharmacy. Nobody would know her here.

She handed the prescription to the pharmacist behind the counter.

He read the slip of paper and squinted. "Do you have your photo ID?"

"Yes, I do." Her eyelid flickered as she fumbled for her driver's license.

The man stared at the picture, then at her, and lifted the bill of her cap. "Carol Mason! I didn't recognize you. My wife and I attend Apache Pointe Community." He returned her license and waved the doctor's prescription. "It'll take a few minutes to fill this. I'll get right on it."

Carol slid her license into her billfold and felt a tap on the shoulder. She glanced heavenward. Of course, someone else she knew would show up. She turned, and there stood the impeccably dressed JoAnna Foster. What were the odds of running into her twice in one day?

"Hey, girlfriend!" JoAnna pushed her shopping cart closer. "What are you doing on this side of town?"

"I was trying to pick up Dad's meds, incognito." Carol shrugged. "I'm so embarrassed to be seen like this. Andy and I had a long day cleaning the stockroom and taking inventory."

"Don't worry about it." JoAnna laughed. "It was good seeing your mom today."

"I'm encouraged she's growing stronger every day. All things considered, she's still perky and determined to get better."

"Sylvia's always been a happy lady."

"That's my mom." Carol pushed limp curls from her eyes.

"I'm glad we met again because it saves me a phone call." JoAnna touched Carol's arm. "Russ and I are going to the cabin to bring in the New Year, and we'd love to have you and Frank join us for a couple of days."

"Sounds wonderful. With the stress of Mom's stroke and the Christmas rush at work, I'd *love* to get away."

"Oh, Carol, I have a super idea." She narrowed her eyes and glanced over her shoulder. "The male spit-and-scratch club kicks back to watch football on New Year's. They expect us to fetch and carry snacks all day, while we'd rather watch Sound of Music and scarf down Grizzly Bars. So let's do something entirely for us on New Year's Eve."

"I love the way you think." Carol's hands went to her hips. "We shouldn't be the only ones to suffer. What do you have in mind?"

"Why don't we surprise them with a romantic candlelight dinner?" The devious grin resurfaced on her face. "You guys come all dressed up, and we'll have hors-d'oeuvres and fizzy grape juice." She rubbed her hands together. "Your pale blue evening dress will be perfect."

Carol nodded vigorously. "I love it, but we only have a couple days to set this up. Is that enough time?"

"Don't worry." JoAnna flipped her auburn curls in mock pomposity. "I got peeps."

"Well, aren't you special?" She laughed. "What fun. What can I do to help?"

The pharmacist returned to the counter. "Here's your dad's prescription, Carol."

JoAnna turned to leave. "I'll call you tomorrow and we'll compare notes." She lifted her fist and called over her shoulder. "Let the games begin."

CHAPTER THIRTY-FOUR

A GROVE OF SILVER SPRUCE CAME into view. Carol released Frank's hand as he skillfully maneuvered the car up the snowy mountain slope. The frosty forest sent her mind to Vermont and the blessed life she'd shared with Bob. So much had happened since losing her husband and son nearly two years ago. Her mouth dried. Had it really been two years? She lowered the visor to block the late afternoon sun streaming in the window.

The car swerved on an icy patch, catapulting her thoughts to the present. She gripped the armrest and glanced at Frank. His smile offered reassurance. She adjusted her position and straightened her beaded light blue gown.

Frank's stomach growled. "Hope Russ has his Moose Knuckle Stew ready when we get there. I'm starved." He yanked his tie. "What sane person gets dressed up to go to a log cabin?"

"I don't know what you're grumbling about, Frank. You look handsome in that suit."

"All I can say is Russ Foster had better be wearing a tie with his sweats."

"How tacky would our New Year's pictures be if JoAnna and I were all dolled up and you guys were getting your grunge on?"

Frank shrugged. "Who cares what we wear?"

"JoAnna and I care, silly. December has been a rough month, and we haven't had a romantic evening in a long time. Besides, we have a change of clothes for later." She smoothed his tousled hair. "I've been thinking. Mom's getting stronger so maybe it's time to reset our wedding date."

A slow grin grew across his face. "Our marriage license is good for ten more months. Let me check my calendar, and I'll get back with you."

She punched his arm. "If you change your mind, Skeeter Swakhammer's interested."

A snort burst from Frank as he pulled the car into the Fosters' driveway. "Carol, he's twenty years older than you and still lives with his mama. And Gertie Swakhammer is a lot like your Aunt Penny." He reached over and squeezed her hand. "My New Year's resolution is by this time next year, we'll be married."

"Can we make it a little sooner, like, maybe next month?"

"That can probably be arranged." Frank helped her from the car. Ice crunched beneath their boots as they made their way to the cabin's front door. He knocked.

Carol scanned the beauty of the moonlit property while they waited to be welcomed in.

The cabin door opened and a scent of logs burning in the fireplace greeted them. JoAnna's emerald chiffon dress fluttered as she stepped aside to usher them in. "Welcome to our New Year's celebration. I'll take your wraps and phones."

A glow from many candles, warmth from the crackling fire, and soft music gave a romantic ambiance. Russ, in a three-piece suit, stood next to the hearth with an open book in his hands.

JoAnna pointed to the fireplace which was embellished with pine branches, red berries, and white lanterns. "Frank, stand by Russ." Then she handed Carol a small clutch of crimson rosebuds, baby's breath, and cedar fronds. With a smile, she carefully tucked Bob's bookmark into the bouquet.

Carol drew in a quick breath. "They're beautiful, but what's going on?"

"Someone's gonna get mar-ried!" She sang. "Russ and I set it up with your family. Andy and Ethan gathered the rings, marriage license, and your mom's pearl necklace. Turn around and let me put it on you."

Following her instructions, Carol's stomach clenched. "Wait! What about our families? We can't get married without them."

"They're watching via Skype." JoAnna pointed to the laptops on a nearby table. Their phones were placed between them.

The cyber attendees on both screens cheered across the miles. "Surprise!" Voices were loud and clear.

Eyes wide, Frank grabbed Russ' arm and searched all three screens. "Is this for real?"

Ethan stepped from a side room, and beside him was Andy, sporting a toothy grin. Sprigs of mistletoe adorned their lapels. "A lot of work went into this, so you better believe it's real."

Max leaned into the picture of one laptop. "Millie and I are here at the rehab with your mom. We're wishing you the best. Here's Mom."

"Don't see . . ." Sylvia's face grew larger as she moved closer to the screen.

Carol laughed when the monitor displayed a lone blinking eyeball.

"Back up a little, Aunt Syl." Millie repositioned her at the proper distance. "Now they can see you."

"Oh . . . fancy." Sylvia's mouth puckered while struggling to speak. "P-proud of you."

Tears fell as Carol watched her mom settle into the wheelchair, exhausted.

Max patted his wife's shoulder and bent closer to the

computer screen. "I hope you're not upset with us for springing this on you."

"I appreciate everyone setting this up, Dad." Carol wiped her eyes. "It means the world to me that all of you will see our wedding."

"Hi, Carol. I told you I wouldn't miss your wedding." Sue laughed with tears in her eyes and pointed to her daughter. "Rikki is here with me. We're both excited for you."

From another laptop, little Shea squealed and clapped her hands. "Ith Gwampa gonna kith Cawol on the wipth, Mommy?"

Lisa hushed her daughter. "Let's watch and see. Congratulations to the happy couple." She pulled her younger sister into view.

"It's about time you tied the knot." Gwen blew a kiss. "Love you both."

Immediately, Carol's phone lit and Mendelssohn's Wedding March filled the air. JoAnna took her place next to her husband, while Ethan and Andy escorted their mom to her groom.

Carol stole a look at her equally shocked betrothed. The poor man's eyes were glazed over, and perspiration beaded his upper lip.

When the music ended, Russ cleared his throat. "Who gives this woman to this man?"

Ethan puffed out his chest. "My brother and I."

"Frank, please take Carol's hand. We've gathered to witness the much anticipated union of Francis Bailey and Carol Drake Mason. Out of the pain of losing a spouse, the extraordinary has happened for this couple. They met, fell in love, and are now pledging their commitment before God. In Ecclesiastes 3:1 we read, 'To everything there is a season, and a time to every purpose under the heaven.'"

Carol squeezed Frank's hand and eyed Bob's bookmark in her bouquet. Once again, tears formed as she sensed affirmation of their union.

Russ turned to Frank. "Francis, do you take Carol to be your wife? Do you promise to love, honor, cherish, and protect her, forsaking all others and holding only unto her as long as you both shall live?"

"I do." He winked at her.

Russ turned to Carol and repeated the same vows.

She lifted her chin and gazed into Frank's eyes. "I do."

Russ held out his book as JoAnna and Ethan placed the rings on it.

"Rings represent an unbroken circle of love, signifying the union of this couple in marriage. It symbolizes your faithfulness to one another with the same kind of love Christ showed the Church when He died for her. Love each other as a part of yourself because in His sight you shall become one.

"Frank, repeat after me. Carol, please wear this ring as my promise . . . that I will always love, cherish, and honor you all the days of my life . . . With this ring, I thee wed."

With a smile, Frank slipped the ring on her finger and kissed it.

Carol echoed the vow. Her hands shook as she pushed the gold band onto his finger.

"By the power vested in me by the state of Arizona, I now pronounce you husband and wife. Frank, you may kiss your lovely bride."

Frank claimed Carol's lips and dipped her into the circle of his arms.

The brothers each threw a handful of rice while hoots came from the Skype audience.

"That's long enough." Russ released his off the wall laugh, tapped Frank's shoulder, and turned the couple to face the laptops. "Presenting the Reverend and Mrs. Francis Bailey."

More cheers came from the crowd. After all the congratulations, well wishes, and thank yous were shared, the computer monitors darkened.

As Russ went to the coat closet, Carol and Frank thanked the boys for helping.

"I'm happy for you, Mom." Ethan gave her a kiss and shook Frank's hand. "I know you'll take good care of her."

Following his brother, Andy embraced his mom and new stepdad. "Love you guys. Remember Pops, if you get in trouble, *you're* sleeping on the couch."

JoAnna hugged the newlyweds. "We're going home. Dinner's in the oven. A small wedding cake is on the counter." She wiggled her eyebrows. "And you know where I keep the Grizzly Bars. By the way, your room is upstairs, second door on the right."

"We'll give you plenty of time before the chivaree commences." Russ closed the door behind them. His high-pitched cackle could be heard as he walked to his car.

"Let's go over here, Mrs. Bailey." Frank pulled her to the fireplace and held her close. "Tonight was a total surprise, but I did promise we'd be married by this time next year."

She stood on tiptoe and kissed his lips. "You're definitely a man of your word."

A Sneak Peek at Book Two
The Promise of Spring

CHAPTER ONE

July

"Your momma wants to meet me?" A sharp twinge of panic made Millie Drake's heart rate speed up. She plopped down on a park bench and covered her warm face with her hands. "What have you told her, Lou?"

"She knows I think you're pretty special and that we've been dating for six months." He cracked his knuckles, then sat down and draped his arm on the back of the bench. "I'm kind of surprised your parents haven't asked to meet me."

Millie lifted her head and gazed at him while her mind waded through a quagmire of emotions. Mother would be infuriated when she finally learned of their well-guarded romance.

Millie had labored over forty years to stay on her mother's good side. Today she was faced with the difficult task of coming clean about her secret relationship with Lou Blythe.

She flipped her hair over her shoulder and opened the back door. "Dad. Lunch is ready."

"Millicent!" an angry voice growled. "Close the patio door. You're letting hot air in."

"Sorry." Millie's shoulders drooped as she pulled the glass door shut and headed to the kitchen table. Their mother/daughter relationship had always lacked warmth and closeness. Even as a child she was required to call her 'mother'— any other title was deemed highly undignified.

She nervously smoothed her raspberry-colored blouse. In the best of times soul-baring conversations with Mother never ended well. She'd take your naked soul and ram it through the meat grinder. At least she could trust her dad to stay cool, calm, and clever.

Millie scooted her chair closer to the table. The Lou bomb had to be tactfully dropped during lunch because she had a date with him tonight. The Grand Ol' Duchess needed to be carefully primed before any favors were asked. She grinned. Dad's royal title for Mother was very fitting. Thanks to him, she learned to start the groveling process with a compliment. "Umm. Mother, I'm glad we're having tossed salad today." Not much of a rave review. Seconds passed. Finally, inspiration hit. "Have I ever told you how much I love your homemade salad dressing?"

"You sound like your father when he wants something, Millicent." An annoyed sniff followed as she plopped into her chair. "Where is that man, anyway?"

"I'm coming, Penny." Stuart Drake joined the family. He pushed his sunglasses on top of his balding cranium. "Everything smells delicious. Let's thank the Lord for our lunch."

With head bowed, Millie gripped the hands of her parents while offering a silent prayer for courage to complete her mission.

". . . and bless this food for our nourishment. In the name of Jesus we pray, amen." He looked at his wife. "You were at the flower shop this morning, Penny. Did you happen to notice anyone lurking around the desk?"

"Stuart, please." She jabbed a slice of roast beef. "Do you think I pay attention to every little thing that happens there? I'm not a store detective, you know. All I remember is your niece haggling with the mayor's wife."

He cleared his throat. "Carol called and said several raffle tickets were missing. If they don't turn up, I'll have to pay for them."

"Hmm." Penny's eyes met his. "Have you checked Carol's pockets? That woman has been known to take things that don't belong to her. Do the words Pastor Frank ring any bells?"

Millie shook her head. "Let it go, Mother. Carol didn't take Pastor Frank from me. He was never mine in the first place." She bit into a carrot. "By the way, Dad, what's the raffle for?"

"The Chamber of Commerce is trying something new this year to raise money for the hospital. The KAPP-TV news team has agreed to be auctioned off as dates."

"Just think, Millicent, some lucky girl will win a date with that hunky head anchorman, Kent Sheridan." Her chin lifted. "We'll make sure to get several tickets for you."

Stuart's eyes narrowed over his drinking glass. "Penny, did you—"

"This topic is boring me." She waved her hand dismissively. "Let's talk about something else." After pouring blue cheese dressing on her salad, she covered the delicate container.

Great. Millie closed her eyes and took a deep breath while doom circled overhead like a vulture. All signs pointed to Mother manipulating the raffle to win the newsman for her. But, how could she ever think of dating someone other than Lou? She swallowed. The time had come to drop the bomb.

With hands shaking, she clenched the napkin on her lap. "I turn forty-three next Saturday, and I only have one birthday wish." She nervously zeroed in on her mother, sitting across the table in a flamboyant purple lounging robe.

"What is it, Millicent?" Her brow puckered above her red-rimmed glasses. "Did your subscription to Bleeding Hearts in Duluth expire?"

"I've been too busy to read lately." Millie stared at the fluted meat platter and nibbled her bottom lip. Could she pull this off? "Since we usually have a cookout for my birthday, I'd like to invite a guest this time. Dad, you make the best grilled steaks in the world, and Mother, everyone knows there isn't a better cook than you." Did that sound more sincere than her last compliment?

"Why, thank you, dear." She smiled, took a sip of lemonade, and set the glass down. "It's not your cousin, is it?"

Millie swallowed a bite of roast beef sandwich. "Don't worry, it isn't Carol."

"Well, that's a relief. What's your friend's name? Do I know her?" A string of creamed spinach dangled from her fork.

"You know of *him*. He goes to our church." She squirmed in the chair, adjusted her blouse, and gauged her mother's reaction. "As a matter of fact, Carol and I sit with him during morning worship when he's in town."

"You mean that odd man in the church balcony? Oh, Millicent, that heavy brow makes him look like the missing link."

Her reply hit Millie like a sack of fresh fertilizer on a sweltering day.

Stuart frowned. "That remark was totally uncalled for, Penny."

Peace-loving Dad rarely called her out. Millie winced

and waited for creamed spinach to hit the fan.

Her mother's fork clattered to the plate. With a lowered voice, she pecked her finger on the table. "Your daughter and Carol made spectacles of themselves when they sat with him in the church balcony last winter. They giggled, dropped things over the ledge, and shamed our family. Do we want Millicent involved with such a bad influence? Of course, we don't."

"His name is Lou Blythe, Mother. He's wonderful, handsome, and loving. It would be nice for you to meet him." She smiled at her dad. "We're going to celebrate six months of dating this evening, and I'd like to invite him to the cookout."

"I'm your mother, Millicent Marie. You've hidden this for half a year? Didn't I warn you as long as you live under my roof; you were never to hide anything from me?"

"When will I gain the right to my own life?" Millie gulped when she realized she'd blurted her thoughts. She'd never stood up to Mother before. Her eyes searched the ceiling for lightning bolts.

"Maybe when you start making intelligent choices." Her mother sneered. "He's just a plain, ordinary repairman who looks like a mangy orangutan." She pushed her plate away. "I don't want to discuss it anymore. It makes my stomach hurt."

Her dad cleared his throat. "We're getting off topic, ladies. The question was if she could invite Lou to the cookout."

Millie crossed her arms and focused on her mother. "He not only has a good business repairing office equipment, he's also in a gospel quartet." She grinned. "Carol said his voice is so deep, it'll melt the polish off your toenails."

"Millicent! Watch your mouth in front of your father."

"You know, she's right." He chuckled. "I heard his group sing at one of our men's breakfasts. I guarantee there wasn't a speck of polish left on my toenails. Lou's a nice guy but kind of backward."

"Don't encourage her, Stuart."

Millie sent him an appreciative smile. "Lou is shy, but once you get to know him, I'm sure you'll love him, too. His mom's coming for a visit, soon, and he wants us to meet her."

"Meet his mother? Stuart, do something. This relationship is moving too fast." She glared at Millie. "Did that knuckle dragger even notice you before you started wearing Carol's war paint? Of course, he didn't. He's used to all those worldly hussies in the music industry, and you're fitting right into their mold."

"Mother, please. It's gospel music." She finished the last bit of her salad.

A teasing smile tugged at the corners of her dad's mouth. "Hardly a hussy haven, Penny."

"Be that as it may, he'll have his way with our daughter and then bolt like a bat out of you know where." Her gape locked with his, and her voice raised an octave. "And then no other man will want her because she's been soiled like Fanny Woolsey on Frontier Passion."

"Penelope, drop it. Millie has a nice young man who loves God and is interested in her."

She pinned him down with eye daggers. "Hush, Stuart. Next thing you know, Fred Flintstone will take her to some liberal church that prays to goddesses with rainbows and unicorns circling their heads. They'll have those cheesy fish crackers and wine coolers for communion. I *demand* you put your foot down."

Millie fork-jabbed her baked potato right between its eyes. Her dad's good-natured belly laugh was the only thing that protected Mother from a similar fate. Would she ever be out from under that woman's thumb?

"The boy has my complete blessing, dear." He patted Millie's shoulder. "Lou's in love with our girl, so are you going to deal with it, Penelope?" He frowned. "Of course you are."

She pushed back from the table, and rose with her hand pressed to her stomach. "Stuart Thomas Drake! Are you using a *tone* with me?"

Coming November 1, 2017

Author Note

Dear Reader,

Because we live in a fallen world, pain is inevitable. Tragedies, mistakes, and illness pull us down. Often our burdens are too heavy to carry, and it shakes our faith. Sometimes when we stumble we forget to take His hand and get back up.

In writing Carol's heartbreaking story, we wanted to share how God's love can sustain us even in our darkest hours. Her spiritual journey deepens as she grasps His lifeline, regains her equilibrium, and finds a new normal for her life.

We hope Carol's experiences reach into the hearts of our readers and remain a source of encouragement.

Many people are curious to know how we became writing partners. In 1989, Linda and her family moved to the same area as Debbie and her family. We went to the same church and it wasn't long before a friendship developed. We've worked, laughed, and ministered together ever since.

Early on, we talked about writing a book just for the fun of it. We first dabbled with a children's story, but common sense quickly told us that writing for kids wasn't our true calling. But the time spent on it unlocked the door to the fascinating world of writing.

So...we started over with a different storyline geared for grown-ups. However, our plans were put on the shelf when we were asked to lead a combined mature adult ministry for three churches, and for 12 years, we thoroughly enjoyed our time with the seniors. Later, we were appointed the senior adult ministry co-directors of

Indiana North District of our church denomination. We rolled up our sleeves and had a ball for another five years. The District Superintendent even called us the "Darlings of the District."

During the last year, we had reached senior adult status ourselves, and due to physical complications, we realized it was time to step down. It was a difficult decision; however, a twenty-year-old unfinished manuscript was screaming our names. We were unsure about our writing abilities but dusted the cobwebs from our humble beginnings, and set out to learn more about the process.

One of the most frequent questions readers ask is how do we write together? They assume we take turns writing chapters or paragraphs. That may work fine for some co-authors, but not for us. The storyline goes in different directions, and if we're not working together each step of the way, it's like putting two kinds of wall paper on one wall.

So, our joint effort goes like this - we have computers and phones with headsets which allow us work together on the dialog and every other aspect of the story...word by word.

Brainstorming is a big part of the writing process. Sometimes it helps to get away from the computer, go out for coffee, and take notes the old-fashioned way—with pen and paper. By the way, we find the working conditions at Arby's are much quieter than McDonald's where too many kids break our concentration. We lob ideas back and forth, and by the second or third cup of coffee, it's narrowed down to one, and then we run with it.

Once in a while, real-life situations might influence our plotting, but generally, it's just pure imagination. Putting characters in difficult and sometimes humorous predicaments, is a necessary part of our stories, and to do that we play the "what if" game. *What if this happens – or what if that happens?* Before long, the story emerges.

Most of Come Next Winter is fiction from the town of Apache Pointe to the characters. A notable exception is the extra protein that appears in the baked beans. True incident. One of us will never buy veggies in a can again.

We hope you enjoy *Come Next Winter* and look forward to reading *The Promise of Spring*, book 2 in the Seasons of Change series.

We love to hear from our readers. Feel free to contact us on Facebook at:
www.facebook.com/groups/Thebooknookoflindaanddeb

Linda Hanna and Debbie Dulworth

Book Club Discussion Questions

1. Carol struggled emotionally and financially after losing her husband and son in a tragic accident. This led to a desperate situation with Grady. Do you think the timing was coincidental? She learned to depend more on God for strength and direction. In what ways did He manifest His will for her life?

2. Grady North lived to please one god. Have you ever felt there were times in your life that you strayed from serving God and got your eyes on yourself, or on power, pride, money, etc.? Have you ever had to intervene in a family member or friend's life when you saw them going off the path? Was the intervention received, and if not, why not? If so, what made it work?

3. How did the friendship between Carol and Millie serve as a support system, spiritually, emotionally and physically? Have you ever had this kind of friendship where you were like either Millie or Carol? What helped you about the relationship?

4. Millie got her focus off what the Lord could be leading her to—a love that could be real—because she focused her attention on romance novels that weren't reality. Have you ever been in a situation where something took your attention away from the direction God wanted you to go? What helped bring you back?

5. Aunt Penny took a malicious letter to the church board. Has anyone ever hurt you by sharing something personal with others? How did it make you feel? Have

you ever listened to gossip and passed it on as truth? Were you sorry? What steps did you take to heal that relationship?

6. Frank asked Carol to forgive his rude accusations. In her anger and hurt, she held onto a grudge. Do you think her reasons were valid? What helped her release the pain? Do you find it difficult to forgive those who have wronged you? What does the Bible (Colossians 3:13) say about forgiveness?

7. Carol had difficulty getting along with her Aunt Penny. Have you had to deal with a temperamental relative or friend? Occasionally, even our closest friendships turn down a bumpy road. Have you had this experience? How did you resolve the disagreement in order to continue the relationship?

Made in the USA
Middletown, DE
29 January 2017